Dreaming of

First

Dreaming of First

book one of the **HOMERUN SERIES** by
Kay Lucas

Acknowledgments

A big thanks to all that helped with this project! First to my amazing husband, Lucas. Not only did you read and advise me as I ventured down this path, but you also encouraged me, tolerated the late nights when inspiration would strike, and didn't get too mad when I put off housework so that I could focus on this crazy idea of mine. I love you, "three million-thousand!"

Next to Michelle Flick, for inspiring me to do anything besides reading books. You were the first author I personally knew that published a book. I would have never even dreamt of being an author if it weren't for you!

Kirsten Milliron for her beautiful work on the cover design. Jennifer Stewart for my portrait, and all the ladies who helped me through all my editing stages: Kim Trott, Gloria Cernoch, Rebecca Gettelman, Linda Knauer, Nica Kimbrell, and Elizabeth Mauldin.

Last but not least, the biggest shout out to Leslie Parrish for putting so much time into revising the original story into this new and expanded version. And to Raven Peace, for your constant support and inspiration. Both of you have advised me since I started writing in 2019, and I couldn't ask for better besties!

"Never let the fear of
striking out
keep you from
playing the game."

~Babe Ruth

Chapter 1

Fall 1998

~Millie

"Eww, stalker alert," Danika, one of my two best friends, whispers a little too loudly. I follow her gaze to the right and see Dalton James staring at me before quickly looking at his cup.

"That's just Dalton; he's not a stalker," I reply.

Dani says, "He's cute, I'll give him that, but the guy is always watching you. It's a little creepy."

Cute is an understatement. Dalton has a strong jawline and a long narrow nose. Under the signature ball cap he hides behind, he has the most amazing blue eyes that are almond-shaped and crinkle into narrow slits when he smiles. He is tall and broad-shouldered, muscular in a way you only get when you spend all your time working out—I may or may not be guilty of watching him exercise from time to time; it's one of the perks of living across the street from him. Unfortunately, that is too far away to see the faintest impression of a V definition in his lower abs. That's something I noticed once during track season when he lifted a duffle bag, and it caught on his shirt. Who's the stalker now?

Angie, my other best friend, adds her opinion, "Aw, I think it's sweet. He's had a thing for you since fourth grade, Millie."

Rolling my eyes, I repeat for the hundredth time, "He isn't a stalker or in love with me. Remember that was the summer I broke my arm? We were playing in my backyard. He just feels bad because he was pushing the swing when I fell off."

Dalton's family had moved into the house across the street from mine a week after I finished third grade. It had taken nearly all summer before his mom brought him over to play. Calling him shy was, and still is, an understatement. His mother had to stay for half an hour to make him stick around and persuade him to say more than "Hi." He probably hasn't spoken more than a handful of sentences to me in the last eight years. Yet, I get a prickle of awareness every time he's near—I swear the arm I broke tingles, telling me to look towards Dalton, and by then, his eyes have always found mine first. It sounds odd, but I've never gotten a creepy vibe from him.

Unlike Bobby Stevens, who my mother keeps trying to persuade me to date. I guess she doesn't see through his 'good boy' act.

There's something about Bobby. Maybe it's that he seems just a little too flawless. His straw-colored hair is always perfectly groomed, combed over to the right. He dresses preppy all the time—which isn't bad in and of itself, but his clothes are always absolutely perfect—no mud, no smudges, and it doesn't even seem like they have wrinkles from sitting. He always wears collared shirts tucked into khakis with a matching belt. The worst is watching him paint it on really thick in front of teachers and other adults. Wholesome, as long as you like fake and plastic.

Shit, I hope he isn't here tonight. I do not want him to ask me out again because my "Just friends" excuse *will not* change in his favor.

Tonight, we are at a senior bonfire, the traditional last hurrah before school starts next week. It's always hosted by one of the farm kids, providing us a field outside town. A couple of trucks are parked next to each other in the middle of the field with the liftgates down for food and drinks. To the left of the trucks is open for dancing, but most of the area is covered in lawn chairs. Someone always sneaks beer and pot in; therefore, all of us athletes usually try to show up (and get done) before that side of the party starts. Heaven forbid we risk our season.

This makes it extra odd that Dalton is here. He usually doesn't come to social gatherings; plus, there is the fact that he is so good at baseball -he could probably go pro after graduation. Add that to his shyness, and I don't understand why he would risk it.

Angie smirks a little and says, "*Riiight*, I'm sure he's always watching you because of the one time you got hurt *eight years ago* playing with him. The guy looks at you like a puppy that wants attention. Why don't you go say 'Hi'?"

Angie's the one with the big-dark-brown puppy-dog eyes with all her hopeless romantic stuff. Angie is part Thai and has beautiful golden-brown skin and dark-brown hair, newly highlighted.

"Because that's as far as the conversation will go. I will say 'Hi' and ask him a couple of questions, in which he will mumble some short reply." I like Dalton and usually try to talk to him when I see him. When he smiles, his whole face lights up. I often challenge myself to make him smile; it's rare to see a genuine smile from him unless he's playing baseball. Even then, he's super serious.

"What a weirdo," Danika reiterates, taking the last word as she blows the argument off and changes the subject. "Anyway, let's get something to eat; I'm starving!"

"How are you still hungry? We just had pizza!" Angie moans and clutches her stomach.

I have to agree; I definitely over-ate at 'The Hut.'

"Coach had us run three miles today and lift after practice. I need to refuel already," Danika shrugs.

"We did the same workout, Dani, but I don't know where you put all the food you eat," Angie shakes her head.

Danika has a willowy build and tends to have trouble putting on weight. I am more of an athletic rectangle, while Angie has all the curves with her hourglass figure.

We walk over to the food table and lay down the extra pizza we brought. Most of the kids bring something to share.

Even though I'm stuffed, I snag a chocolate chip cookie—my guilty pleasure. Meanwhile, Dani loads a whole plate with treats.

As I'm enjoying the perfect combo of crisp and chewy sweetness, I hear the high-pitched giggle that can only belong to one girl, Carrie Appleton. I look towards the laughter; I'm right. Carrie, easy to pick out with her freshly bleached hair, is standing in a group listening to a story Bobby Stevens is telling.

Ugh, why did I come to this party???

-Dalton

Why am I here? This isn't my thing. I don't even like most of the people, and the smoke from the fire burns at my eyes. But I

4

know why. I'm here because I promised Grandpa Jack I would come to more of this stuff.

The last time Gramps talked to me with much clarity was in his fishing boat. Sitting next to each other with our lines in the water, his quiet rumble came slightly unexpected as, like me, he wasn't much of a talker. "Listen, son, I know you eat, sleep, and breathe baseball, but you gotta get out there and live a little. Make your last year in school memorable; get into a little trouble. Make some friends that aren't just teammates." Grandpa looked at me and gave me a wink. "Ask out that girl you've had your eye on." He died a week later.

I'm brought back to the present when three girls walk up to the party carrying a pizza. The tallest of the trio is in the middle. She has a smooth stride and a slight sway in her hips that I know all too well. It's her; Millie Wilkins finally showed up to the party. Her long curly hair has a life of its own, and her eyes always sparkle with laughter. Was she the girl Gramps was talking about?

As they come closer, her friend says something to her, and she looks at me. Damnit, I've been busted staring at her already tonight. I don't know how, but she always catches me. I look down and take inventory of whatever's in my hand—the sourest lemonade I have ever tasted. My cup is three-quarters full, but I head off to fill it back up anyway.

A girl with the fakest bleach-blonde hair I have ever seen offers to pour me more. As she hands it back to me, she brags about how she made it from scratch. Yeah, I bet she did. I see chunks of powder floating in it, and it has a fake yellow tint. But my mama raised me to be a humble gentleman, probably because she doesn't want me to turn out like my father, so I nod and take a drink anyway. I can't be held responsible for the look my face makes, though, so I quickly turn away.

As if she is a magnet to my eyes, I see Millie again. Her long, brown hair cascades down her back. She's wearing a white school sweatshirt and faded jean shorts that show off her rounded ass and tan, well-defined legs. I take a long deep breath in and catch myself. I better look away before I get caught ogling again.

I turn to see a couple of teammates over by the fire and head their way. I know Gramps wanted me to make friends outside the team, but I'm already taking a huge step out of my comfort zone just being here tonight, so I'll play it cool and hang out with them.

"Bro! I can't believe you're here," Kyle says, giving me a fist bump.

"Dude, wassup?" Jason says with a nod.

"Not much, just checking it out," I reply.

"Well, the first rule is not to eat or drink anything Carrie brings to a party," our catcher, Nate Rodgers, says. Then he gets a water bottle from the cooler he's sitting on.

"Oh good, this stuff is foul," I say, dumping out my solo cup and accepting the bottle. They all chuckle at me.

"What did you think of the new line-up Coach tried today?" Jason asks, and everyone groans in frustration.

"I guess he's just hoping to find the right spot for the new guys," I say, trying my best not to step on anyone's toes. He moved me from first base to shortstop. I've played almost every position, but I prefer first base. He had me pitch some today, too. I'm an alright pitcher but I can't throw as fast as Kyle.

"At least Bobby isn't on the team; he ran away to be a lawn fairy," Kyle ridicules. Soccer has never been a favorite of mine, either. I prefer to hit a ball out of the park than to kick it into a net.

"Good riddance," Jason cheers.

"Yeah, I took over a couple of the batting lessons he was giving," I add.

Not that I need the money anymore. I had been saving for some wheels, but that was before Gramps left me his truck.

Kyle is fast to quip, "That guy was giving lessons! He has the worst form on the team!!"

Everyone laughs because it's so true, but somehow even with a terrible form at the plate, Bobby manages to have a pretty good batting average.

"Tell me about it. Sometimes I feel like I should give the parents a discount because they've been paying for crappy coaching, but I'm working twice as hard trying to clean up their kids' swings."

The guys keep chatting ball and making fun of what a wannabe Bobby is. My eyes wander around the crowd that has gathered. This isn't my first party, but I'm surprised by the number of people that have come out tonight. Someone has turned on their truck radio and is playing country. The song that comes on is popular and upbeat, and it's just a touch twangy for my taste. A group has even started line dancing. Once again, I spot Millie. She's dancing with her friends. She spins and kicks along with the beat.

I must be smiling because Nate calls me out, "Man, go ask her to dance."

I stammer, "W-what?"

His white teeth stand out against his dark skin as he chuckles. "Millie. I know you've got the hots for her. Go dance with her before some douche decides he likes it and wants more of it."

I immediately think of Bobby. He has a reputation for being a smooth talker and getting girls in the sack, or so he brags. And just as I speculate it, I see him head to the dance area. Millie also seems to notice him because as the song changes, she walks over to the food. Time to take Nate and Gramps' advice. I grab a couple of new waters and walk over to her.

~Millie

I love dancing, but when I spot Bobby heading in my direction, I duck behind some other kids and make my way over for a drink and more of the chocolate chip deliciousness at the table. Ugh, Carrie's lemonade or beer. Lovely, the party has really started now. I guess it's about time to head to 'Movie Haus' with Angie and Dani to rent the latest chick flick.

As I reach for a cookie, I hear a guy clear his throat; in a low voice, he says, "Hi, Millie."

I turn with two cookies in hand. "Oh, hi, Dalton. I'm surprised to see you... here... tonight." I start stammering when the full power of his attention paralyzes my soul. "Having fun?"

"Um, yeah. I guess. Just gettin' the full high school experience, or whatever." Thrusting a bottle of water at me, he says, "Here, that lemonade is terrible." I'm momentarily taken aback by his sudden offer and the fact that he just spoke more words to me than he did all of last year.

"Thanks. I had some earlier; it doesn't exactly hit the spot," I say with a cringe and a glance at the so-called lemonade. "Have you tried the cookies? They're the best."

"Yeah..., my mom made them," he says, sounding a little embarrassed.

"I should've known. She always makes the best cookies." Even if he has been a practical stranger living across the street, his mother hasn't. Mrs. James is always friendly. Sometimes she and my mom will get together for coffee, and she always brings baked goods.

Beyond the embarrassment, I see a little pride in his eyes when he agrees. He has his mother's eyes. They are so blue they sometimes look a little violet, unlike his dad's cold gray eyes.

I only met his father once, and that was enough for me. They all came over the day after I broke my arm. He seemed to be preparing a countersuit if my parents pressed charges. Maybe that's his nature because he's a lawyer, but my parents are much more laid back and down to earth. They knew it was an accident and said, "Kids will be kids," and all that. Yet, Mr. James didn't seem to take it as well. Right in front of us, he told his son that there would be no more playing on our swing set. He said Dalton couldn't risk breaking his arm, too. Dalton was supposed to be playing catch with a neighbor kid, not fooling around on a swing set. He asked if I had a brother Dalton could play ball with, but it's just my older sister and me. Dalton hung his head the whole time they were over.

The thing of it is, Dalton wanted to play catch and even brought over an extra glove for me, but I didn't have any interest in that. I have never been very coordinated at catching a ball. We tossed the ball for about two minutes until I got tired of having to go find the damn thing and throw it back. I was the one who talked him into going in my clubhouse, then down the slide, and eventually to the swings.

I hear Danika call out for me to come back and dance, then see Angie grab her to give her a pointed look. I know what that look means, but Dani doesn't take the hint to shut up. She pulls out of Angie's grasp and jogs up to me.

"Come on, Mill, I have our favorite song coming on next," she says with a wink. We don't have a favorite song, and the wink confirms what I know she is thinking. She believes she's being helpful by rescuing me, but come on, why couldn't she save me earlier when Bobby put his arm around me and wouldn't shut up. I would have welcomed the help then.

Just to poke at her, I turn to Dalton and say, "Come dance with us. Our *favorite* song is playing next."

9

For a brief moment, Dalton gets that dear-in-headlights look, but then in a very hesitant voice, he says, "Um, okay," and walks up the small hill to where everyone is dancing. Just as we get there, Billy Ray Cyrus sings "Achy Breaky Heart." Dalton stops at the edge of the clearing, gives me a weird look, and asks, "This is your favorite song?"

I laugh and deny it as Dani loudly insists, "YES!!" and tries to prove it by dancing her butt off. Her high ponytail of dyed black hair swings to its own beat. It's a stark contrast to her porcelain skin. Dalton and I laugh together. It feels nice to share a moment like this with him.

Before the end of the song, which I've bopped around to even though Dalton just stands still, he asks, "What's that smell?"

No girl ever wants to hear that. Every insecurity starts going through my head before I catch a whiff of what he smells. "Pot." I sigh, "Party's over—for me, at least. I won't risk getting caught."

"Me neither."

With reluctance, I turn to the girls, giving them the signal that we need to get out of here, and then we head towards Dani's car. Dalton walks along until he reaches his pickup truck, and I feel his eyes track us through the dark mass of vehicles. As I open the passenger door, I finally turn to see if it's just my imagination. I can barely make out Dalton's silhouette through the windshield, but his wave is clear as day. With giddiness, I take my seat and think about Dalton for the rest of the night.

Chapter 2

-Dalton

With the start of school, the teachers pile on the homework. The whole class groans as Mrs. Fisk assigns a paper due by the end of the week. Out of the corner of my eye, I watch Millie pass the handout with the assignment criteria to the person behind her.

I'm not surprised to see Millie in most of my advanced placement classes. Most college-bound kids are taking as many AP classes as possible. The more college credit out of the way, the faster I can earn my degree. Of course, college is plan B because the dream is to get drafted right after high school.

Week after week, my time fills with schoolwork on top of all the practices, games, and lessons I have been doing all summer. Travel ball is a serious commitment, but it's over in October, and then it will be indoor track season.

Not that I like running. My dad repeatedly tells me how important it is to find another sport to show that I am coachable.

Running is so dull, but it does help my speed and conditioning. Dad constantly compares me with his college record in the fifty-yard dash and reminds me that I won't break it if I don't buckle down and work harder.

Blame it on my antisocial tendencies or my busy schedule, but I don't even realize homecoming is a couple weeks away until Rodgers calls me out for being an idiot.

In the parking lot before practice, Nate looks at me and shakes his head in disappointment. I'm clueless about what I did to earn his disapproval, so I seek him out at warm-up.

I throw up my hand. "Dude, what was that look for?"

Nate shakes his head again. "Man, if you don't even know, I don't have the heart to tell you."

Immediately I think it's news from the coach. Something about the team or the future my dad has planned for me. But he surprises me when he asks, "Whatever happened after the bonfire? I saw you leave with Millie, and now I hear she is going to the homecoming dance with Stevens!"

I'm so shocked that the ball he throws hits me in the shoulder. "Ow," I say as I rub my shoulder and lean down to retrieve the ball. "I didn't leave with her; I walked with her and her friends to my truck and drove home."

Having had enough eavesdropping, Kyle butts into our conversation, "You mean to tell me you had that smokin' hot girl's attention, said goodnight, and haven't taken her out since? You really are a fart-knocker."

I stop throwing to Nate and face off with Kyle. "What'd you call me?"

"Fart-knocker. It's from a tv show—means you're an idiot," he informs me.

"Um, yeah," I trail off. They're right, though; I should have asked Millie to at least hangout or study together.

Then the image of my grandpa winking at me, telling me to "Ask that girl out," pops into my head. Shit, now she's going to the dance with Bobby Stevens, the biggest douche I know.

~Millie

With Homecoming coming up, I have been avoiding every guy that looks my way. I hope Dalton will ask me, but I know the odds aren't in my favor; I'd have better luck if I asked him. With all the classes we have in common, you would think I could get a chance to talk to him, but I don't even catch his eye much. I'm thinking of pretending that my car won't start just so I can ask him for a ride to school. Then I would have a reason to make idle chit-chat that could lead to Homecoming questions. So far, I have chickened out. Angie is in on this plan, but Dani told me it is manipulative; she's right, I guess. Besides, I'm a terrible liar.

After church, Mom talks me into getting lunch and doing a little shopping for her upcoming anniversary trip with Dad. We are talking about her plans at an outdoor cafe when I see Bobby. Ugh, how am I going to avoid him with my mom here? She has fallen for all his smooth-talking since he was in her first-grade class. That's what worries me the most about him; all I hear is bullshit when he speaks.

As Bobby walks by the café, he sees us. "Oh, hello, Mrs. Wilkins, Millie. Funny to bump into you here." The way he says it and the look my mom gives him tells me this is a setup. I can't believe she would do this to me! I have made her field all calls this week. Gah! How could I have been so stupid?

She is cheery (and suspiciously stilted) when she says, "Good morning, Robert. How are you on this beautiful day?"

"It certainly is a nice day. That's why I decided to go for a walk; I just love fall."

"How is school? And soccer?" my mom/betrayer asks the Casanova-wannabe.

"I love soccer, and my team is undefeated!" Bobby's smile is just a bit too cocky, his tone just a touch condescending. I can't believe my mother doesn't see through it. But then, adults never seem to.

"That's wonderful, Robert!" My mother says—dear lord, is she simpering? I am trying not to gag while I eat my chicken sandwich. "Well, you will have to excuse me. I need to go to the ladies' room," Mom informs us, leaving me alone with Bobby. Subtle, she is not.

"So, Millie," Bobby starts, "Do you have a date for homecoming yet?" He has the audacity to swipe a fry off *my* plate, dip it in *my* ketchup, and pop it in his mouth.

"Um, ah, no. I actually wasn't-"

He cuts me off, "Well, that's great because I would love to take you."

"As I was saying, I'm not planning to go this year."

My meddling mother returns just in time to say, "Don't be ridiculous; it's your senior Homecoming. Millie, go with the young man." She must have been lurking, just waiting to jump in.

Taken aback by being blindsided by my own mother, I stammer out, "Okay." Not an 'Okay, I will go with you,' but an 'Okay, what the hell is going on here?'

But Bobby takes it as confirmation I will go. "Awesome. I'll pick you up at six, and we can get dinner at the new steakhouse before we go to the dance."

Mom asks, "When is the big day? I can't wait to see you two all dressed up."

"October 10th," Bobby tells her.

"Bobby, that is one of the nicest places in town; they're probably already booked up," I say, trying to find a reason not to go.

"Don't worry about it; I already have the reservations," he says with a wink. *A wink. Really?* What an idiot.

"Oh no," my mom cries. "We will be gone that weekend." She bites her lip, thinking, "Maybe your father and I can reschedule our trip."

Seeing a way out of this, I chime in, "It's okay, Mom. I don't have to go, and your 25th anniversary needs to be celebrated."

"Don't be silly, Millie, you should go. Dad and I will work something out." Isn't your mother supposed to be your ally?!

"I promise to take good care of her, Mrs. Wilkins," says Bobby with a devious smile. Gag me with a spoon. Undoubtedly, he is thinking about how I will be home alone.

"I'm sure, Robert. We will work it all out," Mom says.

Well, this is just great, not. My head hurts, and Mom beams the rest of the whole damn day. "I can't believe you hung me out to dry like that," I grumble.

"What do you mean, Millie?"

"Why do you think I've had you screen my calls this week?"

"You told me you were busy with homework."

I roll my eyes, "Mom, seriously? Maybe I was waiting for the right guy to ask me?"

She laughs, "Oh heavens, who would you rather go with than Bobby?"

"ANYONE!" Well, almost anyone, but the one exception, my ex, graduated years ago. "Bobby is slimy," I shiver.

Tuesday rolls around, and I get butterflies when I catch Dalton staring at me for the first time in a month. I also feel trapped because I'm still stuck with Bobby as a Homecoming date. If we weren't in calculus, I would try to communicate with him somehow, but this is my hardest class, and I need to pay attention.

Dalton doesn't seem to be worried about schoolwork. His brows are furrowed, and he's chewing on his pencil, but he isn't looking at the problems on the board. I wish I had time to ponder what he is so deep in thought about, but Mr. Schmidt is talking about variable rates and water emptying from a pool—I'm sure I got that wrong on Friday's test. My pondering will have to wait until I run today. I may not be the best on our cross-country team, but I love the long runs when I'm able to work out life problems during that time of solitude.

Chapter 3

~Millie

Homecoming week is here. Every day we dress up funny and attend as many sporting events as possible to support our classmates. It's announced that I'm on the court, so I guess it's a good thing I was already talked into going. My mom and dad still go on their trip because my grandma is in town, should I need her. She's even going to help me get ready and take pictures for my mom.

Bobby hasn't been so bad, either. He came to cheer me on at my meet, so I felt obligated to go to his soccer game. Danika, Angie, and I found dresses last week. Everything seems to have come together.... except my confusion over Dalton. He hasn't said much more than hello since the party in August. But I guess that's been the norm with him for as long as I've known him.

In the crowd at the pep rally on Friday, I hear some guys say, "Mill Will." My chest tightens, and my head whips around as I search for the offending party, but I can't spot anyone even glancing in my direction. I don't hear it again.

Mill Will was a nickname from my freshman year, a time in my life I would prefer to forget.

My boyfriend that spring was Cory, a handsome, popular senior. He talked me into doing a lot of things I wasn't ready for. Unbeknownst to me, he would then brag to his buddies about all the stuff we did. Like, "Hey, does your girlfriend give you blowies because Mill Will." Of course, I didn't know this until it was too late. My reputation, heart, and body were ruined. I thought we had something special; I wanted to give him everything I had because I foolishly thought I was in love and afraid of losing him after graduation. But I gave him too much of me and ended up losing everything to him. He laughed in my face when I told him I loved him, that I wanted him to wait for me so we could move away to college together.

Since then, I've barely dated, and I make sure to keep all my dates PG. Dani and Angie stood beside me through all of it and helped me to clean up my reputation. I haven't heard those terrible words in years. Besides, most of the guys that knew that nickname graduated my freshman year, so why am I hearing it now?

After the rally, I think it must have all been my imagination.

-Dalton

We have a scrimmage on Saturday afternoon. It wasn't supposed to be on the schedule, but Coach knew it was our Homecoming, and with all the school spirit, he thought it would be fun. Playing is always more fun than drills. The crowd isn't bad, but no one I'm looking for is in the stands, not even my parents.

After the game, we change out of our cleats and pull on our hoodies. Most of the guys are in a hurry as we head to our cars so they can get cleaned up in time to pick up their dates and go to the dance, but Nate pulls me aside. After a quick glance around to make sure no one is listening, he informs me that the soccer fairies have been talking.

"I know you are as oblivious as an ostrich with its head in the sand, so I wanted to let you know Bobby-the-Douche has been bragging about his plans for tonight." My stomach drops, knowing I'm not going to like the rest of this conversation. "There's a bet on whether he will close the deal with Millie. He has even been using that old, hurtful nickname she worked so hard to erase." Calling Booby "Douche" may be too kind of a name for the asshole, but I know Nate rarely calls anyone dirty names. "He's saying it is a sure thing since Millie's parents are out of town."

I feel all the blood rush to my face, and I grip my bag a little too tight as my hands tighten into fists. My vision tunnels and I have to take deep breaths.

"Sorry, man, I just thought I should tell you. I know how you feel about Millie." Nate puts his hand on my shoulder and gives me a quick squeeze. I manage a mumble of thanks, and I walk away. Once in my truck, I sit staring out the windshield until I pull myself together enough to drive.

My brain is in a red fog the whole way home, and the only words that come out of my mouth are four-letter ones. After imagining multiple scenarios (all of which involve Bobby bleeding or losing the use of certain parts of his anatomy), I come to the conclusion that it's not my place to do anything. I feel helpless and angry, but I don't have any kind of relationship with

Millie; we aren't even friends. It sucks he's doing this, but if she agreed to go out with him, maybe I misjudged her.

Speak of the devil; I arrive home just in time to see Stevens knocking on her door. Instead of going in, I sit on our porch swing and watch. He seems to be the perfect gentleman, offering his arm to walk her to his car (or rather, his daddy's car) and even opening the door for her. I watch them take off and notice her grandmother waving to them, camera in hand, from the front door. Maybe this isn't as bad as Nate said.

I go in and see a note from Mom, reminding me she and Dad had a work dinner. When she took a new position in hospital administration, she warned me they would have lots of shindigs to attend. At first, Dad was happy she got the promotion but not so pleased about having to play the role of doting husband. When they go, she is in the spotlight, and he doesn't do well sharing that. It has never been a secret within the family that they have an unhappy marriage. I'm sick of the constant bickering and fighting; it's one of the reasons I have devoted so much time to baseball. They only married because she got pregnant. It's the one time in his life he didn't get his way on something, and he makes her life hell for it every day. I'm pretty sure they are only staying married for me, and I bet they will finally get a divorce as soon as I graduate. As if raising me in a two-parent home means they are doing it right. A stable home isn't the same as a loving home.

I'm watching the highlight reels on the ten o'clock news when I see headlights coming down the street. I can admit, only to myself, I have jumped at every car that has gone by since I've been home. I couldn't concentrate on anything I tried to watch, and doing homework was even worse. When the car pulls into her driveway, I slip out to sit on the swing. They are in the car

20

for over five minutes. I feel a headache starting and realize I have been grinding my teeth. But, fuck, how long does it take to say, "Thank you, goodnight?"

Suddenly, the passenger door is thrown open. Millie doesn't shut it as she runs for her front door, but her dress and heels slow her down. Before she gets it unlocked, Bobby gets out and follows her up the stoop. I see him grab her, and she tries to push him off, giving up on the lock. I am on my feet and crossing the street before I know it.

"Go home, Bobby," she shouts, "I told you NO!" Millie's voice sounds like she is trying to exude authority, but it's laced with too much panic to be commanding.

"Oh, come on, baby, I know you had a good time tonight," Bobby sneers at her. Even before he says it, I know what is coming next. "Now, it's time for me to have a good time."

She slaps him—the sharp crack carries through the whole neighborhood. He doesn't even flinch, just puts his arms around her in a bear hug. I hear fabric tear and see his mouth on her neck.

"Doesn't look like the lady's interested, Stevens. Maybe you should let her go and leave," I manage to say evenly, even though my whole body is thrumming with rage.

Bobby whips his head around but doesn't let Millie go. "This doesn't concern you, DJ. *You* go home," he says. With a lecherous grin, he adds, "Unless you want to watch." Then he proceeds to grind into her with his hips and slowly licks her face.

"UGH! LET ME GO, ASSHOLE!" A combination of disgust and fear paints Millie's features in the soft glow of her front porch light.

Bobby smiles a predator's smile and whispers, "Oh, Mill Will, this is happening. Call off the guard dog; I can still make this good for you, too." I hear every word; he means for me to.

I focus on remaining calm, even though my stomach is rolling and my adrenaline is pumping. There is no room for my emotions at this moment.

Millie looks at me with pure panic—the disgust is gone; so much for this not being my problem. I grab him by the wrist, twist, and pull his arm back, yanking his elbow to wing up and hear the satisfying sound of a seam rip.

When she is free, Millie runs back to the door, managing the lock this time, and shuts herself inside.

Even though a considerable part of me wants to beat the bastard's face and break every one of his fingers, I let him go and shove him toward the car. He stumbles, but as he regains his balance, he says over his shoulder, "It doesn't matter. I'll still tell everyone that she was a lousy lay."

I stand in front of the porch steps, arms crossed, feigning a cool that I don't feel. If I don't hold myself in, I might go after Bobby. Instead, take an unintended lesson from my father, and use my words. "You do that, and she'll file charges against you for sexual assault. Keep your mouth shut, and so will we." I am going to encourage her to press charges anyway.

He springs back toward me. "Fuck that, you asshole! I'm not going to lose out on a hundred bucks because of that bitch." As he reaches me, he starts to pull his arm back like he's going to hit me.

"Go ahead, but you'll lose more than a hundred bucks. Hitting me will only guarantee my dad takes the case, gives us credibility, and adds more charges against you," I condemn. It works; he drops his arm and starts backing away.

Before he gets in his car, though, he points at me and adds one last jab, "You're going to regret this, James." Then he gets behind the wheel and peels out of the driveway.

I watch his taillights go down the street. His tires squeal at the stop sign, and then the engine revs as he turns onto the main road. If he gets in an accident in his father's car, he will have more to worry about than us. I've met his father; the apple doesn't fall far from the tree.

I turn back to Millie's door, unsure what to do or say, but I have to see if she's okay. I raise my hand and pause, taking a deep breath before gently knocking once. I can hear her crying on the other side.

Clearing my throat and trying to soften my voice, I talk to her through the door. "Hey Millie, it's Dalton. He's gone. Are you okay?"

There is a long moment before Millie slowly opens the door and looks around. Then, all of a sudden, she clings to me. She is shaking and doing that little hiccup thing that happens when you've been crying hysterically. She sniffles, "Thank you, Dalton. I don't know..." she trails off, shakes her head, and with a small gasp, starts crying again.

A moment passes with me just standing there like a statue, so I awkwardly put my arm around her and rub her back. "Shh, don't even think of the what-ifs. You're safe now. He won't come back," I say, trying to calm her.

She gasps, "Come back?"

Did I just put that in her head? Damn it. I'm shit at this stuff. "Don't worry about it. Just get inside and lock the door. I only wanted to check on you before I go."

She pulls back and crosses her arms, trying to protect herself from the events of the evening. Then she looks up at me. Her makeup is all smudged and running down her face. "Do you have to go right away? Can you stay for a little bit?" She pauses before adding, "I..., I would feel better not being alone."

I can't explain how her emotion-filled eyes make me feel. It tugs at my heart, so I nod and follow her inside.

Chapter 4

-Dalton

I follow Millie into the living room, where she sits on the couch, still holding herself like she's afraid of falling apart. I just stand there, not knowing what to do or where to look. This isn't a game, no rule book, and I don't know what the play is. I have lots of training and conditioning, but none of it is for personal stuff, especially not with girls. When my mom gets upset, the only clue is her locked bedroom door. I've never witnessed one of her breakdowns, but I know my dad has made her cry with his words and actions. He has never touched her in anger, but I haven't seen him show her any kind of affection, either.

Millie breaks the silence and my train of thought. "I bet you think I'm a fool. A weak, pathetic fool." Her voice is so soft I can barely hear it, and there is an edge to it that I've never heard from her before.

My head whips around. "I don't think that at all," I say immediately. "I think Bobby is the biggest jackass at our school."

I spit out "jackass," and my voice is a bit louder than I intend it to be. I don't want Millie to think I'm yelling at her, so I take a breath to cool down. In a lower voice, I say, "I could have...should have told you that before and prevented this...this whole... night." I feel somewhat responsible for this whole mess.

"I didn't want to go with him tonight, but I got blindsided by my mother." Millie looks at her hands and then suddenly stands up. "They planned this whole 'chance' meeting, so I would be forced to accept his invitation." Her voice climbs in pitch and volume as she continues. "She insisted I go with him, knowing I was trying to say no and wanted to back out of it." I watch as scared Millie is replaced by angry Millie. I don't know if this is a good thing, but at least she isn't using her arms to hold herself together anymore.

Now I see how torn her dress is. The left strap isn't attached to the back anymore, and that isn't the only part that is ruined. I step closer and pull the delicate strap of her dress back in place. When I reach for her, though, she flinches. I see a touch of fear come back into her beautiful green eyes. Instead, I pause and hold my hands where she can see them. Then I speak as if I'm talking down an injured animal, "Easy, I am not going to hurt you. I was just going to right your dress."

She looks down at the broken strap and the dipping of her neckline. Nodding, she grabs the blue string and pulls it up. I see a tear trickle down her face. I guess scared Millie wasn't gone after all.

Sniffling, she says, "Yeah, he did that when I got out of the car."

"You should call the police and file a report," I tell her.

Her eyes go wide, and she says, "I can't do that. Nothing happened. You stopped it from getting that far. No, I don't want to relive it. I... I don't want anyone else to know."

26

"You think that ass is going to keep his mouth shut?"

"I can't," she says, shaking her head. A fresh tear slips down her face when she closes her eyes.

Slowly reaching out, I brush that tear and cup her face. As gently as I can, I say, "Look, I can see what he did to that pretty dress. If he left any marks on you, too, you need to tell someone, and they will need to take pictures for evidence."

She looks up at me and says, "You think my dress is pretty?" Then I get the closest thing to a smile I have seen from her all night.

This makes me smile back at her. "Well, it *was.*"

We both laugh a little, but it dies quickly. There's a pause, and Millie looks at her feet, and I register how close we are standing to each other.

"I saw him pick you up and your grandma taking pictures," I admit quietly, and Millie's face turns up to me.

She just stares into my eyes for a moment...and then the moment is gone. Millie steps away and fans out her long, dark blue skirt. It shouldn't fan out. It was a straight skirt, but that bastard tore it there too.

"I think it's time to retire it. Will you stay here while I change? I'll be quick."

I nod, and she runs up the stairs. With nothing else to do, I walk around and look at all the pictures on display.

They are mostly candid shots, but there are two of those 'through the years' frames, each showcasing every school picture up to the larger senior portrait—one for Millie and one for her older sister, Michelle.

Despite living across the street, I haven't been inside the Wilkins' house in over eight years. Not much has changed. The layout is similar to ours, probably because the same construction company built the whole subdivision, but theirs is much more homier. I remember even at ten years old, I could feel the love in this home. The furniture is still all in the same place, and though there have always been family pictures on the mantle, they have updated most of them.

Mr. Wilkins is balding but maintains a long gray ponytail and a gray goatee; his wife looks like an older version of Millie with gray streaking her curly hair. Neither of them colors their hair to appear younger than they are, like my parents do. Michelle has the same brown hair as Millie, but hers is straight and cropped short. The girls are both taller than their mother, but their father maintains a couple of inches on everyone.

Millie comes back down in soft, stretchy pants and a t-shirt. She has taken her updo out and has her curls hanging in a ponytail.

It looks like she has washed most of her makeup off, too. This is the Millie I know best. She isn't usually all done up fancy, and I think that's what I like most; she is real—when so many other girls aren't.

"Wanna watch TV?" she asks. She's calmer than she was when she went upstairs. Maybe because she feels more like herself too.

"Sure." I cringe at my one-syllable word because it sounds more like a grunt.

Millie grabs the remote and sits on the couch, curling her legs under herself, making her look smaller. She isn't short compared to most of the girls at school, probably only three or four inches shorter than my nearly six feet.

"You can sit down; I won't bite," she says.

"Um, yeah," I say, looking around. Do I sit in the rocking chair or next to Millie on the couch?

"Dalton?"

She looks at me with big, pleading eyes, and it seals the deal to sit on the couch. I lie to myself that it's not so I can be close to her but to be more comfortable. It's an L-shaped couch, and I can put my legs up; it's just more practical.

Millie turns on music videos. We sit there awkwardly, staring at the television. Although we both seemingly watch intently, I'm pretty sure I won't be able to tell you a single artist that was on later. I concentrate on not touching her because I'm sure that is the last thing she would want after the night she had. Three videos play, and then the commercials start. She leans into me, and I can feel her deep, shaky breathing. Turning to her, I ask, "You doin' okay?"

"Yeah, it's just a lot. Ya know?"

"Sure." It has been a lot for me, too. My emotions have been all shaken up today. "Adrenaline."

Millie asks, "What?"

"The shakes and the weird empty feeling. It's the adrenaline high that you are coming down from. Well, that and a lot of other stuff."

"Oh. I guess so," she meekly whispers.

"It always takes me a couple of hours to calm down after a game, especially if I'm pitching." Stupid thing to say—baseball, at a time like this? I'm such an idiot, but I'm emotionally stunted due to my home environment.

But Millie doesn't act like she minds. "How is baseball going this year? I wanted to come to the game today, but I had so much to do to get ready for…" she pauses, takes a big swallow, and chooses her next words carefully, "the dance."

"It's going good." This is territory I know, and it relaxes me. "We had a couple of scouts at our last tournament."

"Is that what you want to do when you graduate? Go pro?"

"That's the dream, Millie," I say with a shrug, trying not to let on just how much of my dream it is.

"Then, why all the AP classes?" Smiling, she continues, "Don't the outstanding athletes just get good grades because the coach works it out for them? They skim by not having to take the hard way out of school?"

Laughing with her, I say, "I guess I'm just not that good, then." But I know I am. My mom has never let me boast about it. My dad is more prideful but agrees calm confidence is always better than a showboat.

They both have very good, respectively high-paying jobs, but we live modestly. Stuff like a reasonably sized house, no flashy cars or showy vacations, not that my parents would take time off work to go on a nice vacation. They always buy the best quality, but they don't flaunt their wealth. They also both believe hard work is what it takes to get to the top; Dad especially won't accept anything less. No handouts, period. They may not have the best marriage, but I will give them that they are usually a united team regarding how they raise me.

"No, really, if you plan to go pro, why are you taking so many college-level classes?" she asks.

I shrug, not knowing how much I want to tell her about what it's like at home. "I've already signed intention papers with a scholarship to Florida, but if I get drafted, I can turn them down. My choices are to get a job and give up the dream or go to college. But if I go to Florida like planned, I'll have to be a junior before the scouts look at me again. If I start my credits now, I will be that much closer to my junior year." "Wow, you really have this all worked out." She says this without sarcasm, just a bit of surprise in her voice.

Not entirely my plan, but I have never wanted anything else. My dad has planned my life just like he plans a case. Feeling more peaceful, I stretch my arm out across the back of the couch—her side of the couch. She's right beside me, and it feels nice; comfortable. We watch the next set of videos without talking. When the commercials return, I ask, "So what's your dream, Millie? What are you taking all your AP classes for?"

"I want to be a physical therapist. I've applied to KC, Columbia, and Springfield."

"Sounds like you have things worked out, too," I say with a smile.

"Yep. I have known I wanted to go into PT since you broke my arm," she jabs.

"*I* broke your arm?!" I widen my eyes in mock indignation. "As I recall, you were the one squealing that I needed to push you higher. You just weren't hanging on tight enough for the ride." We are both laughing now, causing my arm to slide down from the couch and around her shoulder.

I hold my breath, afraid of her reaction. After the night she had, I should respect her boundaries, but this feels right. She feels right.

Millie lightly slaps me on the chest and says, "And I thought you were so sorry when you came over to apologize!"

I ponder making another joke about it all being a show for my parent's sake or being sincere, then choose sincerity. "I even hand-picked flowers from Mrs. Bailey's garden and left them on your doorstep." The mood seems to have suddenly turned solemn.

"I got them. I think the glass soda bottle they were in was a nice touch." Millie swallows as if hesitant to continue. "I still have it." She bites her lip, showing her perfectly straight teeth from the braces she used to wear.

We go quiet again, focusing on the television. Millie yawns, rests her head on my chest, then murmurs, "Why didn't you ask me to the dance? I hoped you would," her voice trails off from either exhaustion or shyness.

"You did?" Blown away by her admission, I trip all over my thoughts and words, "I…I didn't…," I didn't… what? I didn't know? Didn't think? Didn't have the courage to ask her. "I didn't realize I wanted to until it was too late."

I don't think I've ever been this honest with anyone. This moment is priceless to me. It's like everything in my life has led me to this. I don't want to do anything to break it, so I don't ask any questions during the next commercial set. She doesn't either. Eventually, I look down to see she has fallen asleep. I should go; I did my job keeping her company until she calmed down. The jackass never came back for me to scare away. But I am *cuddling* with Millie Wilkins. This is a dream I never thought would be possible with the way Dad drives my life so hard; he doesn't give me time for girls.

My gramps, on the other hand, would be proud. With that thought, I envision him winking at me again. I'll just stay for a little longer in case she wakes up.

I have her face etched in my memory from all the times I couldn't stop myself from watching her. But now that she is sleeping, I can gaze all I want. Her skin is bronze from all the time she spends in the sun. She has prominent cheekbones and a pointy chin, making her face shaped almost like a heart. There is still some glitter shining in her toffee-colored hair; her eyebrows and lashes are slightly darker. I've never noticed how long her eyelashes are, but I have never had this unabashed view before. Her lips still hold a pink shine from the makeup she had on.

She looks so peaceful while she rests, so much better than when I first came into the house tonight. It just about killed me seeing her green eyes rimmed red.

I have also never paid much attention to her hands. Both are tucked between her jaw and my chest. Like the rest of her, they are long and slender. I bet she plays the piano.

Something on the TV wakes me up. I look around and realize I am not in my house. Something heavy and warm is on me. I look; it is actually two things: Millie and her cat. I smile and then glance at the time— 3:22 a.m. Shit, I better get home. My dad is probably pissed, and my mother could be worried.

Of course, they would first have to realize I'm not home, which truthfully is fifty-fifty.

Even though it's late, I'm slow and gentle as I get up, ensuring not to wake Millie. The cat jumps as soon as I move, but Millie sleeps like a princess. I pull the blanket from the back of the couch over the captivating girl that was just in my arms. Then I carefully put a throw pillow under her head. With my face this close to hers, I can't resist kissing her forehead and whispering goodnight. I turn off the TV, and all the lights, save one lamp, lock the doorknob, and leave.

I jog across the street and sneak into my house. Dad is passed out in front of the TV, much like I just was, but he has his arm wrapped around a liquor bottle instead of a woman. He must have had a terrible night; for all his faults, he doesn't usually drink that hard. I creep up the stairs, but Mom catches me before I reach my room.

"Dalton? Where have you been?"

Most teenage guys would lie to their moms, but I have never been that kid. Not because I'm close with my parents, I just don't do anything to get in trouble. "I, uh, I saw Millie come home from the school dance," I tell her everything that went down with Bobby and that Millie needed the company to calm down.

"Aw, Dalton, you did the right thing," she tells me with a hug. "That little shit has it coming to him." Before mom got into administration, she worked as a social worker at the hospital. She knows more of what's going on in this city than Dad pretends to.

"Has he done this kind of thing before?"

She smiles sadly, telling me everything I need to know. "You know I can't tell you that."

Thank the Babe, Nate gave me a heads-up, and I was there to stop it.

Finally, I get to my room. When I take off my shirt, I smell Millie's vanilla perfume on it, so I throw it on my pillow instead of in the dirty basket with my sweats. I have never fallen into a more blissful sleep.

Chapter 5

~Millie

Body aches wake me before I even open my eyes. "Ugh," I've slept on the sofa; no wonder I'm in pain. I sit up and stretch, recounting what led to me not making it to bed.

Bobby.

Dalton.

"Oh. My. Gosh!"

I stand up with a start. Zinny, my cat, gives me the kind of disgruntled look that only a cat can manage as he is unceremoniously dumped on the floor and runs off.

I look around and listen, wondering if I'm alone, but I end up walking through the house just to make sure. A quick search confirms I'm by myself, leaving me feeling oddly relieved and slightly disappointed.

If I go for a long run, it'll work the soreness from my muscles, and I can figure out what I'm going to say to Dalton before I see him again. As I head upstairs to grab my workout clothes, I let myself smile just a little at what happened with him last night as I push away thoughts of everything that happened to bring him here in the first place. Once I get into my room, though, I change my mind. My bed looks more inviting than my sneakers do.

The next time I wake up, it's about 9 a.m. I stretch and head for the bathroom with more drive than before. Getting dressed for my delayed run, I start thinking about Dalton, which gives me butterflies in my stomach. Although I tell myself it would be his M.O. to avoid me for the next couple of months—or years, I shake my head.

When I see my damaged, discarded dress and bent tiara tossed in a heap on the floor, Dalton's words come back to me, "Look, I can see what he did to that pretty dress. If he left any marks on you, you need to tell someone, and they will need to take pictures for evidence." At the time, I only wanted to concentrate on his compliment on my dress. In the light of the day, I see more clearly just what Dalton was talking about.

Just then, the doorbell rings. "Who the hell can that be?" I mutter to myself. Fear nearly freezes me, but I manage to look out my window to see the driveway and road are clear in front of our house. Whoever is at the door didn't drive here.

Excitement and nerves fill me expecting to find Dalton at the door, but when I get downstairs and peek through the peephole, I find his mom. "Mrs. James?" I ask as I open the door.

"Hello, Millie." Her eyes are filled with pity, and I know she knows what happened—or rather, what almost happened. "I thought we could talk."

I swallow and nod, opening the door to let her in.

"I always love how warm and homey it is here," Mrs. James says as she walks in. "It's what I had hoped to achieve, but...., anyway," she takes a seat on the sofa and pats the spot next to her for me to join her, "I'm sure you know that's not what I came to talk to you about."

With tears burning the backs of my eyes, I sit where indicated. This may be my house, but she is guiding the direction of this conversation. Evie James is the epidemy of authority, but not in a tyrannical way. She is likable, confident, and put together—definitely role model material. "Dalton told you."

"Yes, I caught him sneaking home at 3:30 in the morning." She gently lays her hand on the middle of my back. "How are you feeling?"

"Fine," I sniffle. "Nothing happened. Dalton scared him off."

"You are both very lucky about that. But in Dalton's version of the story, more than 'nothing' happened." I start to protest, but she cuts me off.

"Where is your dress?"

"Upstairs."

"Can I see it?"

Nodding, I stiffly stand and quickly retrieve it. Mrs. James holds it up, examining where it was torn. "I don't see any blood on it. Do you have any scratches or bruises?"

I shrug but hold out my arms for her to look at. There are small fingertip bruises on my forearm, a line on my collarbone from the dress strap, and Mrs. James points out a couple of spots on my left thigh, just above my knee.

"First and foremost, none of this was your fault." She clasps my hand. "Millie, look me in the eye and repeat that." I do as she says. "Good; tell yourself that every time thoughts of last night creep into your mind." I nod with a shaky breath. "Okay, so let me give you the rundown on how this can go." She explains, "I have great connections and know exactly which officers to call. Unfortunately, Bobby's dad is also very well connected, and it will turn into a he-said-she-said ordeal."

"But Dalton saw," I interrupt.

"Yes, and I'm sure he will testify what he witnessed. But Bobby's friends will collaborate on his behalf."

"They weren't even here," I argue.

"That won't matter. They will lie, say you were leading him on before you left the dance."

I gasp, "No. I didn't lead him on. He got handsy, and I wanted to get out of there."

She softly says, "Which will translate as you wanted to go somewhere more private." I feel stabbed, and the tears that flow are like blood gushing from the wound. "I'm not saying I agree with that. I'm just warning you how everything gets twisted."

"So, I shouldn't report it."

"Yes, you should. Boys like Bobby get away with too much in this world. For women everywhere, I urge you to stick it to him. I am just warning you how it could go so you can be prepared for the battle."

She passes me a tissue, and I dry my face remembering an incident last year when a girl cried rape, and in the end, it didn't matter if it was true or not; the rumors of what happened got out of hand. The guy she blamed played the victim, and she was dubbed a slut. It got so bad that she switched schools. I strain my brain to remember what happened to him—did he get prosecuted? All the attention unfairly went focused on her. "No, I don't have it in me," I shake my head vehemently.

After a while without any conversation, Mrs. James pats my back again and stands. "Take some time to think about it. You don't have to do anything today, but don't wait too long to do the right thing."

I walk her to the door, sniffling. "There isn't a right way out of this; whatever I decide will have consequences." I just wish I wouldn't have gone with him, then none of this mess would have happened.

"Sadly, you can have all the right reasons and still make the wrong decision—you just don't know until you have picked which path to go down."

Nodding, I open and hold the door for her. "Thank you, Mrs. James."

"Please call me Evie," she pats me on the cheek. "And I am just across the street if you need to talk about anything. I will always respect your choices, even if I don't agree with them."

"Thanks, Evie."

Mrs. James—Evie gave me a lot to think about, so I need to run more than ever now. Maybe I can just outrun this problem? I have a few favorite paths, but the park by Grandma Bea's house calls to me. And once I'm good and exhausted, I will spend some time with her.

Grandma still lives in a ginormous Victorian home. It's way too big now that it's just her living here, but she won't let go of it because she raised her kids there. The home sits at the end of a cul-de-sac, and the backyard bumps against a big park. I have so many memories of playing with my cousins there, like discovering my love for running when we raced around the perimeter path.

As I pull into her driveway, I admire the fancy scrollwork with pretty paint on the outside, or as she likes to call it, "gingerbread." It has been lovingly and meticulously cared for, and the inside is just as beautiful with all the natural hardwood and polished woodwork. I've always loved it here, like a second home. I already know what it will smell like when I walk in, a combination of oranges (because she makes her own cleaner with them) and cinnamon (because she makes coffee cake every Sunday morning).

I walk in the front door into the foyer and grand staircase. To the left are a small sitting room with a bay window and Grandma's prized Persian rug. The family room and a den with Grandpa's roll-top desk are on the right. The kitchen is past the stairs, and just as predicted, Grams is wrapping a coffee cake. She looks up and beams at me, "Dear, I am so happy you came by, but you aren't exactly dressed for church."

"No, I'm not." You don't wear anything less than your best for church with Grandma Bea, so my ripped-up shirt and running shorts are definitely not going to cut it. "I'm going to go for a run and thought we could play scrabble when you get back."

"I'm honored that you want to spend your day with an old lady."

"You are my favorite person in the whole world; there is nowhere else I'd rather be." In fact, I wish I had stayed here last night, wish I would have gone with my gut about Bobby and not gone out with him…. but then I wouldn't have fallen asleep on Dalton's shoulder.

-Dalton

When I come down to breakfast, Dad is reading the Sunday paper at the dining room table, and Mom is standing at the kitchen counter waiting for the coffee to brew. As usual, the room is cold and unfriendly, and I can't wait to get out of the house. I grab three large bottles of water from the fridge to make it through the day.

"Thirsty?" she asks with a smile just for me.

"Yes, Ma'am. I also have a couple of lessons today before practice."

"Good. You have grown into such a responsible young man," she says with warmth in her eyes. "After our conversation last night, I was thinking of calling on that friend you were concerned about. Do you think she would be receptive to that?"

I try to pull off a casual shrug, but I can feel the heat creep into my face. Thankfully, Dad comes in to refresh his cup, stopping any more questioning from her. "What friend?"

All compassion drains from Mom as she answers, "It's a confidential matter, Michael."

"If something is bothering my son, you need to take care of it before it sidetracks him from his priorities." Here we go again.

Mom crosses her arms and, even in a silk bathrobe, looks ready to rule the world. "Being a compassionate human is always a priority. Maybe you should look into it."

Shit, this is not going to end well. Our house is crumbling because of power struggles and broken dreams. The best way to distract them from this argument is to focus their attention on baseball, and that's fine with me because it's one of the few things we can all connect on.

"We won 11:6 yesterday." Before Dad can drill me on every play-by-play, I add, "I hit a homer in the first inning. My second time at bat, I hit a double bringing Rodgers in on a line drive into left field. I got up a third time, but they walked me—didn't help them much since I stole second and third and made it home on Burnett's pop fly. My field game was on point, too."

"What do you mean 'on point'?" he replies.

"I didn't have any errors."

Mom cuts in, knowing that Dad will grill every second of the game out of me. "Wish we could have been there."

For as absent of a father as he is, he usually makes it to my games. Mainly to make sure everything I do meets his standard of perfection. Dad played in college, and when he couldn't play anymore, he projected his dream on me. Before I could walk, he had a ball in my hand, and I've always had the best coaches and equipment.

"I know," I wave it off. "It wasn't on the schedule until last week."

With that, I make my protein shake, grab a granola bar and a banana to eat later and head out the door, sliding my backpack on my shoulder as I go. It's only eight, and my first lesson isn't until ten. I don't need to leave yet, but I don't want to stick around the house for more inquisitions. As I pull out of my driveway, I look over at the Wilkins's home. I wonder how Millie's doing and if I should check on her. But our front curtains are open, and Dad has a clear line of sight from the table if he looks up from the paper, so I shift into first and drive off before my dad suspects anything. Mom will talk to her; she will know how to handle things better than I do.

At the park, I get some homework done and then hit the ball on my own. I practice hitting to every position, dropping it into all the pockets the imaginary team is leaving.

Benny, the first kid on my schedule, is one of my newly acquired players. Not many kids take lessons all year round, and I am happy that he gets here ten minutes early. As his dad talks to me about my calendar, I have Benny run around picking up all the balls on the field.

While Benny and I are in the batting cage, I notice a young woman running on the far side of the park. Her ponytail is light brown, and she is built just like Millie. Is it really her, or am I just hoping it is? I shake my head at my thoughts. When she gets closer, I can clearly see it's the girl I dreamt of all night. I still have time left on this lesson, so I shouldn't do more than wave. I will just have to talk to her later, I guess. I'm nervous and excited at the same time.

Millie is still running the park's perimeter when the lesson is over. There is an excellent trail there, and her stride hasn't slowed. Benny's older sister, a junior at my school, picks him up. I'm spacing on her name, but she is overly friendly. Usually, this doesn't bother me, but today I find it excessively annoying. When Millie passes by again, I can see her stance has changed, and her eyebrows are all scrunched up. Benny's sister greets her, and Millie stops to talk to us.

"Hey, Millie! Congrats on being crowned queen of the Homecoming!" Benny's sister says a little too cheerfully.

Wwhhhaat? How did I not know this?

"Oh, thanks, Britney," Millie smiles. She isn't even that out of breath from her run, and I notice her smile doesn't reach her eyes.

"Why didn't you tell me you won?" I ask.

"Um, I don't know," she shrugs and continues cryptically, "There was so much going on when I saw you."

"Oookay," the girl, Britney, says, looking between us. She obviously can tell there is more to what Millie is saying—that she is missing something, but she doesn't ask. "Benny, are you ready?"

He nods, and they take off.

With them gone, I turn back to Millie. Her eyebrows are scrunched again, and it's adorable. "Your mom stopped by this morning."

Inwardly I cringe. "Sorry, she stopped me when I got home."

"That's what she said."

"She's dealt with this sort of thing at work before. Are you mad I told her?"

"No, how could I be mad at you?" Millie's lips twitch like a half smile. "I don't think I thanked you for last night."

"No thanks necessary, ma'am." I give her what I hope is my most swoon-worthy smile and adjust my hat. She gives up the stern face and flashes me a lop-sided grin. Somehow, it's even more adorable than the scowl. "How ya holding up, Millie?" I say with more affection in my voice. I want to reach out to her, but I fidget with my glove instead.

Looking around the park, she says, "Oh, you know." I can tell she is going to try to play it cool. "Your mom gave me a lot to consider. I'm a little embarrassed it happened, but deep down, I know it's not my fault. I had bad feelings about the whole thing but went against my instinct. I'm also really embarrassed that I fell asleep on you." Now she is biting her lower lip and looking down.

Somehow, I find the courage to act on the feelings churning in my gut. "Come here," I say as I pull Millie into a hug. "Don't feel bad about that. I fell asleep, too." I don't add how much I enjoyed having her sleep on me.

She willingly comes to me, takes a deep breath, and says, "Thank you, Dalton. I don't know what I would have done without you last night."

I take a deep breath, too, hoping my next words don't ruin this moment. But when I see my next lesson show up, I have my out. And a way to see her again. I pull away and say, "There is something I need to tell you, but I can't right now." I nod toward the family that's getting out of the car. "What are you doing for later?"

Eyebrows raised, she says, "I'm spending the day at my grandma's," pointing to the pretty Victorian house on the other side of the park.

Disappointed, I say, "Okay, but I want to tell you tonight. Can I stop by when you get home?"

She smiles and agrees. Then she takes off, running another four laps while I try to concentrate on correcting everything this kid has been taught.

Chapter 6

~Millie

What's another mile at this point? I only just come down about last night, but now I'm just running to keep watching Dalton. Was he flirting back with Britney Shaefer? Did I read last night wrong? Is that what he wants to talk about tonight? So I keep running for however long it takes to calm my mind.

I get in that cadence of only feeling what my body needs. I'm not sure what is louder in my ears, my heartbeat or breathing. When I round to my grandmother's backyard, I crash into the cool grass and stare up at the sky. Despite my emotions, it is a beautiful day; only a few white puffy clouds break up the endless clear blue yonder. Once my panting subsides, I stretch and head inside.

Grandma gets home while I am standing under the hot spray of the shower, cueing me to finally get out.

"Have you eaten, dear?" Grams asks as I walk out of the bathroom.

"Na, I haven't even thought about food."

Grams stops looking at her newspaper and looks me up and down. "Sit down, and I'll make you a sandwich while you tell me all about your date."

If reading between the lines could be a superpower, my grandmother is a hero. Her food sure tastes magical when you are down about something.

"Well, the date didn't go so well." I cringe, not sure how much I want to tell her. Clutching the bag stuffed with my ruined dress, I choke, "Bobby wanted more from our time together than I did." I trust Gram completely, so I don't hold back. I tell her about the staged setup, all the lewd comments Bobby and his buddies said to me, every perverted touch Bobby attempted, the car ride home, the confrontation at my door, and how Dalton saved me from things I don't even want to imagine. By the time I am done, tears are running down my face, and I show her my dress.

Grandma is very still for a minute. Her hand rests on mine, and her soft grey eyes show worry as they caress me. "That boy sounds like a real piece of work," she says about Bobby.

She looks the dress over, tracing her fingers over every rip and tear. "This dress tells the story all on its own. Did you call the police, dear?"

"No. I know Bobby will just lie about what happened. The dress is the only evidence I have, and that could have all happened in the heat of passion. I know Bobby's dad is on the city council. Who is going to believe me over Bobby?"

"That's how my generation felt, but times have changed."

"Not enough. I'm afraid I will be dragged through the mud, and it will haunt me forever." I just want to forget about it, but here I am, reliving it all over.

"What about the neighbor boy? He is a witness."

"Dalton," I sigh, "His name is Dalton James." I must give something away, just saying his name because Grandma picks up on it.

"Tell me more about him. You like him, don't you? I can tell by the twinkle in your eyes."

She winks at me, and I gush to her about the rest of my night. How perfect and safe it felt to hang out with Dalton, and I fell asleep with his arm around me.

Grandma smiles warmly for the first time since I began my story. Her eyes are bright when she says, "Dalton sounds like a keeper."

"I'm not even sure he's interested, Grandma," I say with a sigh.

"Oh honey, of course he is, and why wouldn't he be? He didn't have to sit with you like that on the same sofa until you fell asleep, dear." She has a point, I suppose.

At the end of our Scrabble game, Grandma surprises me. "I have a great idea!"

"What's that?"

"Let's go get cell phones."

This tickles me pink—my anti-tech grandmother with a cell phone! The laughter this gives me shakes my worries away. "Grandma Bea, I thought you were against those newfangled gadgets?"

"Well, my friend Susan got one from her daughter, and we have had so much fun with it."

Dalton knocks on my door shortly after I get home. Instead of the tracksuits he usually wears, he's in jeans, a plain light blue t-shirt, and a flannel. It's a typical casual look on most guys, but since it's Dalton, he looks HOT. The shirt makes his blue eyes stand out. He even skipped the hat and styled his super-short hair with a little gel. I stand in the open doorway, a little stunned.

Dalton's strong jaw frames his crooked grin, and it only takes one word, "Hi," to make me swoon.

"Hi," I answer back, not moving. I wanted to play it cool, but I don't think I'm very successful.

He chuckles and asks, "Can I come in, or do you want to go somewhere?"

"Oh, come in." I move out of the way, and a whiff of CK1 clouds my senses as he passes. "If you want to go somewhere, we can. My parents are still out of town," then remembering the last guy that knew I was home alone didn't have good intentions. I add, "But they are due back at ten." I mentally kick myself. Dalton is not that guy; I can trust him.

"We can just stay in," he says with a poker face. Does he want to hide from the world, like I do? I even avoided my best friends today, only calling Angie and Dani briefly to give them my new number and a heads-up about what Bobby did before any rumors spread.

"Would you like something to drink? Or anything to eat?" I offer.

He shrugs his shoulders slightly and says, "I'm a guy; I can always eat."

With that, I lead the way to the kitchen, where we check the pantry and fridge, agreeing to make nachos. He doesn't talk, so I fill the void with nonsense about my this and that as he sits on a stool at the breakfast bar, watching me warm up the cheese. Then I join him on the seats so we can share.

"So, spill. What is it that you need to confess to?" Yep, cool is not in the cards for tonight.

He plays coy. "Confess? Why would you think I had something to confess?" Those blue eyes look so innocent as he raises his eyebrows at me.

I play along. "Ha! I didn't, but you just confirmed it. What is it, Dalton? Did you go through my bedroom after I fell asleep?" I am secretly nervous about that, especially with Dani's stalker talk.

He laughs at me but takes another chip before answering. "You want a confession?" He playfully pretends to think about it while he chews. "Let's see...., okay, I got one. My mom didn't make the cookies for the party."

Caught off guard, I say, "What? You lied to me about those delicious cookies!"

"I did. While my mother used to make the best cookies, the sad truth is she is too busy at work these days. Her skills are rusty, and the title has slipped." He says this in a tragic voice. "You deserve the truth, Millie, and I can't keep it from you any longer." Dalton pauses for a dramatic effect. "I made the cookies."

My stool tips over because I jump up so fast, but Dalton's quick reflexes enable him to grab it before it can hit the floor. "Get out of here!" I say. "Really?!" Then I go around the kitchen, pulling out bowls, flour, sugar, chocolate chips, and all the other ingredients I can remember off the top of my head to make cookies. Dalton shakes his head and laughs at me harder than I have ever heard him laugh before; it satisfies me in a way I didn't expect.

"What are you doing? Think you can prove me wrong?" he challenges.

"Nope, I just want cookies!" I grin at him like this is the most brilliant idea in the world.

The shortening is on the top shelf of the pantry, and I stain to reach it. I can just get my fingertips on it when it gets warm behind me, and a large hand grabs the can. I turn to face Dalton, realizing I am trapped between the shelves and his rock-hard body. Startled at the unexpected closeness, I stumble and brace myself with my hands on his chest—yep, exclamation point on ROCK-HARD.

Alarmed at the placement of my hands, I stare at them, willing them to move, but I'm frozen in place. Gradually my eyes rise to meet his, and he gazes back so intently that I feel like he is silently speaking to my soul. We stand there for what feels like an eternity with my chin tipped up and his head bent down.... when I can't stand the tension between us any longer, I ask, "Dalton?"

"Hmm?"

"Are you going to kiss me?" I blurt.

"I'm thinkin' about it," his deep rumbling tones send thrills through me just as much as their meaning.

"Think faster," I breathlessly plead.

His soft breath from a snigger brushes my cheek, but other than that, Dalton doesn't act on my encouragement. His gaze flickers between my eyes and lips and then back again—it's all so intense my eyes involuntarily shut. Only then does Dalton slowly close the last few inches between us, and I feel his mouth meet mine.

His lips are soft and almost hesitant, but when I kiss him back, the slow burn suddenly explodes and sparks fly. His arms wrap around me, and I take that as an invitation to touch him, too. Raising my arms, I run my fingers through his short, velvety hair, imagining its dark-honey color. It's all wet lip-smacking until I open the slightest bit more to run my tongue along his bottom lip. Immediately, Dalton repeats the movement, and when our tongues glide against each other, I melt into his arms just a bit more. I feel treasured in his embrace, as if this is where I am supposed to be for the rest of my life.

He stops kissing me but doesn't pull back. We are both breathing hard, and he presses his forehead to mine. Then he whispers, "You have no idea how long I have wanted to do that."

"I'm glad you finally did."

-Dalton

Millie zooms around the kitchen as if she can stump me on making cookies. She doesn't know that making cookies with my mom was as much of my childhood as playing baseball with my dad. Of course, he turned baseball into a career path for me, and by the time I was 12, I was only baking by myself.

It's no surprise that my height is going to be needed at some point on this ingredient hunt, so I am ready when Millie strains to get the Crisco. But something happens when she turns and touches my chest, a power I cannot deny, nor do I want to. I have wanted this moment with Millie since I first started thinking of girls as something more than aliens. And it has always been this girl—the one right across the street.

I went from not wanting to talk to her to not knowing how to talk to her. Now she is within reach, and no words are needed to tell her how I feel about her.

But how will she respond? I don't want to be rejected or, The Great Bambino forbid, be anything like what she went through last night.

I've never even kissed a girl, not like this, at least. The closest I have to experience is playing Spin-the-Bottle at Kyle's birthday party during our freshmen year. Kissing the girls there didn't count because I didn't have all the feelings for them that I have for Millie.

Millie's voice cuts through all my thoughts, "Dalton?"

Suddenly all I can think about are how clear her green eyes are. "Hmm?"

"Are you going to kiss me?" She asks as if she can hear my inner turmoil.

"I'm thinkin' about it."

"Think faster," she whispers, almost in a plea. It's amusing to me, but I'm still puzzling out how to do this right.

It's now or never, Dalton, I hear in my grandfather's voice and go for it. I kiss Millie Wilkins, like really, really kiss her. She lightly moans and molds herself to my body.

I feel a slow, cat-in-the-cream smile spread across my face. This night could not get any better. Warmth radiates from somewhere inside me. It's almost a buzzing; it starts in my chest and burns down my arms, making my fingers tingle. Is this euphoria? Because I couldn't imagine anything giving me a greater high than being able to hold and kiss this girl.

"I have another confession," I say, feeling a bit sheepish.

Breathlessly, she answers, "Yeah?"

"I kissed you last night too, but it was only on your forehead." I pause to make sure she isn't upset.

Millie still has her hands on my neck and pulls me back in for another kiss. Nope, not mad, then. This kiss is shorter but just as intense.

After, she puts her head on my chest, and we cling to each other. "Having you kiss me back is way better," I tell her; my voice is low and just a bit raw with emotion. Considering where she is resting her head, I'm sure she can hear my heart racing.....and I'm aware she might feel the other parts of my body reacting to our closeness.

I ask, "Do you still want to make cookies?"

"Hmmm. That is a tough decision. I do want cookies," Millie hesitates, biting her lip, enticing me to kiss her again, "but I think I like this better. Wanna see what's on TV?"

"Sure. We'll make cookies another time," I promise.

We walk back to the family room, fingers entwined, and sit on the couch. We're in the same position as last night, her head on my chest and my arm around her. She asks if there is anything, in particular, I want to watch as she turns on the TV and flips through the channels, but I am thinking more about how I feel at this moment than what we are watching. I'm on cloud nine.

This is what Gramps wanted me to man up for, what has been missing in my life. He always told me he knew Grandma was the only woman for him from the moment they met. He was a big believer in not wasting time because you never knew how long you would have on this earth. I never knew my grandmother because she passed away before I was born.

After an hour or so of comfortable silence, I ask, "What did you do with your grandma today?"

Laughing, Millie sits up. Instantly I miss her warmth, but her eyes are full of mirth, and I'm interested to see where this is going. "We got cell phones!" She leans to grab the bag on the other end of the couch and pulls out a phone. "I can even play some kind of worm game on it."

"Mine has that game."

"You have a cell phone, too? Give me your number; I want to add you to my contacts." Her excitement is adorable, and I find that I'm inordinately pleased she wants my number.

"I got it so I can keep in contact more easily with the parents of the kids I work with." I give her my number, and suddenly my phone rings in my pocket.

"Now you have my number," she says, the smile on her face playful. "I got to pick it. The last four numbers are 2181, my birthday. I'm going to keep this number forever!" Settling back in against me, she asks, "When's your birthday?"

"August 8th. I turned ten the day before we broke your arm," I say, stroking the long-ago-healed arm.

She picks up her head and looks at me. "How did I not know that?"

"The only way you would have known is if my mom told you." Mom had been sad that I didn't have any friends here yet, and I had been going stir-crazy in that house. She kept telling me to go out and meet the kids in the neighborhood, but I was too shy. "Anyway, eight is my lucky number, and I have always insisted that my jersey number is 88."

She seems deep in thought for a few minutes, then asks, "You like coaching kids?"

"Hell yeah. Kids are fun. They always make me laugh, too. I have one boy who is as smart as a whip and constantly has a sarcastic comeback. Like I'll say, 'What's up?' and he will answer, 'The sky.' Lessons are good because, one-on-one, I can focus on what the kid needs to improve. I'm an assistant coach for the little league, too. That's more fun because you get the dynamic of a team of boys. I used to ump for the city, but the parents were brutal. They always think their kid can do no wrong and that they have a better view than me when they are behind me looking through a fence." I bring my hand to my face and shake my head, thinking of some of the things that get yelled.

She asks, "Is it just boys? No girls allowed?"

"There are a few girls every year, but most girls usually like to play with a big yellow ball." She looks confused. "Softball," I say with a wink.

"Oh, duh." She grins and looks embarrassed. "I liked that unit in gym class, but not all the balls were yellow."

"No, you can probably buy them in any color you want these days, but neon yellow is the most common."

"When's your next game? I want to come," she says, then quickly adds, "If that's okay with you."

I can't hold in the grin that splits my face. "I'd like that. We have a tournament next Saturday; the first game is at 9 a.m., but we'll probably play four or five games, depending on how we do."

"I have a meet that day, but I should be able to make it before your last game." Then she holds up her new phone, "And I can call you to get more details when I'm done."

"That sounds great."

"Can you hang out again before then?" she asks.

As if there's anything I would like to do more. "Of course." I give her a little squeeze, pulling her in for another kiss. I'm not sure life gets better than this.

I don't want this night to end, but there is school tomorrow, and her parents will return soon. In a serious tone, I say, "There is something I need to tell you, and it might change your mind."

"So, the cookie confession wasn't what you came over tonight to talk about," she says in a mock shocked tone, but then she sees my face, and the smile that had started freezes, half-formed.

"No, but it was an easier confession." I look away for a moment, trying to figure out how to say this in the gentlest way possible.

I'm nervous, so I sit up, ready to leave if this goes badly.

She sits up, too, takes my hand, and says, "It can't be that bad." She tells me, but I can hear in her tone that she is also looking for some reassurance.

I take a deep breath and look straight into her eyes. If I don't tell her, she will hear it from someone else. "There was a rumor I heard—before everything happened. Bobby was going around telling everyone he was going to," I don't want to use the word I'm sure Bobby used, "screw you after the dance." I inwardly cringe because I know my phrasing isn't much better. "There was a bet, but he was so sure of himself because he knew your parents would be gone, and you would be home alone."

Millie's eyes fill up, and for a moment, I think she will break down. Her hand slackens in mine. She takes a deep breath, sits up a bit straighter, and gives her head a small shake. The tears don't fall. She grabs my hand again. "That is not your fault, Dalton. That is Bobby's, and I guess mine." She looks deeply into my eyes, and the whole thing becomes even harder. "Why would you think I would be mad at you for it?" she asks me.

I look down at our entwined fingers. This sucks so much. "Because I knew before he took you out."

Her eyebrows shoot up just before her legs do. She lets go of my hand and stands up. "You're saying you could have prevented it? All of it?"

With my hands free, I cover my face and look down at the floor before I continue, "Nate Rodgers told me Saturday afternoon. I was going to tell you, but when I got home from the game, the dickwad was already here. Your grandma was taking pictures. I just watched him take you out, knowing his plans."

"I see I have some things to think about," she finally manages to say.

I nod and, without really looking at her, head for the door. Quietly I make my last confession, "That's why I was here so quickly when you got home. I sat and waited for you. I didn't know he was going to be so forceful. It looked like everything was going okay when you left..... I didn't want to intrude."

I open the door and risk one glance back. The happy girl I was kissing earlier is gone, and tears are now coursing down her face.

Millie finally makes eye contact with me again. "Thanks for telling me," she says in a tone that I can't read. Her expression is now closed and guarded.

I let myself out, turning to say, "I'm so sorry," but the door has already shut, and I hear the deadbolt click.

That may have been the shortest relationship in the history of the world. Maybe I shouldn't have told her... No, I should have punched Bobby's perfect face off as soon as I found out about his plans.

All alone, I walk across the street, back to the house that should feel like home.

Chapter 7

-Dalton

I wake up feeling terrible physically as well as emotionally. I'm sure it doesn't have anything to do with my extra hard workout at 10:00 p.m. because I was so pissed at how my date with Millie went.

The lowest level of our split-level home is an exercise room, so I was able to go at it for hours. I'm moving slowly because of it, but I still manage to get to school on time.

My first period is public speaking. Millie is in the same class, sitting in the front row. Per usual, I claim a desk in the back and have my hat pulled down low over my eyes. Mr. Parker tells us about our upcoming assignment, listing the requirements on the whiteboard. I jot down a few notes and get to work on it until the bell rings. I hang back, but Millie walks out the door like she doesn't see me.

Like I don't exist.

Like we didn't share the last two nights together.

That is pretty much how the whole day goes. It's like before the senior bonfire, only worse—at least she used to make eye contact and give me a small smile.

I watch Millie at lunch, but she's unapproachable. She's at a small table with her friends, and they are in deep, whispered conversation the whole time. Every now and then, the one I can never remember the name of will look at me with sad eyes. The other friend, Danika Parrish, scowls at every guy in the room. Yikes, I do not want to get on her wrong side.

I'm crap at practice—lack of sleep and sore muscles. Kyle comes up to razz me about it as we are leaving. "Dude, what is up with you? I've seen freshmen perform better." I make a half-hearted retort about him needing glasses. He laughs, slaps me on the back, and gets in his car, oblivious to what is really going on.

Jason is, unfortunately, more observant.

"I know that look. Someone finally has girl problems," Jason says with a commiserating grin. I look straight at him and say nothing, loading my gear in my truck. Suddenly there seem to be more guys around than there were just a moment ago. I hear a couple laugh, and someone makes a comment about girls being more work than they are worth. This is not how I wanted my afternoon to go.

Nate steps in to save me from my tormentors, "What's up, bro? Wanna grab a burger? After those drills, I think I need some fries and maybe a big milkshake too."

"Aiight! Miss Patti's Diner?" Jason chimes in, inviting himself.

"Sure, meet ya there in an hour," I reluctantly agree, giving myself time to get home and shower.

Maybe it won't be so bad. Miss Patti's does have amazing burgers, and their malted chocolate milkshake is, hands down, the best thing in town.

At the diner, I confide in the guys about what went down with Bobby on Saturday night. I don't share the parts about cuddling or kissing because that isn't public info. I can't just leave it at chasing Bobby away, though, so I simply say that I hung out with Millie Saturday and Sunday.

"You like her, then?" Jason asks.

Nate slaps him across the back of the head, "Of course he does, dumb ass."

"Ow!" Jason says and rubs the back of his head. "I heard about the bet, too. Didn't know it reached a hundo."

"Did either of you see Bobby today?" I ask.

"Nope," they both say in unison.

"Let me know what you hear. If Stevens starts running his mouth, I want to know," I tell them. They both fist-bump me in return with their promise. They might be a bit obnoxious at times, but Nate and Jason are good guys.

"That's a good story you tell, DJ, but that doesn't tell me why you're having woman trouble," Jason says.

"Or why you played like crap today," Nate quips.

Okay, so maybe they are more than a bit obnoxious. And just too observant.

Nate continues like he wasn't interrupted, "If you got to hang out with her again on Sunday, that's a good thing, right? What went wrong?"

"It was.... until I told her I knew about the bet. How I could have stopped her before she left," I admit.

"Damn," Jason says, shaking his head. "Why'd you go and tell her that?"

"I don't know," I say with exasperation, throwing up my hands. "Maybe because I like Millie, and if I want to have a relationship with her, it should be open and honest." Unlike the example my parents have set. Bad role models still teach good lessons.

Cool, calm, and collected, Nate says, "And there it is." He has a stupid gloating look on his face.

"Where what is?" I ask, not entirely positive I want his answer.

"You sure you didn't do more than hang out? You sound invested," Nate says, placing extra emphasis on "invested."

Jason slaps the table. "Did I miss something? You aren't holding back the good details of this story, are you, DJ?"

Yeah, really obnoxious.

"Don't call me that. I hate that nickname," is all I can say without incriminating myself. I'm getting angry again, and I don't kiss and tell.

Thankfully, that's when our food arrives. The waitress is my student, Benny's sister. Becky? Bethany? No, wait, her name is Britney. She passes out our burgers and asks if there is anything else that she can get us. She isn't the waitress that took our order, so she's surprised to see me at the table. Cheerily, she says, "Oh, hey, Dalton."

"Hey," I reply. I can't even fake any enthusiasm.

"Hel-lo" comes from Jason, definitely not faking his interest.

Britney mostly ignores Romeo here next to me but doesn't leave. Instead, she fidgets, brushing at her apron and tucking her hair behind her ear, obviously gearing up for something. "So, um, are you seeing Millie?"

I'm taken totally off guard, and my head snaps up, meeting her eyes for the first time. I quickly school my face, though, and look at her with a blank expression instead of answering.

"Well, I was just wondering—because I saw you two hugging, and if you aren't with her or anyone else, I would...."

Before she can finish, our original waitress steps in and asks us how everything is while shooting Britney a you're-in-for-it-now-quit-bugging-the-customers glare. Then she pulls the poor girl back to the kitchen with her. They aren't entirely hidden by the doorframe, and I can see Britney getting her ass chewed out. Now that she's out of my hair, I feel bad for her.

"Damn, Dalton," Jason says. "That girl is fine and into you, too. I think you should ditch the neighbor drama and take out that sweet ass." Okay, Jason is the more obnoxious one.

Nate kicks Jason under the table. "Shut it, Jay." Then to me, he asks, "So when did our fine-lookin' waitress see you huggin' Millie?"

Busted. "She's the sister of one of my players. I hugged Millie at the park after his lesson. They must not have left yet."

Jason gives me a look. "I know you're still holding out on us, dude," Jason tells me, but the food is hot and more tempting than gossip.

We scarf down our dinner and take off. I carefully avoid Britney. I don't know where I stand with Millie, but I know I'm not interested in anyone else.

It's dark when we leave the restaurant, and I'm nearing my truck when I recognize Bobby's car parked on the street.

There's a shuffle behind me, and I turn just in time to dodge a baseball bat to the back of my head. As I regain my balance, I feel a blow to the gut. Lucky for me, Bobby doesn't get a full swing coming back at me.

I'm in pain, but I fully anticipate his third strike.

Distantly I hear someone, Jason, maybe, shout, "Dalton, look out!"

Before Bobby can connect the bat to my hip, I step in towards him and punch his face. My right hook is as strong as Gramps taught me to use. As a veteran of war, he wasn't keen on fighting and told me he had seen enough violence to last him three lifetimes. But he also said every man needs to know how to defend himself.

I grab the middle of the bat, overpowering Bobby for control. When he doesn't let go, I clinch the end by his hands, giving me leverage to push my weight against him, using the bat crosswise to pin him against the hood of my truck.

"What the fuck do you think you are doing, Bobby?" I snarl.

Bobby struggles to get free, but I outweigh him by a good twenty pounds. "You owe me, James," he grunts out. "If it wasn't for you, I..., I,"

Nate's voice calls out, "Hey, what's going on? Dalton, you okay?"

Then Jason exclaims, "Holy shit! Is that Bobby?"

My attention is entirely on the scum beneath me. "You want to finish that sentence?" I pause, offering him a chance to tell everyone what a bet-losing rapist he almost became. "Didn't think so."

Nate's voice is closer now. "Let him go, Dalton. He isn't worth it."

Oh, but it is. Between clenched teeth, I say, "I don't owe you shit, asshole. Unless you want me to give you the ass-kicking that I should have given you Saturday night." I push down on him a little more.

Bobby struggles and whimpers. He knows I'm proving what a weak little douche he is.

"Hell yeah! Do it, Dalton! Open that can of whoop-ass!" Jason cheers.

I stare down into Bobby's frightened face. The eye I hit is already swelling. I want what Jason says so bad. The kid deserves much worse than a bruise and being pinned down. Filled with a rage that I'm only barely containing, I speak so quietly that only he can hear. "Is this what you wanted to do to Millie? Hold her down so you could have your way with her?" I punch him again, breaking his nose this time.

He gasps in pain, letting go of the bat to hold his bleeding nose.

My hands are shaking, and my voice crescendos when I growl out, "Because of a fucking bet?!"

I hear more voices, and I feel a hand on my back. Without letting Bobby up, I look over my shoulder at Nate.

Nate sounds like an adult, a voice of reason. "Dalton, let him go. What he did was wrong, but violence isn't going to make it any better."

I respect the Hell out of Nate. Otherwise, my body wouldn't back down so easily. As my tunnel vision starts to dissipate, I notice the crowd of onlookers. I give Nate the bat, step back, and look down at Bobby. He is disheveled, blood trickling down his face, hair standing at odd angles, shirt half untucked, and a piss stain on his khakis.

With Nate in control of the weapon, he steps between us to end the fight. Bobby manages to scurry away to his car. He peels out into traffic, almost sideswiping a minivan.

I hear Jason holler, "Boo-yah!" at Bobby's retreat.

Without a word to either of my friends, I nod to Nate and get in my truck.

Chapter 8

~Millie

"**I** refuse to let you play the victim," Danika, my assertive best friend demands.

"I'm not," I mutter.

"Yeah, because you had a hero rush to your rescue," Angie says with moons in her eyes.

"She didn't need a hero, Angie; she would have taken care of it if he didn't show up."

"Guys, quit talking about me as if I'm not here," I beg. "And please drop the subject; I am so sick of rehashing it." I've tried keeping my head low and focusing on school; that is all I want to concentrate on right now. I just wish the whole thing would go away.

"I'm just saying," Danika crosses her arms and leans back in her chair, "Bobby better not cross my path, or his balls will match his eyes."

Thankfully, Bobby wasn't here on Monday or Tuesday, but today (Wednesday), he came to school with two black eyes and a taped nose. One rumor is that he couldn't pay up on his bet to screw me, so he got his ass kicked. Another is that Dalton beat him up, fighting over me. Someone else said he wrecked his dad's car. None (that I have heard, anyway) are about me sleeping with him.

I ignore anyone that asks me questions. Danika and Angie are my only confidants, and they are sworn to secrecy. The gossip train has traveled through the teachers all the way to my mom, who teaches 5th grade in a different school. I had already told her, though, when they got home Sunday night. Bobby's reputation isn't so squeaky clean anymore.

I'm still avoiding Dalton, despite the fact that I know he didn't do anything wrong. But I just haven't let my guard down yet. I know I'm going to cave soon. We only hung out twice, but I miss him.

Angie is Dalton's biggest champion, and she keeps trying to get me to talk to him. Dani hates all boys on principal now and wants the three of us to enroll in self-defense classes.

The longest week of my life is over, it's Friday, and I'm getting ready to go out to dinner with my parents (because there is no way I am going to the high school football game) when the doorbell rings. I'm sitting in the living room, playing Worm on my phone, so I'm the closest to answer the door.

I open to find someone dropped something off, and he's running away. One inhale, and I can smell what has been dropped off—cookies. Fresh-baked. Chocolate. Chip. Cookies.

I call out to Dalton, who is running back home. "Hey, you just gonna ding-dong-dash me?"

He stops, turns, and walks back. I pick up the plate and see the note, "Sorry."

Standing at the base of the stairs, he says, "Mrs. Bailey is all out of flowers for the year. I had to improvise." He is a sight for sore eyes in his track pants, hoodie, and ball cap. It's pretty much what he always wears; if I hadn't seen him Sunday night, I wouldn't have known he owned anything else.

I bite into a cookie; it's pure bliss. "Yummm, these are perfect. Flowers don't taste nearly as good."

He smiles and says the very thing that has been on my mind, "I miss you. I know that must sound weird 'cause we didn't really spend that much time together."

I walk to the steps where I'm slightly taller than him on the ground. "I know what you mean. I miss you, too."

He takes one step up. "Do you forgive me, Millie?"

"There's nothing to forgive. You didn't know how it would play out, and when you saw it going bad, you jumped in and stopped it." I wrap my arms around his neck and hug him, and he squeezes me back. "I'm sorry I didn't talk to you this week."

Still standing on the stairs hugging, my dad comes around the house. He passes us on the stairs and steals one of my cookies. Then he goes inside. Dalton and I laugh—I think it's the first laugh I've had this week.

My mother opens the door saying, "Well, who's at the door?"

Dalton pulls back and answers, "Hello, Mrs. Wilkins."

"Hello, Dalton. We were just about to head out for dinner. Would you like to join us?" She looks back and forth between us, "Or do you have other plans now, Millie?

"Umm," I look back at Dalton. He seems a little panicked. "I think we'll just order a pizza." He looks back at me with relief in his eyes.

Mom smiles, "Okay, you two have a good evening. And Dalton?"

"Yeah?"

"Thank you for, well, you know." Then she turns back inside. A few moments later, they are driving away.

"Want to come inside? We don't have to order pizza."

Following me in, he says, "Pizza's good, but let's go out."

"Alright, but not the game," I request. "I don't want to be harassed by the gossip train." Dalton stands in deep thought for a moment, and I repeat my words back to myself. "Shit, that came out wrong. This week has been nonstop, with stupid questions that I don't want to answer or correct. It has nothing to do with being seen with you."

A slight nod of acknowledgment or agreement, I'm not sure which, is Dalton's reply. We really need to work on his verbal skills. Then he holds out his hand and speaks. "Come on, I know just where to go."

"Where?" I ask as I slip my palm into his.

"First pizza, then I'm going to take you where I like to go after a rough week."

Intrigued, I follow him across the street to his truck. He calls in an order for a pepperoni pizza for pickup. Then we hit the road, first to get our food—which we eat on our way to the mystery location. There isn't much conversation, so I sing along with the radio. Dalton's lips move to the music, but he isn't belting it out like I am.

We are on the edge of town when he pulls down a long gravel driveway and parks in front of a warehouse. "Um, Dalton?"

Turning off the engine, Dalton says, "Don't worry, I've got keys," as he twirls the key ring around his finger.

"That doesn't exactly reassure me." I stay put, watching Dalton shake his head with a grin as he walks around the front of the truck to my door to open it.

"Come on," he says without moving out of my way.

I pivot so that my legs are dangling, but he still obstructs my path. "Where do you expect me to go? You are blocking my way." Before I finish my sentence, Dalton's hands are on my waist, assisting me down. It's not necessary, we both know it, the drop isn't high from this pickup, but the gesture crosses that invisible barrier of not touching to an intimate closeness that he must be craving as much as I am.

Looking up into those incredible violet irises, I expect him to kiss me. Instead, his lips twitch into a smirk. "What's the matter, Millie? Don't you trust me—out here, all alone?"

"After the week I've had?"

"Touché. Here," he reaches into the bed of the truck, pulls a bat out of a duffle bag, and hands it to me, "now you have protection." Something tells me that's not the kind of protection I'll need if I keep hanging out with Dalton.

-Dalton

My cheeks burn from that little Freudian slip, so I grab the bucket of balls and tee as if nothing is amiss.

"What's all that?" Millie asks. She really has no clue about baseball, does she?

"What's with the 20 questions?" I walk to the door, unlock it, and hold it open for her to follow me in. There is one light that we always leave on, but it's pretty dark in here. I would probably be hesitant if I were her too.

"You don't talk much," she whines, gripping the bat with both hands across her chest. "Do you expect me to read your mind?"

"I don't know," I mumble, turning the lights on to the whole warehouse with one switch. In the light, you can see the nets, equipment, couch, and kitchenette. What you don't see is all the blood, sweat, and tears or the hours I have put in under this roof. "Welcome to the Batcave."

"Batting cages?"

"Yep."

"Umm, you know I am not coordinated enough to hit a ball, right? I can't even catch one."

"You doubt my coaching ability?" That shuts her up. "We will start by hitting off the tee."

Millie still looks unsure after I get everything all set up. For a good reason, too; she really is terrible. She swings and misses, and swings and misses.... more times than I can count.

"Like this," I demonstrate.

"You make it look too easy."

"It is easy."

"Not for me."

A lightbulb clicks on in my head. I don't know why I didn't think of it earlier. She isn't a student; there aren't the same boundaries that I have with the boys. "Here," I call her back to the tee. But this time, I stand at her back, and we swing the bat together. Feeling her move with me, especially her hips... I clear my throat and step back. That is not why we are here.... alone. I set the next ball up for her to hit on her own, and she hits it. "Wazir of Wham, you got it!"

Laughing, she asks, "What did you just say?"

"Wazir of Wham," I repeat with less enthusiasm. "It was one of Babe Ruth's nicknames. I guess it's kind of a weird habit, but

Gramps used to get after me for taking the Lord's name in vain, so I started using The Babe's nicknames."

"Oh... that's... creative."

Yep, she thinks I'm a weirdo. "What did you think about that time? Before you hit."

"I don't know. I guess I was just imagining what you showed me and trying to replicate it."

"That's good, but it's not what I really brought you here for."

"It's not?"

Shaking my head, I tell her, "This is what I do to clear my head, and I can take all my aggression out on the ball."

"This time, I want you to try that. Think of a problem and hit it away."

Millie winds back like she is going to hit a whopper, and she misses, hitting the tee instead of the ball. I chuckle. "Feel better?"

Millie nods. "Again."

I set the tee back up with a ball, and she swings with all her might again. We do this ten more times. She is panting, and I'm starting to fear for my tee.

"Better than therapy, isn't it?"

"I don't know; I think I still prefer running." A shit-eating grin spreads across her face. "But imagining Bobby's face on that ball felt pretty good."

"I hope that was one of the times you actually hit the ball."

Millie's laugh is incredible. "I don't even know; I just wish I could actually do that."

"Do what? Smash his face in?"

"Yeah....but apparently someone already did that." A long pause passes without any word from me, but it must be written on my face because Millie's jaw hits the floor. "So that rumor was true?"

Balls are scattered all around us, so I start picking up, and Millie joins me. Finally, I confess, "Losing control wasn't something I'm proud of, but yeah, hitting that son-of-a-bitch was one of the highlights of my week, and I refuse to feel guilty for it."

Millie's voice is weak, but I can hear her clearly, "You got in a fistfight with Bobby over me?"

"Why does that surprise you?" We are face to face, about a foot apart, and suddenly it feels really hot and heavy in this big empty building.

Millie's eyes are wide and glossy. "I don't want you getting in fights because of me."

Shrugging it off, I try to look away; what were we doing before everything got serious? "He came at me first, and I ended it for good."

Her hand clasps around my forearm. "I mean it. If you got hurt because of me," she shakes her head with her mouth ajar like she can't finish her sentence and exhales.

"Millie," looking into her pale green eyes, I want to tell her I already hurt—I hurt *for* her. But that isn't something a man can say.

"Dalton, think faster," Millie taunts.

"Oh, I'm thinking plenty fast. I just know how you react when someone you don't like kisses you, and now you have a bat." Is it too soon to joke about it? I chuckle nervously.

Millie rolls her lips together as if she is fighting a smile. "But you also know how I reacted when the guy I like kissed me."

In a million years, I did not expect to hear that, and it makes me a little lightheaded. "The guy you like?"

Red flushes Millie's face, and she lets go of my arm to fiddle with a lock of hair. She is also biting her lower lip so hard that I should rescue it before there is a hole, and I do, with my thumb.

Then I slide my palm to the back of her head, threading my fingers in her hair to urge her face closer to mine and claim the lips that haunt my dreams.

Chapter 9

~Millie

The lock on the bathroom door doesn't lock, but I guess it's just Dalton and me here. And when I wash my hands, the water is ice cold, like it doesn't get used often.

I walk out to ask Dalton about this place, but I get sidetracked when I see him hitting balls off an automatic pitching machine. His movements are as smooth and graceful as a dancer's. Is it weird to compare him to a dancer? Shaking that thought away, I watch Dalton hit ball after ball, and each flies away from a perfect hit.

Dalton shed his hoodie while I was in the bathroom, and the t-shirt he has on is fitted, but the sleeves are creeping up due to the fact that his arm muscles are bulging..., and that isn't the only bulge I see. Suddenly I'm a big fan of track pants because they show everything—and I mean *everything*. While Dalton's ass is mesmerizing, especially with the sway of his hips, another part of his anatomy has my attention.

I am a dirty, dirty perve.

When the machine is out of balls, Dalton turns to me. His chest rapidly rises and falls, and his skin shines under the lights from perspiration. As soon as his eyes land on me, he grins with radiance, making me blush.

"Do we need to pick up?" I ask.

"Na, I'll get it later."

"We can do it now. I don't want you to get in trouble for us being here after hours."

Dalton chuckles, "In trouble with who?"

"Whoever owns it," I look around the large empty space.

"You mean my dad, who doesn't come out here unless he wants to bust my balls?" My eyebrows shoot up at that, and Dalton cringes. "I mean, when he wants to tell me I can't live up to his dreams."

"I'm not sure that's much better. Are you saying this is your own personal clubhouse?" That actually explains a lot.

"Yep. Dad bought the land with the building on it ages ago and fixed it up for a place I could train all year round."

"Wow."

"Yeah, there are nicer batting cages, but they can be crowded, and you said you didn't want to be around people. So, I brought you to my secret hideout."

I approach the trophy cases, realizing they are all Dalton's trophies. Holy shit. There is a second case filled with awards for Michael James; Dalton's father must have also been a big-shot baseball player when he was young. "Do you get trophies at all of your tournaments?"

Dalton shrugs, "Depends how good we do." His hands are hot and sweaty, and when he takes my hand. The heat travels all the way up my arm and through my whole body, causing me to shiver. "You cold?"

76

"Not really."

"Don't be silly; you have goosebumps." Dalton lets go of my hand and jogs back to where he was batting moments before. The sudden absence of heat gives me chills. Great, now I am cold.

Dalton returns in less than a minute, his hoodie in hand. Without waiting for my approval, he plops it over my head. I'm lost in a dark sea that smells like cologne and detergent—I'm sure there are other things, too, like sweat and deodorant. Summed up, it's purely Dalton-scented. It makes me feel safe and warm... and dizzy in the best way.

My head emerges from the neck hole, hair stuck to my face, and Dalton attempts to push back the unruly tendrils that slipped from my ponytail while I slide my arms in the oversized sleeves. Once he has dubbed me free enough, he gives me a quick peck on the lips. At least he didn't need an invitation this time.

Continuing to play with my hair, Dalton asks, "Better?"

"Yeah, thanks. I'll give it back when we get home."

"Don't worry about it." With a slight yank on my ponytail, my curls are released. "I'll just keep this for collateral." Dalton holds up his wrist with my lemon-yellow scrunchie. "Let's go."

When we step outside, I'm instantly thankful for the warmth of Dalton's sweatshirt. With a big shiver, I hunch my shoulders and tuck my nose in the neck hole, taking in the intoxicating smell of Dalton while he locks up. As soon as we are in the truck, I crank the heat as high as it will go, and he laughs at me.

"What? Aren't you cold?"

"Maybe a bit." Dalton holds out his forearm and flexes, turning it back and forth. His hair is standing up with goosebumps, but that isn't what catches my eye—his arms are *ripped*. I've never imagined forearms could be sexy until now. How have I never noticed that? I want to trail my fingers along his muscles, but they are currently bawled in fists and tucked inside the sweatshirt..., and I'm chickenshit.

Forcing my focus away, before I do something to embarrass myself, I start flipping through the channels on the radio until I find something worth signing along to.

The drive home is shorter than the ride out, and when we get back to our neighborhood, Dalton parks on the street instead of his driveway. Wings flutter in my tummy as he walks me to my door. "I guess I should give this back to you now," I start to take off the hoodie. "Thanks for letting me borrow it."

Large hands grab the hem of the sweatshirt on either side of my body, making me freeze instantly. Dalton tugs the shirt down, and his hands linger loosely at my waist. "Don't worry about it. I have more hoodies. Besides, it'll probably get cold at my game tomorrow; you can wear it then." He clears his throat, "That is if you're still going."

My lips creep up into a grin. "Are you going to wear my scrunchy at the game too?"

With a cringe, Dalton says, "I don't have enough hair for a ponytail, and it might be against regulation to wear it on my wrist."

"I guess you'll have to get creative then," I challenge him, and then with all the bravery I can muster, I lean in on tip-toe and press my lips to his.

My intentions are to be quick, say goodnight, and go inside. But when Dalton's fingers curl around my waist, and he holds me close, my plans slide, and I fall deeper into the kiss.

Danika wrinkles her nose when I suggest we go to the baseball tournament in Kansas City. "Why would I want to go watch a bunch of pigheaded athletes play a game after spending most of the day with the same sort of meatheads?"

"Because she wants to see her knight in shining armor, Dani," Angie argues.

"He's not—ugh, whatever. If you both want to go, I will too," Dani agrees.

"I'm going either way, but thank you," I tell them.

"I will be your wing-woman anytime you want." Angie goes on, "You and Dalton are going to fall in love and live happily ever after. I just know it."

Angie's positivity makes me feel light and happy, but Dani rolls her eyes at our hopeless romantic friend.

We navigate our way through the ballpark. "Dalton said they are on field four."

"Okay, but let's stop at the concession stand first," Dani demands.

Evie James walks past us while we wait in line. "Millie," she leans in for some kind of hug/pat thing. "I'm glad you came."

"Hello, Mrs. James."

She smirks at me, but I can tell she wants to correct me for addressing her formally. "Let me get that for you girls."

"That's okay," I try to stop her, but it's too late, she pays, and Dani comments something about free food.

"Nonsense. Dalton's game is about to start over here." She pauses, "You are here to watch Dalton, right?"

"Yes, ma'am," Angie answers.

Walking with her to the bleachers, she quietly asks me, "So did you decide what to do about that little problem?"

"Yes. I'm not going to be a victim. Nothing happened, and I just want to forget about it." Besides, I have brighter things on the horizon.

"I can respect that, but can you live with any consequences that may happen from your decision?"

"Nothing happened," I repeat. "There won't be any consequences." Does she think more happened and that I'm pregnant?

Evie smiles, but it almost looks sad. I know she doesn't like the path I chose. "Maybe not for you."

I catch sight of Dalton warming up. I don't know how I know it's him from this distance; I just do. And when we get closer, I realize track pants have nothing on baseball pants.

-Dalton

While we wait in the dugout for the officials to start the game, Nate Rodgers asks, "Hey, man, did you see who just showed up?" He points to three girls sharing a blanket in the stands.

She showed up; Millie actually came to my game. I try to fight the feeling, but goosebumps still spread down my arms and legs, which have nothing to do with the drop in temps.

"Maybe they just came to see me," Nate says cockily, "Angie's kinda cute—so is Danika, but she kinda scares the shit out of me."

"Yeah, and what about Millie?" I ask.

"Oh, Millie is gorgeous, but I don't want you to beat me up like you did Stevens."

"You're my bro," I brush off his observation. "I wouldn't do that to you.... unless you touched her like he did."

Nate whistles, holding his palms up as if in surrender. "Memo received. So is Millie your girlfriend then?"

Completely clueless, I look at my buddy, "I don't know."

"I don't have experience in that department, but you should figure that out."

Jason butts in, "Figure what out?"

"If he and Millie are official," Nate answers. "Have you taken her out?"

"Sorta. I took her to my Batcave."

Jason gasps, "Dude, you promised to take me to the Batcave."

"Yeah, Zeek has been wanting to go, too," Nate adds, referring to his cousin. "He even drew up a poster of a wooden bat wearing a mask and cape for you to hang."

I snort at his antics. Nate is the one that named my barn the Batcave after I took him there in the spring, and it stuck. "Book a lesson, and I'll take you there."

"Oh, is that what you were doing with her at the Batcave?" Jason asks suggestively. "Giving her a *lesson*."

"Man, that's not cool," Nate chides. "Don't you remember pulling D off Stevens for talking smack about his girl?"

Ignoring that comment, I say, "I figured she needed to hit something after the week she had, so I turned it into a constructive activity."

"Dalton, don't take this the wrong way," Jason whispers, "but you sound like an old man. Please tell me you at least made out."

Jason calling me out for being an old man makes me think of Gramps, so I don't answer even though part of me wants to brag about all the sweet kisses Millie and I have shared.

"Look at his face!" Jason points and cheers, "That's a yes!" I try my best to wipe the silly smirk off my mug and glare at him.

"Well, Dalton, it's not a no," Nate argues. "But you took her to your secret spot, so I'm guessing there is more physical activity than you admit. Not to mention everyone knows you've had eyes for her for years."

"No kidding," Jason agrees. "We know where Dalton sits on the issue; the question is if Millie feels the same way."

"And she is here with her beautiful friends," Nate comments.

"WOULD YOU LIKE TO QUIT YACKING LIKE A
BUNCH OF LITTLE GIRLS AND TAKE THE FIELD?!"
Coach yells.

The three of us jump, grab our gloves, and run out of the
dugout with the rest of our team.

A little distracted, I miss the first ball off the bat. This is the
championship round; both teams have been undefeated today.
We will walk out of here as failures if I don't get my head in the
game. Even if Coach lets us rest tomorrow, Dad won't give me
the day off if we lose.

When I get up to bat, I can't help checking to see if Millie is
still in the stands and if she is wearing my sweatshirt like she
promised.

I have her hair thing in the pocket of my jacket. It's not on
show, but I have been fiddling with it between my games today
without anyone being the wiser.

"STRIKE ONE!" the ump yells, waking me from my brain
fog.

Shit, Dalton, get it together, I tell myself, stepping out of the
batter's box to shake it off. When I get back up to the plate, I
reposition and touch the tip of the bat in the dirt, scribbling an
M. If I get a hit, I'll grow a pair and ask her to be my girl. If I
miss...., fuck it, I'm not going to miss.

The ball flies out of the pitcher's hand. It looks like it will be
outside, but I know this kid has a wicked curve ball, and I'm
ready for it. The crack of the bat when they collide is music to
my ears. I start running at full speed, watching for the first base
coach's signal. He is mid-air from jumping, so I look to see where
the ball landed. The guys in the outfield are all the way back at
the fence, and their arms are waving that the ball went over.
Slowing my pace, I round the rest of the bases; it isn't until then
that I hear the crowd going wild. My eyes wander to Millie, who

is bouncing up and down with her friends—and she is definitely wearing my hoodie. That means something, right? She said she liked me, and she is wearing my sweatshirt for everyone to see.

A few rows away, Mom and Dad are sharing smiles for once. I don't have time to enjoy that for how much that means to me because my team has left the dugout to welcome me home.

It's an odd feeling, but I'm settled for the rest of the game. No nerves, just calm focus. Kinda what Dad harps about, but he seems to balance control against anger rather than anxiety. Of course, Gramps was never breathing down his throat.

The scoreboard reads 6:2 final; we won. The cheering is so loud that I might lose my hearing. There is a short awards ceremony that Millie stays for despite Danika looking pissed about it. Why is that girl always so bitchy?

Grabbing all my gear from the dugout, I sling my bat bag over my shoulder and set out to find Millie before her grumpy friend talks her into leaving. Luckily, I find Millie waiting for me, her friends a slight distance away.

"Hey," she says as I approach.

"Hey. You are my girlfriend, right?" I blurt out and feel my face burn from embarrassment. *Smooth, Dalton. Real smooth,* I chastise myself.

Millie's eyes are wide in shock, but she handles it better than I did. "Are you asking me if I want to be your girlfriend, or are you telling me I am your girlfriend?"

Nervously, I ask, "Do you want to be my girlfriend?"

"Yes," Millie answers with a brilliant smile.

"It's settled then. You're my girlfriend." To break the nervous tension, I grab my phone from my pocket, her hair-tie wound around it, and start punching buttons.

With a perturbed tone, Millie asks, "What are you doing?"

I show her she is now listed as 'Girlfriend' in my contacts. Without missing a beat, Millie jumps, wrapping her arms around my neck, and I catch her, clutching her to my body. Just as I'm about to kiss her, a catcall whistle rings through the air.

"I called it!" Nate hollers.

Chapter 10

-Dalton

Things with Millie have been going well—actually, make that fantastic. Our fall season sports ended shortly after we started dating. Now, we are both on the indoor track team, so we get to see and support each other even more. She still likes the long distances, while I'm only doing it to work on sprinting and speed. Most evenings, we spend at my house since there is hardly any parental supervision. We've gone out on several dates, even doubling with Nate and Angie once. They had a good time together but didn't hit it off as a couple.

Tonight, we are at my house working on our public speaking assignment. We have to write a paper about a person we admire in the career field we are interested in. Then, for our semester final, we will give a speech on him or her. This is easy for me, but not so much for Millie.

"UGH!!! This is so hard. Who did you pick again?" Millie asks.

"I picked George Herman Ruth, Jr," I reply.

"Okay, I'm guessing that is some famous baseball player?"

"That's it. We are done." I throw my hands up and lean back on the couch, exaggerating my dismay. "If you don't know him, you are no longer my girlfriend." It still makes me giddy to call her that. We have been dating for two months, and it hasn't gotten old.

She pouts out her lip and bats her eyes. "I can't get by on my looks; I have to have brains, too?" she teases.

"Hmmm, let's see. Are those lips good for anything else besides pouting?" I lean over to kiss her, sucking on that pouty lip, and soon our tongues are entangled. Then I try to cop-a-feel of her boob, but her sweatshirt is too bulky—because it's one of my hoodies. I swear she has more of my clothes in her closet than I do.

Millie giggles. "Is it my lips or something else you are interested in?"

Looking into her green eyes, I growl, "I am interested in all of you." I claim her mouth again.

First base is kissing, especially the open-mouthed tongue action I'm getting right now. I've even made it to second base on a handful of occasions, no pun intended. With that thought, I slide my hand up Millie's shirt and gently squeeze. Maybe tonight I can steal third.

"Dalton," Millie gasps, "we are supposed to be doing homework." Her lips find their way back to mine, contradicting her complaint.

"Nobody is here to stop us," I say between kisses.

"Not the point," she barely finishes the sentence because she is just as horny as me.

"Ten more minutes," I beg.

The papers on Millie's lap fall to the ground, and she shifts from sitting next to me to straddling my lap. Millie is wearing tight stretchy pants, and I'm in athletic joggers, so there are only thin layers of fabric between us. I can feel the depression between her legs, and I'm sure she can feel how hard I am beneath her.

Fuck, ten minutes are not going to be long enough.

With my hands still under her shirt, I lift my arms, thus pulling the shirt over her head.

Seeing Millie in a sheer, navy bra is breathtaking. "Oh, Millie," I murmur. She blushes, and a giggle emerges from deep in her throat. I feel her fingers run up my arms, over my shoulders, to the back of my neck, where she strokes up and down along my spine—it gives me tingles.

Wanting to make her feel the same, I trail my lips from her ear to her collarbone. Millie deeply inhales with a shutter, causing her chest to rise, and I take that as a cue to continue my journey south. When I reach her cleavage, I gently tug the flimsy fabric, exposing a rosie nipple.

Millie's fingers curl into fists behind my head, and she holds me close as I focus on that puckered bud. She moans, arching her back and rocking her hips. Shit, I'm not ready for her reaction, and I have to grab Millie's hips to stop her movement against my loaded bat. "If you keep doing that...."

"Don't stop," Millie pleads, and I know that she is as close as I am.

I would do anything for this girl; if that means cumming inside my pants and wearing it the rest of the evening, I'll do it with a smile.

My hands slide down to cup her ass, each cheek fitting perfectly in my palms. Then I guide her up and down against my erection until our bodies reach the ultimate peak of fulfillment.

Warmth spreads in my lap at a pulsing rate. Part of me is embarrassed, and the other is very pleased. That doesn't exactly count as getting to third base; more like an in-the-park home run. That's gotta be better, right? Millie and I tend to do things out of order anyway.

"I think our ten minutes are up," Millie teases.

Shrugging, I joke back, "I'm not the one struggling with the assignment."

Millie's jaw drops with a loud scoff. It's absolutely adorable, causing me to pull her chest against me and kiss her again.

All too suddenly, Millie pulls away in a gasp, "Oh, Ruth! You're doing your paper on 'Babe' Ruth!"

"And now you have brains, too." I wink at her, and we fall back together like magnets, only stopping when we hear the garage door open.

"Shit," we say in unison. Millie hops off my lap and scurries to put the hoodie back on.

I look down to see a wet stain on my warmups. "Agh, I need to change." With wide eyes, Millie looks at my lap and nods her agreement.

I rush up the stairs to my room, overhearing Mom as she enters the house through the kitchen. "Hello, kids. Brrr. It is getting cold out there." Mom calls out. "They're calling for another snowstorm this weekend."

I sigh in relief that it's her and not Dad that's home first. Still, I hurry to get back to the living room.

Sharing a conspiratorial smile with me as I sit beside her, Millie greets my mom very politely, "Hi, Mrs. James." Looking at Millie, you would never guess what we were just up to.

Mom smirks and waves her off, "Oh please, I've told you to call me Evie. At least when Michael's not around." She is always more laid back when Dad isn't around. "I'm going to go change." Pausing at the door, she adds, "Aw, you two are just so cute together."

I put my hand on my face, "Ugh, MOMM!"

At the same time, Millie giggles and says, "Thank you, Mrs.... Evie."

"Okay, okay, I will let you two be," she finally leaves.

"I am mortified."

"What would she have said if she saw us before she came in? Would she still call us cute?"

Cringing, I admit, "I don't even want to know."

We go back to the homework. Millie's still searching on my laptop, looking for someone to write about in her speech. "I give up. I'm going to give up my dream of being a physical therapist because I can't find anyone to do my report on."

All the lightheartedness in my soul escapes as I see my father pull into the driveway. "Don't ever give up on your dream, Millie," I say, putting my arm around her and kissing her temple. "When you give up on your dream, you resent the reasons and the people that made you do it."

"Wow, that is awfully profound for you to say. Where does this wisdom come from?" she earnestly asks.

"I have personal experience with it," I say sadly. "I'll tell you all about it later. Dad's home. We should call it a night."

Somewhat hesitantly, Millie says, "All right."

Millie knows the drill. When Dad gets home, it's like you are one out away from the end of the inning. He is very rarely in a good mood, and everyone around him must meet his high expectations. Millie gathers her school stuff and has her letterman jacket and boots on by the time he walks in the back door.

"Dalton. Amelia," he says in greeting.

Millie whispers to me alone, "Does he really think that's my name?"

"Probably. I'll call ya later," I tell Millie, wishing I could kiss her one more time before she leaves.

Mom breezes downstairs, correcting him, "It's Millie, not Amelia."

"I thought Millie was short for Amelia," he questions as if he's cross-examining a witness.

"Go now. Before they get into it over your name," I whisper, only half-joking. She waves and jogs back over to her house. I stand in the doorway with only the storm door closed. Behind me, my parents are still arguing. "It's rude to call her by the wrong name, Michael. She is important to our son; you will treat her respectfully."

Dad changes his tactic. "It's rude to leave the door open in the winter, especially if you're not the one paying the heating bill."

I shut the door, longing to leave this house instead of closing myself in it. "Sorry, sir. I just wanted to make sure she made it home safe." Then I turn back to the couch, pack my school things, and head upstairs to my room.

"Great. Now you've chased both of them off," Mom grumbles.

~Millie

As soon as I walk into my room, my phone rings with the screen reading, "BOYFRIEND is calling." I smile, remembering the first time he called me his girlfriend.

"Hey, Boyfriend," I answer.

"I'm sorry you saw that." Dalton exhales heavily, "I'm sorry my dad is such an asshole that he can't get your name right. And I am sorry my mom picked a fight with him in front of you."

"It's not your fault, Dalton," I reassure him.

"Yeah, well, it doesn't make me any less sorry." Dalton sighs before going on. "Mom is sorry, too. She told me she wants to make it up to you, a shopping and nails day or something."

"Sounds fun, but she doesn't have to do that."

"Just let her. Dad's taking me to Florida State on a college visit soon. She says she doesn't want to go because she needs some girl time, but I think she's just looking for time away from him."

"Oookay." Evie never takes time for herself—always working, even at home. I guess part of that is so she can avoid Michael. "Have they always been like that?"

"As far as I know. Dad's dreams of playing professionally were broken because Mom got pregnant."

"Is that what you meant about broken dreams? You said you would tell me later."

"Yeah. Grandpa Jack told Dad it was time for a new dream and made him man up and marry Mom. So, Dad's dream ended, and he never got over it." The line goes quiet, making me think that's all he's going to share. Before I can come up with some words of comfort, he goes on, "I don't know, maybe they had some good years; they worked their asses off so Dad could go to law school when I was young. But nothing is ever good enough for Dad, and he has taken it out on us ever since." Dalton pauses but spills more of the story, "Once when they were fighting, Gramps told me Dad wouldn't have made it anyway. He said Dad was good enough to get into the minors, but he would never make it to the majors. That life wouldn't be the kind of life for a family."

"That's the grandpa you were so close with, right?"

"Yeah. He died last spring," Dalton's voice trails off. I hear a tapping on the other end of the line; I imagine he's knocking the tip of his pencil on the desk. "It's late. 7:15 tomorrow, or do you need to get to school early?"

Now that our after-school schedules are similar, we've been going to school in one car. "7:15 works; I'll meet you at the truck. Goodnight." I want to say, 'I love you,' but we haven't crossed that line yet. Although, after tonight's make-out session, I feel we are getting closer.

"Goodnight, Millie. Sweet dreams."

For the rest of the week, we study at my house. My parents are annoying, but they don't fight, and they adore Dalton. I'm hoping his parents keep to their crazy work schedules so we can have the house to ourselves during the day over winter break because the Batcave is cold, and my mom will have the same break as us.

Semester finals are fast approaching, but I feel more prepared than before. It's good to have a study partner that I want to hang out with so much. Yes, we get distracted—a lot, and it makes me happy. My life is balanced, and I feel the Zen harmony my hippy parents always rave about.

Before I know it, we are handing in our exams and walking out into the snowy parking lot hand-in-hand. Dalton is quiet today, I thought he was worried about the test, but now I'm unsure.

"Wanna go to The Batcave with me? I need to blow off some steam."

I must make the wrong facial expression because Dalton presses, "Come on, I know it's cold at first, but if you work up a sweat, it isn't that bad."

"Fine," I roll my eyes. At least I'll be entertained while I freeze.

It's only a twenty-minute drive to the property with the big old metal barn-type building, so it feels like the heater in Dalton's pickup only just got hot when we park. Then we have to wait for the space heaters in The Batcave to warm the large empty space up. I sit shivering in a folding chair while Dalton hits ball after ball. Occasionally he looks up to laugh at me—like every time he sheds a layer of clothes.

As Dalton pulls his t-shirt off, he says, "Sure you don't want a turn? Activity is going to warm you up faster than sitting there."

Oh, I'm getting warmed up, alright, I think to myself. Dalton's bare chest is on full display for my eyes only. "I'm fine."

"You can work off the tee if you're still too scared of the pitching machine," he taunts.

"I'm not scared of the pitching machine."

"Prove it."

"Maybe later."

Dalton's answering chuckle rumbles low and sexy, and I feel it shake my soul. He loads another bucket of balls into the machine. I'm cozie enough, more from watching my man twist and strike than from the ancient heater, so I stand and stretch as I take my coat off.

Mildly out of breath, with one hand on his hip and the other holding the end of the bat like a cane, Dalton calls, "It's your turn."

Accepting the invitation, I duck inside the net. I don't really want to make a fool out of myself with the bat. Dalton has told me I'm not that bad, but I feel like he says that to be nice. "My turn for what?"

"Anything you want." Dalton is dripping with sweat, and I can't help but watch the trickle drip between his pecs and down his abs. It collects with more beads of perspiration at his naval before continuing its path south through the trail of hair that gets lost behind his waistband.

Dalton clears his throat, and my eyes snap back up to his. "Penny for your thoughts," he says with a cocky grin.

Without breaking eye contact, I press my lips together and shake my head adamantly. "My thoughts are worth more than a penny."

"Let me guess then." Dalton takes a step closer to me so I'm within arm's reach. "You were thinking," his voice rises like he is trying to impersonate me, "Gee, look at how hot Dalton is. I should have taken his advice about moving around."

"Umm, only about half of that." The combination of my guilt and our height difference makes Dalton a bit intimidating—in the most irresistible way possible.

"Half of that?" Dalton's eyebrows shoot up. "Which half?"

I take a step back, anticipating a cat-and-mouse game to ensue. "Well, I definitely wasn't thinking I should have taken your advice!"

Eyes alight with the challenge, he takes a bigger step. "So, you were thinking about how hot I am?"

"Yes, and sweaty," I quickly admit, this time with a sidestep.

"Sweaty!" The sound of the bat crashing to the concrete floor is my cue to make a break for it. I squeal when Dalton snatches and pulls me out of the net I'm about to get tangled in.

"Where do you think you're going?" I'm giggling too hard to answer, entirely trapped in Dalton's embrace. "What's the matter, Millie? Is it my hotness that has you in hysterics or my sweatiness?"

"Both." My heart is pounding a thousand miles per minute.

"Do you think I'm gross?" He asks while rubbing the side of his face across mine like a cat begging for attention.

"Now I do," I tease.

94

Dalton stops moving but doesn't let me go. He looks into my eyes like he is trying to decide if I'm being serious. His face is inches from mine, so I close the gap with a kiss. Hungrily, Dalton reciprocates, taking control of the situation. After several long seconds, he pulls back just enough to demand his earlier answer, "Tell me what you were thinking about when I caught you ogling me."

I'm too dizzy on his spell to guard my words. "I was wondering where the beads of sweat went once they hit your waistband."

I don't know who is more stunned by my reply, but he is the one that recovers fastest. "You're more than welcome to go scouting."

In the most ladylike move of my life, I snort at his word choice. It doesn't phase Dalton one bit; he plasters his lips back on mine and takes my hand in his, dragging it to the place in question and sliding his pants down. I take my time exploring the new territory. Caressing his length with my fingertips and girth between my thumb and middle finger must only tease him because his large hand is back, guiding me to the pressure and speed he prefers.

Dalton's low moans rumble through his chest, piercing my heart to know I'm giving him such satisfaction. Soon, his mouth goes slack so that he can breathe harder, and he whispers my name in a way that makes my toes curl. It doesn't stop me from continuing to kiss his jaw, neck, and collarbone. Wondering what his reaction will be, I give him a little love bite. A shocked broken laugh with a "Hey now" is the answer. I guess that means he doesn't care for the aggressive stuff, and that's fine by me. His skin is salty, and I am enjoying that more than I thought I would. I imagine what he would taste like if my mouth was where my hand is; it makes me want to suck on his skin everywhere I can reach.

Dalton groans, and I feel hot liquid hit my hand. I look down to watch his release. I've never seen a man cum, not like this, at least. There is a lot more fluid than I expected. "Oh my gosh! Dalton, there is so much. How are we going to clean it all up?"

Dalton is out of breath but chuckles. "Grab my shirt."

I get it, and he uses it like a towel. "That's it? Won't your mom notice when she does the laundry?"

"Millie, I don't think my mom has done laundry in the last ten years." The beautiful naked man gets dressed—minus the t-shirt.

"What?"

"Sweetheart, don't worry about it." Dalton wraps his arms around me again and kisses my forehead. Butterflies dance at the term of endearment.

Sighing, Dalton tilts his cheek to rest on my head. "Millie."

I have learned how to translate Dalton's one or two-word answers. For instance, he says my name in a hundred different ways, and I know exactly what he means every time. This time, he is telling me something is wrong—like he is defeated. The butterflies immediately stop their happy dance because all the endorphins flooding my system are replaced with panic. I pull back to read his face as I question, "What's wrong?"

"I need to finish packing, then maybe we can... I don't know, watch a movie or something."

I forgot that Dalton was going on a college visit to Florida with his dad. "That's fine," I reassure him and myself. It's only a few days apart—not a real problem that guys dump you over. This isn't like my freshmen year when I gave my heart and body to someone just to be tossed aside. Swallowing that fear back, I ask, "When do you leave?"

"Tomorrow," Dalton chokes.

"Dalton, it's only a couple of days; what are you so worried about?"

"I'm not worried; I just don't want to go." His blue eyes pierce me, "I signed those papers before we were a thing. I don't want to go all the way to Florida next year if you aren't, and I can't pretend to like it this weekend when Dad is showing me all over campus."

"But if you get drafted, you could be anywhere."

"I know," Dalton deflates. Silently, he gathers his things and shuts everything off, preparing to leave. He finally speaks when we are in the truck, "You could come with me."

"This weekend?"

"No, if I get drafted."

I laugh because surely he is joking. I don't know much about the professional athlete's life, but I'm positive that would mean driving from town to town, living out of a suitcase. "That would be fun for the summer, but I want to attend college."

"Then screw this year's draft. We can go to Florida," he looks out the windshield, more like at the windshield because the falling snow has blanketed us in, "earn our degrees where it is summer all year."

"I can't afford out-of-state tuition. Besides, I love the snow; it's magical."

Dalton shakes his head, knowing we are at an impasse, and starts the engine. We hold our thoughts about the future to ourselves, letting the music on the radio be our only conversation.

Dalton parks his truck in the driveway. I don't like it. We have taken to parking on the street since we could be at either house. Parking in the driveway means I can't look out my window and know he is home and ready to meet me.

We sit there for a good minute, both of us procrastinating the inevitable. I'm the first to push us forward, "Come on, let's get you packed, then we can snuggle on the porch swing and watch it snow."

We don't get the night to ourselves, though. Michael comes home early. He is in a good mood because he closed a case, but I still feel weird around him. He keeps looking out the window at us. At about 7:00, he comes out to *suggest* leaving for the airport tonight in hopes of getting an earlier flight. I feel Dalton tense up at the suggestion but doesn't voice his complaint.

Evie gets home just as we are all leaving. She is livid that Michael tried "sneaking off before she got home." She receives a rushed goodbye hug from Dalton and a three-fingered wave over the steering wheel from Michael.

Despite her anger at her husband, Evie is kind to me and finalizes plans for our girls' day on Saturday.

Chapter 11

~Millie

Dalton calls throughout the night, keeping me updated on the trip. They don't get an earlier flight but stay at the airport, ready for any open seats.

Friday morning at 10:04, Dalton calls again to let me know they have landed and are renting a car. In the background, I can hear Michael bitching about it, "We are on vacation, that means from women, too."

On Saturday, I wake up and stare at my closet for an hour, unsure what to wear. Evie usually dresses to the nines, and her blonde hair and makeup are impeccable. I decide on khakis, a white Oxford shirt under a sweater, and sneakers. After braiding my hair and dabbing on makeup, I realize I've put more effort into going out with her than I do going on a date with her son.

She calls me when she is ready to leave so I can meet her on the street. When I get in the car, I see she is wearing blue jeans! I don't think I've ever seen her in jeans. Her makeup is still perfect, but she's wearing much less than usual.

"Good morning, Millie," she greets me warmly. "I am so excited about today. First, we have appointments for tandem mani-pedis at my favorite salon. Then, I thought we would grab lunch somewhere and head to the mall."

"Sounds good to me. I've never gotten my nails done at a salon."

"You are going to love it," she tells me. I have never seen her this bubbly. The shell she wears as a workaholic and unhappy wife has been shed, and this is the real Evie. It's a whole new side to her, and I'm instantly at ease.

On the way to the salon, I study her profile as we make idle chit-chat. Dalton has her eye color, but that's about it. Her nose is thinner than his, and Michael's, and her face is also rounder than theirs. I never thought Dalton looked much like his dad until comparing him to his mom. I guess since Michael's hair is a lot darker than theirs, and they share the same eyes, I only focused on that.

While at the salon, Evie opens up, "I always wanted a daughter to go do this kind of thing with. My sister, Vivian, has three kids, and she takes the two girls to get their nails done together every other month. I've joined them a couple of times, but they live in St. Louis."

"Why didn't you have more kids?" I realize that probably sounded rude. "I'm sorry; you don't have to answer that."

"No, It's okay." She brushes it off, "I tried to get pregnant again for years. I couldn't understand why I got pregnant so easily the first time, Dalton was a surprise after all, but I couldn't get pregnant when I wanted to. I even went to an infertility doctor. After that visit, Michael admitted to me that he got a vasectomy behind my back while I was pregnant with Dalton. He told me he didn't want kids and that I should be happy to have the one."

Stunned, all I can replay is, "Ouch, that had to hurt." That was way more information than I needed—does Dalton know?

"It still does. I threw myself into full-time work after that. More than full-time. Besides going to Dalton's games, this is the first day I have taken off in ten years." We stop talking to pick out our colors and watch the ladies work on our feet. She goes back to our conversation, "He wasn't always such an ass. There had to have been something I liked about him in the beginning."

Not knowing how to respond, I just say, "Yeah, everyone wears rose-colored glasses in the beginning."

She perks up, "I hope you and Dalton aren't having problems. I am afraid Michael and I have set a bad example." Her face scrunches, and she bites her lower lip in a very un-Evie-like way. I don't think I've ever seen her second-guess herself.

"Oh, no, nothing like that. Everything still looks rosy to me," I say, hoping my cheeks aren't as flushed as they feel.

"Good." She reaches out to squeeze my forearm gently. "I just love seeing you two together. With how strict Michael is, Dalton never had much of a childhood. The day your arm broke was the only day Dalton cut loose; Michael tightened the ship after that. I enjoyed watching you play that day, too. Well, until you got hurt."

"Dalton talks fondly of his grandfather, though."

"Jack was a wonderful man. The only quality Jack passed on to Michael was his work ethic. But when his wife, Grace, fell sick, Jack retired and spent every moment by her bedside." Evie swallows a lump in her throat. "I didn't know she was sick until I showed up on their doorstep looking for Michael. Jack welcomed me in. Grace took one look at me and knew I was pregnant. Michael wasn't there, of course. It was her last Christmas on this earth, and he was out living his best life."

A tear rolls down Evie's cheek. "She was misdiagnosed at first, so when they finally realized the real problem, the cancer had spread too far, and there was nothing they could do."

Evie wipes her eyes carefully to avoid smearing her freshly polished nails. "Michael was so upset he wanted to sue every doctor and nurse that so much as looked at Grace's chart." She laughs without humor. "I guess that's why I fell in love with him; he was so passionate about taking down injustices. We would have made the perfect team—I would help families in medical crisis, and he would prosecute on their behalf."

"Wait—you just said *that's* when you fell in love with him, but you would have already been pregnant at that point."

Evie shakes her head. "You don't have to be in love to get pregnant."

Well, duh. Obviously, I know some people have no-strings-attached sex, but I didn't think Evie would be like that.

This time when Evie laughs, there is humor in the mix. "Don't look so shocked, Millie. It was the seventies," she stresses the decade as sex was a free for all at that time, "and Michael was a star on the field. There were a lot of girls chasing after him; I was just the first one to get knocked up."

"I guess your mom being sick isn't something you mention to a casual hook-up," I regret the words as soon as I say them. I completely forgot who I was talking to. Somehow, Evie has gone from the mother of my boyfriend to that fun aunt you can talk about anything with. I. Am. Mortified.

Luckily, Evie doesn't bat a lash at my indiscretion. "We were casual, but we had been hooking up for years. There was a group of us that would spend breaks together. Someone had access to a beach house, and we would spend the whole vacation... never mind what we spent our time doing." She winks at me, and I instantly put her back in the "cool aunt" territory. "The point is,

102

Michael never spent time at home with his mother when she was sick. He was all about having fun until reality slapped him hard."

Talk about information overload, yet I'm still buzzing with more questions. "Woah. Where were your parents during all of this?"

Evie gives me a look as if to say *you really don't want to know.* "Let's just say my parents are the reason I wanted to become a social worker."

My mind is wandering about everything that could mean, but I keep my lips shut because the services are finished, and it's time to get lunch.

Evie takes me to the same cafe I was at when Bobby asked me out. Luckily the patio is closed, but it still brings back bad memories. She asks me about my plans for after graduation, and I tell her about the in-state colleges I'm debating between. Neither of us brings up how far away Dalton is looking to go, and thankfully, she doesn't give me the "long-distance relationships don't work" speech.

Like the salon, Evie swipes the bill, not letting me pay for a thing, and then we take off down the street and go Christmas shopping. Boy, does Evie know how to shop! She mostly buys for her sister and nieces, but there are some new clothes for Dalton too.

Evie asks, "Which of these do you like better?"

I look over to see Evie holding up two men's hoodies. They are identical except for the color, with the expensive brand logo stamped across the chest. The blue sets her eyes light, and I know the same thing will happen when Dalton wears it.

"I think the blue will look better with his eyes."

"Right, but the green will look better with yours."

in the most unladylike way, I snort. "I only borrow his sweatshirts until they don't smell like him anymore."

"I know," she smugly says, putting both in her shopping bag. "But then he'll wear it until it doesn't smell like you anymore, and then the damn thing is filthy by the time it gets washed."

Dalton is the last one on my gift list because even though Evie has been fun and laid back today, it's still hard to pick out something personal but not too personal for your boyfriend in front of his mother. I finally pick out a hat and new sunglasses for him.

We laugh the whole way home with her stories of Dalton spending time with his Grandpa Jack. "I hate that I've spent more time working than being a mom, but at least Dalton had Jack.... and I'm grateful it was Jack and not Michael."

"If you aren't working tomorrow, we are having a holiday baking marathon. You should join us."

Evie pauses in thought, "Why not?" She smiles warmly, "I need to check on things at work, but I can log in and do that from home. If everything looks okay, I'll come over before lunch."

I hope she does. Getting to know her today has been enlightening.

-Dalton

Spending the next two days with my dad boasting about his alma mater is not my idea of fun. But if I have to have a plan B, I might as well make the most of this visit.

Dad gives me his version of a campus visit on Friday. This includes his favorite hangouts, a drive out to the house he grew up in, his high school, and a sunset view of the Gulf. Apparently, I'm the only one exhausted by the time we check into our hotel because he takes a quick shower and goes out dressed like he is on the prowl with his navy shirt half unbuttoned. I don't mind, though, because this gives me privacy to call Millie.

On Saturday, I get the official college tour with other kids my age. Then I meet with the baseball coaching staff, where my father has been hanging out all morning. Of course, I have met the head coach before, Coach Haas. He is one of Dad's old teammates and has visited us in Missouri several times over the years. He isn't the only college representative who has approached me, but Dad was always very clear that I would be attending FSU.

I'm not sure I want to go to school out of state unless Millie does, too. She seems set on staying semi-local. My mind puzzles out how I can get out of this contract or get Millie a scholarship to come with me. "Do you have a physical therapy program?"

Coach Haas perks up, "Physical therapy? I thought you were looking at athletic training or business."

"I am, but I was asking for," I swallow back the word girlfriend, "someone else."

Dad clears his throat, letting me know he knows where my mind is, while Coach Haas answers my question without noticing Dad's scoff. "In short, no. We don't have that doctorate program, but we have a pre-physical therapy undergrad option."

Dad interrupts, "I hate to cut this short, but we have dinner reservations."

We all look confused, but Dad steps in to shake Coach Haas's hand, bringing an abrupt end to our visit. "All right, we'll see you tomorrow then."

As soon as we are alone in the rental car, Dad scolds me, "Can't you get your head clear of that girl long enough to see the future I have laid out for you?"

"Her name is Millie."

He continues as if that information means nothing, "Trust me, Dalton, you don't want to squander your talents away. Once you have your big break, then you can think about girls. And I mean that in the plural because you don't want to get trapped until you have reached the top of your career."

I bite my tongue back at my fuming rage, knowing that arguing with him will only end in more work and fewer privileges. Neither of us talks while we sit in traffic, and there is no music to cut through the tension. When we finally arrive at the hotel, Dad speaks in a matter-of-fact tone which is actually gentler than the scolding I got minutes ago.

"Look, I have nothing against Mildred; she's a nice enough girl. But girls like that are a dime a dozen. If you get signed, you probably won't be anywhere near her anyway."

We don't talk much after that. Assuming I will be left in the hotel alone again, I kick off my shoes, flop on the bed, and flip on the TV until I can call Millie. "You aren't wearing that to dinner," Dad informs me.

"I didn't think you were serious about having reservations for us."

"They aren't until seven, but we can go early and sit at the bar."

Obediently, I change into the polo and khakis I packed as a just-in-case. We go to a fancy surf and turf kinda place where we sit at the bar watching football until the rest of our party arrives.

Not wanting to interact any more than I had to, I never asked Dad who we are meeting. Hell, I'm surprised we're meeting anyone. It couldn't be the coaches because they would have said something when we parted, and as far as I know, Dad doesn't have any family left in the area.

To my absolute confusion, two women join us. They look to be in their 20s or 30s and are similar enough to be sisters. Both are slim with chocolate brown hair, dressed like money isn't a problem, and are in heels that put them at jaw level on me.

"Dalton, this is Elaine and her daughter Alyssa." Elaine looks sharply at Dad for his introduction, as if she didn't like him pointing out that they were mother-daughter or something. "Elaine and I go way back to when we attended FSU."

"Hi," I retort.

I try to study the menu as soon as we are seated, but Dad thinks it's a great time to get acquainted. "Alyssa will be attending FSU in the fall, as well." Great. Isn't this the same man that just lectured me to get my head in the game and off girls? Does he think he can sway my focus off Millie?

Alyssa beams back at my father, "Well, that is the hope, Sir. I haven't been accepted yet." She turns her bright smile in my direction to say, "We can't all be star athletes and get recruited a year before graduation." Did I think she had a nice smile? Because she seems more like a predator snarling, somehow, it is very familiar.

Gritting my teeth, I focus on the menu again.

"Don't cut yourself short, honey," Elaine says with a sickening sweet southern accent. "What about all the trophies you have for dance competitions, making head cheerleader for both football and basketball, not to mention all the crowns you won in more pageants than I can count? You are a star in your own right." She has a low, raspy voice like someone that's been smoking for the last 30 years; it's the only thing that betrays her youthful appearance.

"Goodness, Elaine, you raised quite the young woman," Dad exclaims. I briefly look to read his expression; he appears genuine. Gah, is he flirting with her right in front of me? By the position of his arm, it looks like his hand is resting on her leg. I

107

know things are bad between my parents, but does he have to do this so openly in front of me?

Breaking my inner turmoil, Alyssa mutters, "She can't take all the credit; I had three step-fathers that helped... in their own way."

Dinner continues in much the same way. Dad flirts with Elaine; Elaine brags about Alyssa; Alyssa pretends to be a golden child yet says snide comments under her breath. And I sit through all of it, wishing I could be anywhere else, preferably with Millie.

Escaping after dinner is no light feat, but I fake a migraine and get cab fare to return to our hotel. Alyssa follows my lead, leaving Dad and Elaine on their own. It's obvious that we are lying, but they don't care.

It doesn't go unnoticed that Dad stays out half the night with Elaine. He is still asleep in the morning, so I leave to meet with the coaches for breakfast and a few hours in their training facility. Of course, Dad shows up to critique every swing and throw in front of them.

Then he drops the bomb that he and Elaine bumped into more college friends last night, and they all want to get drinks again tonight. It's after lunch when I get a moment to myself. The only thing I want to do is hear Millie's voice. But when I call, she doesn't answer. So, I phone Mom.

She is laughing when she answers. "Hey, sweetie, how's your trip?"

"Ummm, hello? Who is this? You seem to have my mother's phone and voice, but you are not her."

"So, it's going how I thought it would. And stop; I've called you sweetie before," she says.

"It has been years, and I have never heard you laugh like that."

"Well, my time away from your father has brought out the best in me."

I know the feeling. "So, what has you giggling like a schoolgirl?"

"I am at the Wilkins' baking. I forgot how much I love to bake."

"Really? Is that why Millie didn't answer her phone?"

"Yes, she has her hands busy rolling balls." Then, my mother starts giggling like she is in 7th grade. "Here she is."

"Nice, my mom and girlfriend are bonding over ball jokes," I say to whoever is on the other end.

A voice I'm not expecting calls out, "Hello, Dalton."

Judging by the echo, I'm on speaker. Now I am humiliated over my last comment. "Hello, Grandma Bea." It feels weird to call her that, but she insisted. "Am I on speakerphone? Who else is there?"

I finally hear the voice that I've been longing to hear. Millie says, "My mom and Michelle are here, too."

Mom is next to chime in, "I made your favorite, gingerbread men. When you get home, I will pull out the book and read it to you while you play with them. Just like when you were little."

They all start giggling. I hear a few "Aws."

Instead of getting embarrassed, I say, "I can't wait. You know my favorite part is the end when the gingerbread man gets eaten."

They laugh even harder.

A voice I don't recognize says, "We made gingerbread women, too. So, you may want to make up a different ending." Then she starts making kissy noises. It must have been Michelle that said that. They are roaring with laughter now.

"That sounds like fun. Well, I am glad to hear you are all having such a great time. I wish I was there, and I can't wait to taste all your hard work."

Millie comes on the line, sounding closer, leading me to believe I'm off speakerphone. "Hang on; I am going up to my room." I hear the door close. "Is everything okay? I didn't think you would call until you got home tonight."

"Yeah, me too. My dad changed our plans." My heart drops just telling her the news.

"What? Why?"

"He ran into some old friends and wants to catch up with them."

"When are you flying back?" she asks.

"He said tomorrow, but he didn't give me a time. Can you tell Mom for me?"

"You bet. Call me tonight if you get lonely again."

"I will. Go have some fun and save me a gingerbread couple. I will write them a story before I get home."

A listless laugh comes through the line, then she softly says, "Goodbye."

Not even an hour later, Mom calls me to say she doesn't want me to be stuck in a hotel alone for Christmas if flights get booked. She couldn't get the same flight arrangements as before, but I'm flying first class tonight. And the even better part, I am flying without Dad. She and Millie will be picking me up when I land.

Chapter 12

~Millie

Dalton comes over on Christmas Eve for a holiday movie marathon. It's a tradition at my house to watch movies all day and then go to the candlelight service at church. But when he walks in, I can see he is upset.

"What's bothering you," I say.

He asks, "Do you mind if we just take a drive for a while? I need to clear my head."

"Yeah, sure. Let me grab my keys."

We drive around aimlessly because Dalton doesn't want to go to The Batcave. He stares out the window, eyebrows crinkled in deep thought for over an hour.

It makes me anxious, and I eventually beg him to let me in. "It will make you feel better to talk it out."

Closing his eyes, Dalton takes a deep breath and leans his head back against the headrest. "My dad got home this morning."

"He just got home? You have been back for days," I say with astonishment.

"I know."

"How is your mom?"

He sits back up and stares out the window again.

"She went from being laid back and chill to angry enough to kill. Not much of a middle ground." Finally, he looks toward me with so much hurt in his eyes, letting me know there is more that he isn't sharing.

"So, he couldn't get a flight home?" I ask.

"That's what he claimed."

"You don't think he's telling the truth?"

"Not entirely."

Dalton goes quiet again, just gazing out the window. "I know he was with someone else. I didn't tell her, but Mom has suspicions."

"You *know*?"

"Yeah, we went to dinner with a woman that he was awfully friendly with—her daughter was touring FSU too."

"Wait, your dad took you on a double date?"

Dalton looks at me in alarm; it's the most expression I have seen out of him since he came home. "It wasn't like that," he backpedals. "I had no interest in even being there. Alyssa, that was the one our age, was like a jellyfish. She looked innocent enough but was ready to sting you if you turned your back on her. Too much like Dad."

I can't help but snort. "A jellyfish?"

"Yeah, we were in Florida, so the imagery stuck." Dalton's lips twitch like they would smile if he had a little more energy. "I bet he would have stayed if it wasn't Christmas. I wish he would have." He pauses, then adds in a hushed tone, "Sometimes I wish Mom would have left him before I was born. She is so much

112

happier when he isn't around—when it's just her and me. She should have just let him go chase his damn dream. We would have been better off without him."

What do you say to that? What do you tell someone that is hurting like this? He would rather have been raised by a single mom than with a man holding onto a broken dream. I can't just tell him things could be worse and list off a bunch of those possibilities. What am I supposed to say to comfort the boy I love? So, I say nothing. I just hold Dalton's hand and drive. Another hour passes before he says, "Let's just go back."

-Dalton

Christmas sucks. It's my first without Grandpa Jack. Usually, I spend the whole break with him because my parents are workaholics. I would help him put the lights outside and decorate the entire house. He went all out for every holiday, but Christmas was his favorite. He would take me to pick out a tree and let me help him chop it down—well, until I was stronger than him, then I was the one doing the majority of the work. On December 6th, we would put something funny in each other's shoes for St. Nicholas' Day. It was always something small and homemade, like the year I gave him a baggie of Cheerios labeled "Donut Seeds." That spring, he put them in a pot with dirt, and the next time I came over, glazed donut balls on sticks were sticking out of the planter. He talked about the look on my face for years after that.

Dad tried to sell a lot of Grandpa's things after he died. I think it was his way of getting back at Grandpa for crushing his big-league dreams. I was able to keep some stuff, including half of the Christmas decorations, which I put around my room.

113

Mom and Dad don't get into the holiday decorating spirit. Dad sees it as clutter, so Mom only insists on a tree, a front door wreath, and candles in every window.

At least I have Millie this year. Hanging out with her family has been the only bright spot. Their house is more like Grandpa's; Christmas practically threw up in and on it.

I stare out my front window at the Wilkins' home. Yesterday was Christmas. I only saw her briefly to exchange gifts, and then she was off to Grandma Bea's. She invited me, but I wasn't in the mood to be around a bunch of happy people.

Today all is quiet, and I assume that's because everyone is still sleeping. Mr. Wilkins' workshop had been nonstop action, but it is dark today. My guess is that he is taking a break from his carpentry job, whereas My parents have already returned to work. It was as if taking Christmas Day off was the hardest challenge of their lives. Okay, that's not quite right. Staying home together as a family on a holiday was the challenge, and everyone remaining peaceful was an out-of-reach goal.

Then it hits me. School is on break + My parents are workaholics, + I have Millie in my life now. What kind of teenage boy am I for not doing this math sooner? I need to plan something romantic instead of moping around.

She's going with her friends today. I didn't go because I'm having a pity party for one. That's about to change.

With those new calculations in my head, I'm packing up the adult problems weighing me down to focus on my youthful hormones. It's time I turn in my V-card.

Chapter 13

~Millie

Since I haven't spent much time with my girlfriends lately, I promised we would hang out over winter break. I never thought I would be the girl who blows off her girlfriends because she got a boyfriend, but here I am. It's just so easy to spend all my time with Dalton since he lives so close.

My plans with the girls even revolve around him. We had a chick-flick movie marathon while Dalton was gone, and today he wants to be alone, so I'm going sledding. I tried getting him to come too, but he shrugged it off. I know he's introverted, but his attitude lately worries me.

There are a lot of kids from school here. Everyone is asking me where Dalton is. I don't want to lie, but they don't need to know everything going on, either. I make vague comments to lead them off.

When the fun is over, I go home, take a long hot shower, change into my fuzzy worn-out pajamas, and check my computer for messages. Dalton emailed me. That's weird; he usually just calls.

When I open the email, I find an invite to dinner at his house. It's cute; he must have been bored because he even added clipart. I shoot a quick reply and start getting ready. Since the message specifically says not to come before 6:30, I take the time to dry and style my hair. Then put on a little makeup, my lucky black stretch pants, and the new sweater Grandma Bea gave me for Christmas.

At 6:29, I dash across the street and raise my hand to knock. Eager to see me, Dalton opens the door before my knuckles hit the wood.

"Welcome, miss. May I take your jacket?" Something has changed since I saw him last because he looks like the weight of the world is off his shoulders.

If he is in a playful mood, I am going to be, too. "Yes, please, fine sir." I giggle as he helps me out of my coat.

"You look lovely tonight, my darling," he says, kissing the back of my hand.

He is also dressed up, wearing a white button-down shirt and khakis. "You look very well yourself. And it smells wonderful. Where did you order from?" I ask.

"I didn't." A proud smile broadens his face. "I cooked for you."

"Really? That is so sweet." I follow him into the formal dining room. He stops and gestures his arm out like Vanna White, showing something on display. I always thought this room was just for show. It's perpetually immaculate as if no one uses it. However, tonight he has two table settings placed. He's lit candles and has a small bowl of roses as a centerpiece. "Wow."

"Do you approve, miss?"

116

"Um, yeah." Then I try to restore my fancy voice from earlier, "I mean, you have done a fine job, good sir."

He laughs and hugs me from behind. "I'm glad you like it," he says, returning to his usual tone. Then he kisses my neck, sending tingles down my spine.

I turn in his arms to face him. "Not that I'm not happy to see your spirits back up, but what has gotten into you?"

"I just realized I wasn't myself and needed to make it up to you. Come on." He takes me by the hand and leads me to the head of the table, pulling out the chair and scooting me into the table after I sit. Then he goes into the kitchen and starts bringing out food.

"If you like your steak cooked more, I can put it back in."

I'm already amazed by what he has done, but this astonishes me. "You grilled steak... in December?"

"Yes. I wanted steak, so I cooked it the only way steak should be cooked, on the grill."

"You bake cookies, cook, and grill? You are going to be a very nice housewife for someone someday."

He stops cutting his steak and looks at me.

Heat rises to my face. Is Dalton thinking about us being together then? I want that, but I'm not trying to say that. Oh my God, why did I just say that? I try to stumble out of the hole I feel like my words have put me in, "What I mean is,"

Thankfully, he eases the tension with a joke, "I'm going to be the housewife?"

I try to follow the humor, "That depends. Do you clean, too?" It works; we laugh our way out of that moment. I vow to shut up and chew.

After dinner, we take the dishes to the sink. I scrape and rinse the dishes while Dalton packs up the leftovers.

"I think we make a pretty good team," he says. "But I don't clean. We have a cleaning lady that comes every week."

"That explains a lot."

"What's that supposed to mean?" he asks, putting his hands on his hips.

"You are the only guy at school that irons his t-shirts." I squeal in laughter when he picks me up and carries me out of the kitchen and into the living room. He dumps me on the floor and puts a movie in the DVD player.

"What are we watching?" I ask.

"It's something I know you've wanted to see," Dalton says with a sly smile.

The coffee table is pushed aside. Instead of using the small uncomfortable sofa, Dalton made a nest on the floor with blankets and a ton of pillows. This is very cozy. He was busy today; more candles are burning in here, too, and they smell amazing.

We settle in the love nest with Dalton lying on his side, behind me, with his head propped up in his hand. I squirm in closer to be the little spoon, and he pulls a blanket over me because he knows I always get cold when I'm watching TV. The movie turns out to be the chick flick I watched with my friends while he was away. I don't have the heart to tell him I already saw it.

Dalton doesn't seem interested in the movie; he is very handsy tonight. It starts with his fingers playing at the hem of my sweater before traveling up under it to my breast. Through my bra, his thumb rubs my nipple while he palms the weight of the cup. I am not chesty, so his hand can easily cover me. Then his fingers dip inside my bra, and he rolls my nipple between them. I'm glad I've already watched the movie because Dalton is quite distracting.

118

About halfway through the movie, the storyline gets steamy, and Dalton picks up his pace too. He kisses my neck while his hand trails lower on my body into my pants. I can't keep my eyes focused on the TV with his fingers gliding through my sex, but when Dalton says, "I want to do what they are doing."

My eyes flash to the screen to see the actress on her back with her legs spread wide. All you can see of the man is his outline under a sheet, his head at her apex.

"Yeeess," I breathlessly answer.

Dalton sits up enough to use both hands to take my sweater off, then watches with anticipation while I reach behind my back and unclasp my bra. His fingertips graze my shoulders, slowly pulling the straps down. He doesn't pause long before he covers my now bare bust with his palm. His other hand cradles my head, and he shifts his body so I have space to lay flat. He kisses me as he eases my body down. Then, his lips travel along my jaw, to my earlobe, and down my neck until he reaches his first goal. Feather-light kisses are placed across my chest until he reaches my left nipple. He gently sucks it into his mouth and swirls his tongue around the tip. He pauses to look at how the little bud puckers.

"Keep going," and encourage him by running my fingertips along the spine at his neck. He licks his lips and drops his mouth on my right side, covering my left boob with his large palm.

Dalton's mouth continues going back and forth between each breast. After a while, he kisses his way back up my neck while his hand goes down to my hip. When his mouth reaches my ear, he quietly asks, "Should I continue?" His thumb and forefinger hook around my waistband, and I know he isn't asking to continue kissing my chest. All I can do is nod my approval.

Dalton takes my mouth with his as his whole hand goes down the backside of my pants. He palms me there, pulling my body close to his so I can feel his hard length on my thigh.

Before tonight, we have only gotten to the point of rubbing our bodies against each other; feeling the friction of him against me is the only relief my body has had or given. Finally, things are going to go further.

Dalton is on his knees, looking down at me. I have seen him without his shirt quite often, but never from this viewpoint. I ache to feel his sculpted body. "Take off your shirt," I order. He complies, opening each button slowly—too slowly. Unable to wait for him to finish, I reach out to run my fingers along every valley and hill of his defined muscles.

Without breaking eye contact with me, as if he's waiting for me to change my mind, he hooks his fingers around the waistband of my pants and drags them off. He repositions me as he does this, so he is no longer at my side but right in line with me. With nowhere else for my legs to go, they fall on either side of him.

His hands drift up to my thighs and then to my hips. Grabbing my panties, he says, "I want to see all of you, Millie. I want to touch and taste *all* of you."

"Oh my God, yes. Dalton, please."

It doesn't take him as long to rid me of them too. This time he doesn't discard them like he did the rest of my clothes. He clutches them while drinking-in his first sight of me completely naked.

"You plannin' on keeping those like a trophy?" I ask, trying to cut this profound moment with humor. But, also because that happened to me before, and I was horrified to know he showed them off and bragged about the stupid freshman I was.

Dalton looks down at his new prize before looking back into my eyes, raises one eyebrow, and says, "I am now."

"But they are my favorite," I plead.

"And now they are my favorite," he says with a devilish grin. "Now quit talking and open your legs. I'm not done committing your body to memory."

Gulp. I do as Dalton commands.

Dalton's gaze on me is hungry; I love it. "Millie, you are so beautiful," he tells me.

He covers my body with his and puts his mouth back on mine. One arm has him propped up, and the other is in my hair behind my head. He dips his hips against my core and grinds in as he kisses me. He slowly retracts slightly, drags his hand down my arm to my hip, and slips it between us. He stops and looks at me sweetly, and I imagine he's telling me he loves me. Still staring into my soul, he dips one finger inside me. I let out a shutter, which makes him smile. He continues pumping one finger in me, then circles my clit. After a while, he does the same rhythm with two fingers.

With Dalton's mouth settled on my boob again, my hand finds its way to the back of his head. I run my fingers through his hair, telling him without words how much I am enjoying this.

He moves his head farther south, using his tongue and lips as he goes. Finally, his face is positioned to replace the work his hand has been doing.

Dalton dips his head in and puts his tongue on my clit. One delightful swirl, and he stills, picks his head up, and jumps to his feet. The door to the garage opens from the kitchen. A blanket is tossed over me, and he starts buttoning his shirt. Then he's handing me my clothes, and I dress as fast as possible.

"Hey guys, it's just me," Evie calls out. I hear her shuffle around to hang up her coat. Her heels start to come closer but pause around the dining room.

"Hi, uh, Mom, we are, uh," Dalton looks down at me to see how close I am to ready, "in here."

She answers, "Looks like you are having a nice night. I'll talk to you in the morning."

Dalton's eyes are wide, almost panicked. Yet it doesn't sound like she got close enough to see us.

"Okay, goodnight Mom."

"Did she see us?" I ask in a hushed tone.

"I don't think so, but she sure knew not to come in. She didn't even look towards me when she went upstairs."

Thinking we got away with something, we grin like we won the lottery. Stepping into Dalton, we wrap our arms around each other and sway to the music from the movie credits.

"Want to actually watch the movie this time?" I ask.

"No, I like our version better. But I'm not ready to let you go tonight."

"Me neither."

He starts it over, but this time we watch until we both fall asleep.

Chapter 14

-Dalton

I don't know if it's the smell of coffee or my aching body that wakes me up. I know the scent means Mom's getting ready for work, but why is my body screaming at me?

When I try to roll over, I realize I'm still on the living room floor with Millie sleeping in my arms. "Shit," I say, rubbing my eyes.

A very sleepy "What?" comes from the beauty beside me.

"We fell asleep."

"What time is it?" Millie asks.

"It's about 6 a.m.," Mom says from the breakfast nook.

"Oh my gosh! Dalton, we slept the whole night! I have to get home; my parents must be freaking out." She jumps out of the makeshift bed.

"Don't worry; I called them when I came down and saw you two all snuggled up. You just looked so cute; I didn't want to disturb you. So, I let them know you were staying over," Mom tells us.

Bewildered, Millie walks over to the nook and asks, "They were okay with that?"

"I think they were just happy you were safe, sleeping on the floor of our living room," Mom says. "Coffee? There is a creamer in the fridge and cream cheese for these bagels."

Did I just wake up in the twilight zone? "What about Dad? Did he see us?" I ask, coming into the room.

"No, he didn't make it home last night." Mom takes a long sip from her mug. "I don't expect we will see him much anytime soon." Then she changes the subject fast. "Did you get to see any of your movie last night? I heard that one is good." The movie's case is on the table next to her.

"Yes!" Millie goes into more detail on the movie than I caught, which is odd because I'm pretty sure she fell asleep before me.

"Aw, it does sound good. Did you get a two-night rental? I want to watch it tonight."

"Sure, Mom," I say.

Mom stands and says, "Well, I better get going. I'll be home tonight at about 8." She looks at me pointedly. Millie gives her a hug goodbye, and Mom is out the door.

"This is so weird," I say.

"Yeah." Millie bites her lips together and snickers.

"I don't know what I am most shocked about, the way you and my mom are getting along, that we just got away with a slumber party, what she said about my dad not expected home, or the details you gave her about the movie."

Millie walks over to me and puts her arms around my waist. "Well, I like your mom; we have become friends. I'm also surprised by our slumber party pass. Sorry, but I am relieved your

Dad won't be around here. And I saw the movie with my sister before Christmas."

"You little minx. I sat through that romantic movie twice, and you already saw it?!"

"Ha. You can barely say you sat through it once."

"I still can't believe you didn't tell me."

"Just a little white lie for your own good," Millie tells me.

White lie or not, I don't like her keeping things from me. I just grunt in response.

After we eat, Millie says, "I should probably go home and make sure my parents aren't upset."

I already feel the loneliness that usually drives me to our home gym. It is a familiar feeling, but today it's unwelcome. The morning has been perfect. I snatch Millie up and whine. "No, don't go."

Millie giggles. "Tell you what, if I'm not grounded, I'll come back after I shower and change my clothes."

A disappointed moan escapes before I think better of it and suck it up. I kiss her goodbye on the forehead.

A half-hour later, there is a knock at the door. I expect it to be Millie, but it's a man at the door.

"Are you Dalton James?" he asks.

"Um, Yeah?"

"We have a delivery for you." He hands me a note and turns back to help another man unload a large box. They carry it in and ask where my bedroom is. Confused, I point upstairs and look at the paper he gave me. It is my mother's handwriting.

I think we will all be more comfortable if you "watch movies" in your own room. Love, Mom

Well played, Mom. The delivery guys are unwrapping a 30-inch television when I enter my room.

"Where do you want it?" the first guy asks me.

"Um, let me clear this off." I quickly make room for it on the chest. They set it up, make sure it works, and go.

Did my mom just give me permission to have Millie in my bedroom?

~Millie

Mom and Dad greet me from the kitchen table with knowing smiles around their coffee mugs. "Good morning, moonbeam. Did you have a nice night?" Dad asks. Why can't they just call me a "night owl" like normal parents?

"Sorry, I didn't mean to stay out all night."

"That's okay," Mom says with a huge grin. "We were pretty sure we knew where you were."

"Yes," Dad agrees, "it's quite handy being able to look out the window and see that your boyfriend's truck hasn't moved an inch."

"So, how was it?" Mom's grin is even bigger—like a cat that ate a canary.

"How was what? We fell asleep on the living room floor."

Dad scoffs, but Mom presses on, "Uh-huh. It's okay, honey. Sex is a normal, natural activity for two young," Dad clears his throat pointedly, and they share a look telling me everything I didn't need to know about what they were up to while I was gone, "people to do."

"Ew, can we please drop this?" I beg. "Dalton and I didn't have sex. Honestly, we fell asleep watching a movie."

"You don't need to be ashamed. Your mother and I started younger than you are now."

"Not with each other, though," Mom corrects. "We didn't meet until we were in our mid-twenties."

"True, but I'm sure if we grew up together, we would have fallen in love a decade before we did." They share another goofy, love-sick look at each other.

"But times have changed since we were your age. Now you can't turn around without someone preaching about safe sex," Mom says, gesturing to the pile of condoms on the table between them.

I didn't even look at what was on the table until now. Along with the rubbers are an assortment of fruits and veggies. "Oh my gosh, what are you guys up to?"

"We thought you could practice," Dad laughs.

"We did that in school with a cucumber."

"We're out of cucumbers, so we have to improvise."

"I get the banana, but what's with the others? A sweet potato? Squash?"

"Well, if the condom fits," Dad jokes.

"What about the eggplant? It's huge!"

Mom's teaching voice rings clearly, "Penises come in more shapes than a cucumber."

"Eww, Mommm!"

"Sorry, Millie, but it's true," Dad informs me. "Trust your mother; she knows all too well."

Mom snickers, as if Dad didn't just call her a slut.

"I grabbed the eggplant because I wanted you to see how much a condom can stretch. There are guys out there that will complain about a condom not fitting, and it just isn't true. I don't want you to be fooled."

To placate them, I grab the banana and condom and get to work.

"Good choice. See the way it bends? If this was a penis, he would hit your g-spot perfectly while in the missionary position."

"MOM!!" Some people think I have really cool parents, especially since I'm not getting in trouble for last night. But this is cruel and unusual punishment. It's mortifying. Pure hell.

As fast as I can, I open the foil package and roll it down the crescent-shaped banana, leaving a little extra space at the top. They give their approval and hand over the yellow squash.

"I can't. This thing is all bumpy. Why does that happen anyway?"

"It's a result of a mosaic virus," Mom answers.

"A what?"

"I bet if it had been wearing a condom, it wouldn't have gotten a virus," Dad jokes.

"Oh my gosh! Can we stop this insanity if I agree to go on birth control?"

Dad quickly answers, "Birth control won't protect against viruses."

"And I don't want you taking man-made hormones. They could do more damage than good," Mom declares. "I have teas you can drink regularly, but safe sex is about more than pregnancy." She hands me the butternut squash.

"He's not *that* big," I complain.

Mom grins like she caught me in a lie, but it's Dad who voices it. "I thought you were just *sleeping?*"

"We were!" I pause, and their expressions say more than words ever could. "Think about it! If Dalton, or any guy, had a..." I internally cringe, "...penis that big, he wouldn't be able to hide it, let alone walk!"

"Well, it wouldn't always be this big or hard," Mom shakes her head in disbelief. "John, she knows even less than I thought."

"Obviously, I know about *that*. But still, that is not a human-sized penis!" my voice crescendos, so by the time I say "penis," I am practically yelling.

"Wow, what did I miss?" Michelle asks with a yawn.

"Your baby sister is paying her penance," Dad tells her.

"Can I please go now?"

"Put a condom on three more times, and you may go." Mom reconsiders her words, "Properly. You can't double or triple-bag the real thing. Best to pick three different vegetables."

My head hits the table, "Please stop torturing me."

Michelle's monster voice says, "Never," as she pats my head. "It could be worse. Dad could have made wooden penises in his shop."

"If only I had the time," he mutters.

Once I have prepared the veggies with protection, I ask, "Is that all; am I free to go yet?"

"That's all," Mom says with a wink. "I'm proud of you, you know?"

"You are?"

"Of course I am. And we really like Dalton too. I wasn't joking when I said I started earlier than you. I loved my wild freedom, and I knew I wanted to experience as much as possible before settling down—and as many men as," I hold my hands up because I don't want to hear more. "Alright, my point is that you have been much easier on us than I was on my parents."

Hesitantly, I ask, "Am I grounded?"

"Good God, no!" Dad exclaims. "Trying to hold you down will just make you rebel. Right now, we know where you are and who you're with. We don't need you sneaking out your window to go to a rave like she used to do," he points to Mom, "haven't you been listening? Now get out of here... and take these with you." He shoves the rest of the condoms in my hands.

When I show up at Dalton's, he asks, "How did it go with your parents?"

"They laughed and started talking about their hippie days. Eww, by the way," I shudder for emphasis. "They also said they just want to know where I am and that I'm being safe." I'm not sharing the double meaning that they meant.

"I will add that to all the other unexpected events of the day. Guess what happened while you were at home?"

"Aliens, it has to be aliens," I joke.

He laughs, grabs my hand, and leads me upstairs. I have never been upstairs. We walk into his room, and he hands me a note from his mom and tells me she had a TV delivered to him. I admire the new TV and look around his room. It's tastefully decorated, like the rest of the house, but he has baseball posters and shelves of trophies. He doesn't have a small twin-sized bed like me. His is larger; I would guess it's a queen. Yep, that will be more comfortable than last night's love nest.

The next few days are similar. We hang out in Dalton's room most of the time. Our make-out sessions progress, but we still haven't gone all the way—yet. Most importantly, we make sure not to be in the middle of anything when Evie is due home. She surprises us one night, another close call, by getting home early and taking us out for dinner.

Even though I think we are in the clear if it happens again, I'm careful not to spend the night.

Chapter 15

-Dalton

Tonight is the New Year's party at the ski lodge. It's the night—the big one I've been planning since I snapped out of my funk.

There are "Party Like It's 1999" banners everywhere. Millie's friends are here, and so are some of the guys from my team. I'm not much of a partier, but tonight has been fun. We dance the night away—or the year, if you really think about it. We countdown to midnight and start the year off with a kiss.

I haven't told Millie yet, but I have a big surprise up my sleeve. She has been so busy dancing with her friends and putting the camera I got her for Christmas to good use that she hasn't seen me sneaking around.

Around 1 a.m., everyone is clearing out and heading home. As we leave the dance floor, I lead Millie to the elevator instead of the car.

"Come here; I have a surprise for you," I tell her.

She waves goodbye to her friends but follows me. "Where are we going?"

"I said it was a surprise," I tease, giving her a wink. I hope I sound upbeat because inside, I am nervous as hell. We get in and take the longest ride of my life to the third floor. My heart is pounding with adrenaline; the thumping of it in my ears is all I can hear until the doors open with a ding, jolting me out of my anxiety.

I squeeze Millie's hand, noticing how sweaty mine has become. "This is us," I stupidly say because nobody else is in here. "I got us a room for the night." We walk down to room 314. I have been in and out of this room several times tonight, ensuring everything is perfect. Yet, when I pull the key out of my pocket, I drop it and proceed to fumble to unlock the door.

"Oh." Then she looks at the door and says, "The room number is pi." Millie tends to make jokes to ease uncomfortable situations, so she must be as nervous as I am.

"We don't have to stay if you don't want to," I say with a hard swallow. Sure, I hope we have sex tonight, but I won't make her.

"It's just that I told my parents we would be home after the party."

"Your sister is covering for you; she even packed you a bag," I say, gesturing to her duffle.

"Wow, okay," she says, simultaneously biting her bottom lip and smiling.

"I wanted tonight to be special." Looking around at the room, I regret the hotel has a policy against lit candles. But I did sneak in a bottle of wine placed next to a vase of flowers, and I scattered rose petals around the room. I also have a box of condoms stashed in the bedside table. I must have moved them from the tabletop to the drawer a dozen times because I couldn't decide if I wanted them on display. "We don't have to do anything you don't want to do, but I brought condoms just in case...." I'm too nervous to say it out loud.

Millie doesn't say anything as she looks around the room, and it's killing me that she's so quiet. She runs her hand on the bag her sister packed, turns her head towards me, and says, "I'm going to go in the bathroom to freshen up and see what my sister packed."

While she's in there, I start my disk-man, double-checking the speakers are attached. I burned a cd of a bunch of slow love songs to play on repeat. Then I take off my jeans and shirt so that I'm standing there in just my boxers when the bathroom door opens. I turn to see her walk into the room.... completely naked.

This is really going to happen.

I swallow hard—again. I'm doing that a lot tonight.

Millie climbs on the bed, standing on her knees, and crooks her finger for me to join her. She's mesmerizing, but I don't wait a second longer to answer her beckoning. Wrapping my arms around her, I kiss her, feeling her body relax against mine. This is more skin-on-skin than I have ever felt, and it's amazing. Millie's body is exquisite, and I'm finally going to know just how perfectly we fit together. This feels so right to me, but before I get carried away, I need to be sure we're on the same page. "You have to say it. Tell me you want to make love tonight. I don't want any regrets later."

"Yes, Dalton. I want to make love with you." She giggles nervously, "I wouldn't have come in here naked if I didn't."

I would make a joke, but I don't have enough blood in my brain to form a sentence. I can only moan a response.

I bring my mouth down on hers again. I want to take this slow, but the anticipation is killing me. I move my hand to graze

Millie's boob and pause before massaging and squeezing all of it.

Looking down, I peek at what I'm doing, and my mouth follows my gaze. Before I know it, I'm sucking on her nipple. While my mouth is busy here, my hand finds a new place.

Slowly I lower my arm down her backside until I get the guts to slip my hand between Millie's legs. My fingers brush her opening. She is already silky with need making it easy to slip one finger into her. "You are so wet."

Her arm is pinned against her side, trapped between my body and hers, but she can move her hand to stroke me through my shorts. "And you are so hard."

"Mmhmm, I am."

I add another finger to stretch her out. She is tight, and I don't want to hurt her. "I want to take my time, but I won't last if you keep doing that."

"Dalton, you have a whole box of condoms, plus my sister packed me some," she snickers. "We can take our time later. I want you now."

Oh my, Great Bambino, I love this woman. "But I don't want to hurt you; I know the first time can be…. uncomfortable for you."

She looks down and says, "Yeah. But this isn't my first time." Her face is red with embarrassment.

"Oh, I didn't realize I was the only rookie." I wince at my stupid attempt at humor.

"I'm sorry. I wish I had waited for you. It was a stupid mistake that I wish I could take back." A tear trickles down her face.

I kiss it away. "It's okay, sweetheart. You are here with me now."

She looks up and kisses me back with more force than I expect, and we tip onto our sides laughing. "Put the condom on. I want this memory to erase the last time."

This is finally happening. I drop my drawers and open the box, then the foil packet. I have never opened one of these things, let alone put one on. Therefore, my hands jitter as I roll it out a little and put it on. It's not comfortable. Now I understand why so many guys complain about having to wear them.

Turning back, I position myself between her legs. I'm still trying not to rush things, so I start kissing her again. I don't push myself in just yet, only rub my shaft against her lips. I'm surprised and thrilled when Millie makes the next move. Her hand wedges between us, and she captures my length, directing the tip of my erection to brush her opening. She's aligned us to cross the line from two to one. I push in just a bit to test her readiness but slip deeper than I intended. I'm not all the way in, but the entire head of my dick is engulfed by her heat. There aren't words to describe how good this feels. I could easily get lost in this moment, only thinking about myself, so I focus on Millie's body language. Mostly because I care about her, and I really, really want to do this again. I pull back slightly, causing Millie to sigh in frustration; it's kinda cute. I ease myself in just a little farther twice more, then drive home. It is so hot and tight that I wonder if I bottomed out inside her. I have to pause and give myself a minute. I try to recite baseball stats, but I can't focus on that while Millie is mewing and undulating beneath me.

This causes me to fall into the pure biological nature of the act. I'm lost to sensation, only brought to when Millie calls out my name. Her muscles are quaking against me, and I know I no longer have to hold back. My balls tingle and tighten until the pressure explodes.

We lay there, still joined together, breathing hard. I start to kiss Millie again, but I can feel the damn condom slipping away. I have to pull out and throw it away. It is almost off when I do. I toss it in the trash and jump back in bed as fast as possible, pulling the covers out from under Millie to tuck us both in.

She curls into my chest. "Hold me. I feel like I'm going to float away." Our heartbeats stop racing one another, and our breathing syncs into a steady rhythm. "That was, wow, that was good, really good."

Kissing the top of her head, I agree, "It was, and it will only get better." I want to tell her I love her, but that just sounds corny to say now. I've tried to say those words to her so many times, but I always chicken out.

We drift off but wake up to do it again. The condom is more comfortable this time, but it still seems wrong. I guess it is just something I will have to get used to.

Our first time was a rush of adrenaline and hormones. We take our second time slower, and it lasts longer. Then we go back to sleep, limbs all tangled together. My feelings for Millie are stronger than ever. This is the best high I have ever had, better than any baseball has given me.

I never want to sleep without her—or with clothes on, ever again

~Millie

I wake up, blanketed in Dalton. It's mid-morning, and we are spooning. I could lay here like this forever—or I would if I didn't have to pee.

I sneak out of bed to take care of business, including brushing my teeth. When I return, Dalton has rolled onto his back and is rubbing his eyes. An impressive erection shows through the sheets, giving me naughty ideas. Even though I'm sore from having sex with him twice, I want to do it again.

"What time is it?" He asks.

Time for me to take charge. "About 9. Do we need to get home for anything?"

Looking at me now, he says, "Nope. The day is clear. We can get some breakfast and hit the slopes if you'd like."

Biting my lip, I answer, "Maybe later. Right now, I want to climb your mountain." I give him a wicked grin and grab a condom. He rips the sheet off, and I climb in. Gently but assertively, I grasp his dick and lick him from root to tip. Then I suck as much of him into my mouth as I can fit.

Dalton places his hand in my hair, "Sweetheart, if you keep doing that—oh, Babe, that feels so good..... I don't want you to stop, but if you don't, I... I won't be able to stop."

I give him one last flick with my tongue, tear the foil wrapper with my teeth, pinch the tip of the rubber, and unroll it down him.

He watches me intently. "Where did you learn to do that so well? Or do I even want to know?"

I giggle. "My parents made me practice on a banana after our slumber party."

"Well, you are a pro. It feels much better done with your skillful hands."

"Do you want my hands and mouth, or can I stick it somewhere else?" I taunt.

Dalton gives me the goofiest grin. "You're the one running the show this time. Put it where you want it."

With that invitation, I straddle him, feeling the fullness once more, and lean my face in to taste his lips. Dalton's hands are all over me as if he can't make up his mind where he wants them most. As my movements increase, he clamps his palms to my hips, adding to the motion. I sit up to bounce more than rock, but he seems to take that as an invitation to flip me on my back and thrust in hard, making me gasp.

"Oh, shit. Sorry, did I hurt you?" Dalton says, pulling back a bit.

"Just a little sore, but I liked it. Do that again."

And he does. Then he's pounding into me quickly. It's too much and not enough at the same time. "More," I desperately breathe.

Instead of giving in to my request, he goes still, and I can feel his hot cum filling the condom. That's all it takes, and I am flying over the edge with him.

"Shit, I didn't mean to," Dalton pants. "Did you...?"

"Yeah," I answer, between breaths.

"But you asked for more."

"I know, but it was like your body knew what I needed more than what I thought I wanted."

Blue eyes, full of wonder, gaze back at me. I expect him to say something equally as corny, but he remains silent. We continue holding on to each other long after he shrinks from me. The only thing stopping us from laying here longer is the warm wet spot from the condom spilling. Hastily, I roll away as if it's a toxic substance.

"Shit," Dalton mutters, "I forgot about that."

"I should go wash off." Half-heartedly, I sit up. "But I don't think I can stand just yet."

"Do you want to take a shower? Together?"

"Hot water sounds delightful."

Dalton kisses my temple and gets up. I hear the water turn on, and a moment passes before he comes back, scoops me up, and carries me to the shower. We stand under the spray, embraced like we are slow dancing. Maybe we are, to the sound of rain.

Eventually, we start lathering each other with soap that smells like rosemary and mint. It wakes me up from our long night together. I don't think I've showered with someone since Michelle and I were kids, but this is much more fun. I giggle as I rub the cloth all over his body. He seems to be enjoying it, too, because I have excited him with my extra attentive care.

"Oh my gosh, Dalton! Again? "

"I can't help it; he has a mind of his own." He gently washes me next, kissing each place he cleans off. "You are so beautiful, and I have an all-access pass now." I blush at his words. "Just ignore it; I know you are sore."

I wash my own hair because Dalton claims he has no idea how to take care of such a mane, but I think it is because he can't take his hands off my tits.

Dalton's hands continue roaming my body while I finger-comb the last of the conditioner out of my hair. It is not helping his hard-on go away. "I know I said to ignore it, but can I just rub myself on you?"

"Yes," I whisper, taking my hands out of my hair to stroke his need against my stomach. I love the attention he's been giving me, and I want to pay it back tenfold.

Dalton's eyes close, and he tips his head back. I watch the enjoyment on his face, but after several pulls, he drops his chin and traps me in his gaze. His grasp catches mine, halting the hand job I'm giving him. Then he pushes his cock between my legs.

He's bare, brushing against my pussy. It's like he is knocking on a door he doesn't intend to enter.

Chapter 16

-Dalton

School starts before I am ready to go back. This was the best winter break of my life. Sorry Gramps, but I know you would be happy for me. I know how much he loved his wife and if they had half as much sex as Millie and I have—not that I want to think about my grandparents that way. I never knew her, though, so it doesn't feel as wrong as it should to think that way.

The point is, Millie and I have sex—a lot, most evenings at my house before Mom gets home, some mornings before school, in the kitchen, the shower, my truck, the Batcave, and on the living room floor. The stairs were a challenge that we happily share rug burns from. For Valentines Day, we make use of the hot tub and have sex outside for the first time. I can't wait for it to warm up so we can roll around the outfield together.

When we aren't humping like rabbits, we have naked cuddle time while dreaming about our future. Sure, mine is all planned out, revolving around baseball. And Millie's coming around to my ideas of traveling city to city with the league. College will still be there if I get drafted. We can always go back to school, and I will have so much money by then that we won't need to take out student loans.

Unfortunately, we don't have as many courses together this semester, leaving me to pay attention to the teacher instead of watching her throughout the class. That's not true; I'm constantly thinking about her, either reminiscing the night before or fantasizing about sneaking away at lunch for a quickie in my truck.

Track season finishes and baseball is on the horizon, so our schedules will be off again. The worst thing about that is Dad will come home more. It has been years, but he has done this before. He always comes back to bust my balls when baseball season starts.

I have only seen Dad once since Christmas. He came home to pick up his mail and some personal stuff. He wasn't happy to bump into me even though I was returning from the batting cages. Millie had gone with me, but he couldn't have known that.

Unfortunately, I am right about him in the most unexpected way. Millie stays over most weekends. It is late February, and we are cuddled up watching something on my new TV when we hear my father come home.

We hear his deep voice from my parent's room, "Hi, honey, I'm home."

Millie looks up at me and whispers, "I should go."

"If you want to. You're probably safer staying put." I check the clock; it's well after midnight. "He won't come in here at this time of night."

Millie nods at my advice, but Dad's voice grows louder. "Why wouldn't I be here? This is MY house."

"Dalton," Millie's tone is hushed but urgent, "I don't feel right being here with your parents fighting."

Mom is loud enough to hear now, too. "I think you should crawl back to whoever's bed you just got out of."

I sigh. "Yeah, this isn't going to end well," I tell Millie.

She gets up and begins dressing. Mom yells as we enter the hallway, "THEN SLEEP IN THE GUEST ROOM. YOU ARE NOT GETTING IN MY BED!"

Their door opens, and Dad has his sight on a new target. "What is she doing here?" He growls at Millie and me, "Coming out of your room at this time of night!"

I put myself between my dad and Millie, holding her hand to give her my support. I tell her to keep walking.

"I asked you a question, son." I feel his index finger jab into my back. "This little relationship of yours is going to cost you EVERYTHING. IT ENDS NOW. IT IS DONE. OVER. DO YOU UNDERSTAND ME??" Dad grabs my arm and jerks me a step backward. "You are grounded until graduation. No girls. If you aren't at school or training, you are here studying. You will eat, sleep, study, and train. There is no room for a social life."

Still holding Millie's hand, I turn to face off with him. "You can't do that. I love her." I finally said it out loud, and not even to her, to the asshole who thinks he can stop us. I squeeze her hand. Since she is behind me, I can't see her reaction. Instead, I look at my mom and plead to her with my eyes to help.

Mom's eyes are full of sorrow. With pursed lips, she walks past me and ushers Millie downstairs.

"You love her?" My father snarls. "Well, if she loved you, she would let you go so you can live your dreams."

~Millie

What just happened up there? Dalton said he loves me, but not to me in a sweet, perfect moment like how it should have been done. He said it in the heat of an argument with his dad.

I am crying by the time Evie gets me to the door. "Is it really over?" I ask her.

"Aw, sweetie, that's between you and Dalton. Michael doesn't have the final say. But he will make it very hard on you two," she tells me, pulling me into a hug and rubbing my back as I weep into her shoulder.

A moment of clarity hits me, pausing the waves of heartbreak. "He's right, though," I tell her. "I love Dalton, and I can't stand in the way of his dreams."

"Oh honey, don't think that way," she says. Then she stops rubbing my back, straightens to her full height, and puts both hands on my shoulders. Pushing herself back to look me straight in the eyes, she demands, "Go home, now, Millie." Suddenly, her grip releases, and she turns to hurry up the stairs.

I can hear the scuffle of a fight, Michael shouting horrible things that I assume are directed toward me. My heart wants me to go back up there, but what would that help? All I can do is yell at them to stop. I'd likely make everything worse. Instead of standing up for myself, I heed Evie's advice and run home.

-Dalton

"Is she in on this? Is your mother letting you fuck girls under my roof now?" Dad snarls.

I have no answer because it is true. There has only been one, but arguing that seems futile.

143

"I understand you're eighteen, and you want to get your dick wet. I hope to God you are using protection because you don't want to make the same mistakes I did."

"Thanks for reminding me how I ruined your life before I was even born. Yes, we are careful-"

"Careful? If you were careful, you wouldn't have had that hickey I saw before Christmas. "

"That was an accident."

"How is hickey an accident? You have to be doing a lot of sucking to get one."

"Sorry, I'm not as experienced at hiding my affairs as you are." That comment gets to him. He stalks closer to me; I have never seen him so angry.

I can hear Mom and Millie downstairs. Millie is crying. I want to be the one holding her as she's upset—no, I don't want her to be sad at all. We should still be in my bed, snuggled under a blanket, not dragged into my parent's war.

"So that's a yes; your mother knows you have a little whore in your room at night."

All I see is red. I grab my father's collar in both of my fists. "Millie is not a whore." Then I push him away from me. "Where have you been? Sounds to me like you are the one out with some whore." I have to stop talking to dodge a punch.

He misses me and puts a hole in the wall.

"What the fuck?" I ask just before he tackles me.

"Michael! Let go of him!!" Mom screams.

Dad stops and sits up, "You, bitch! You are as horrible of a mother as you are a wife."

"Don't say those things about my mother!" I say as I tackle him back down.

I'm about to take a swing when my mom yells, "STOP! RIGHT NOW, BOTH OF YOU!"

144

I get up, not near as out of breath as the old man on the floor.

"Dalton, go to your room. Michael, you can have the guest room. We will talk about this in the morning when tempers have cooled off," to my father, she adds, "and you have sobered up."

I get in my room and call Millie, but for the first time in our relationship, she doesn't answer.

Chapter 17

-Dalton

In the morning, I call Millie. Again, she doesn't answer. She didn't leave it here, did she? Na, I would hear it ringing.

As I begin dialing the house line, I realize how ridiculous calling her is when she lives 50 feet away. I don't just want to talk to her; I want to see her. More importantly, I need to know she is alright—that *we* are alright.

Mrs. Wilkins answers the door and tells me Millie is out for a run. So I wait for her at home, watching from the porch swing. When I see her running down the street, I jog to her.

"Hey, how are you today," I ask.

"Um, well, I don't know." She won't make eye contact with me and starts stretching.

"I'll never understand how you can run for miles on end."

"It helps me clear my mind."

"Did it help? Do you feel better now?" I ask.

"Not really." Millie's eyes are bloodshot when she finally looks at me. It guts me to think that she was up crying all night. "He is right. We need to cool things down."

"What?" I grab her and beg, "Don't say that." I feel like my entire being is tearing apart.

She pushes me back. "I don't want to distract you from baseball. You have worked your whole life for this. You hardly go to the gym or the batting cages anymore because you spend all your time with me."

I try to pull her in, but she moves out of reach, heading into her house. "Millie. Please. Don't, don't do this," I choke out.

"We can still be friends. But I can't be the reason you don't make it."

"Millie, I love you. I can't make it without you."

She gives me a sad smile. "Dalton, don't make this harder than it is."

"DALTON! Get home NOW!" my father shouts.

I look over my shoulder to see my dad has come out to get the paper. When I turn back to Millie, she is shutting her front door behind her.

~Millie

I slump against the door as it shuts. Somehow, even though I cried all night, I still have tears to shed. Mom joins me on the floor, giving me what comfort she can with her arms. She stayed with me all night too. I guess I woke them up when I barged in.

"Are you sure this is what you want?" Mom asks.

"No. I want to be with Dalton. But it will never work, especially with his father ruling his life."

"I have never seen you so doom and gloom," she tells me.

The house smells like burnt sage and lavender from all the smudging she's been doing to cleanse the negative energy I've brought down on us. The scent calms me, and I finally stop crying. It's probably more of a pause because my heart feels like it got hit by a train. The Reality Express.

"The relationship was doomed from the beginning. We want different things in life."

"Love always finds a way, child." Mom kisses the top of my head. "Hey, I have an idea! I can make us appointments for a reading. Maybe we can find a crystal that speaks to you."

I get cleaned up from my run, but I don't take Mom up on her offer, nor leave my house for the rest of the day. I lay in bed so empty inside that it makes me sick to my stomach. Mom calls me in sick at school, so I can stay in hiding for a few more days.

Wednesday night, Angie and Danika bring me ice cream. They tell me Dalton has been at school, but he might as well be absent. It's more like a Dalton shell is walking the halls.

Mom makes me go to school Thursday, and I do everything to avoid Dalton. I have turned off my phone because if he calls me one more time, I might break. I don't even log in to AOL chat anymore.

Another week goes by. Weekends are the worst. I am lying in my cold, empty bed, watching a Sandra Bullock movie on my laptop. I have watched it on a loop all day. There's a knock on my door. Assuming it's one of my parents, I say, "Come in."

It's not Mom or Dad; it's Evie. "Hey, sweetie, how are you?"

My eyes well up, "I'm fine."

"You don't look fine," she says honestly.

"Oh, these tears are for Sandra, not me," I say, gesturing to my paused movie.

Evie gives a half-hearted smile. She is too wise to fool. "Dalton's not doing well, either." She sits on the edge of my bed and puts her hand on my foot. "Michael has been working from home. He only leaves during school hours." She shakes her head. "I always wanted him to spend more time as a family, but this isn't exactly what I had in mind." She looks down and fiddles with something in her hands. "I think he's watching to make sure Dalton doesn't run away with you."

"That's not going to happen. Don't worry; I have been staying away from him at school, too."

"That is what I'm afraid of." Evie looks me dead in the eyes, the same lavender eyes that Dalton has. Today they seem a little red and puffy, as if she's been crying too. "Dalton was never a very happy child, but he is positively miserable right now. He was so cheerful when you were together. You were, too." She clears her throat as she chokes up. "You could at least be there for him at school. Maybe then you both will get out of this slump and work something out."

"What's the point?" I shrug one shoulder. "In a few months, he will be going out of state to either go to college or join a team. I can't follow him. I have my own dreams to chase."

"I understand. But-"

I cut her off, "I'm sorry, Evie. But I don't want to end up like you and Mr. James. I don't want Dalton to resent me someday because he doesn't make it in baseball." I stand up, walk to the door, and open it for her to leave.

She follows my cue but pauses to reach out and cup my face. "I'm sorry this happened, Millie. I love you like a daughter and only want the best for you and my son. If that means you'll be happier apart, I will encourage him to give up on you." A tear rolls down her face, and she brushes it away with the hand that is holding a folded piece of paper. Then she realizes it is in her hand and hands it to me. "Dalton asked me to give this to you."

I take it, and she leaves. Going back to my bed, I hold the note, not knowing if I want to open it. I fiddle with it as I finish the movie. My curiosity is killing me, so I finally open it.

> *Millie-*
> *Don't give up on us*
> *I love you*
> *- D*

Short and sweet. I fold it back up and put it under the cola bottle that holds the dried flowers he gave me so long ago.

Chapter 18

-Dalton

The alarm goes off. I make a protein shake, go to school, practice, come home, eat whatever, study, and sleep. Repeat. That is what I do every day unless it is a weekend. Even then, it doesn't change much. I don't talk to anyone unless I absolutely must.

Nate tries to get through to me, but I really don't have much interest. Every day, I go to lunch and sit at an empty table. And every day, Nate and other guys on the team move to fill it. I don't even know a couple of them because they are underclassmen, yet they still show up.

"Just go talk to her," Nate encourages. "She's obviously as miserable as you are."

"Yeah, and say what? That it's complete bullshit that she let my father break us up."

"Man, that's not right," Jason says.

"Did you ever hear back from her after the note?" Nate asks.

"How did you know about that?"

"Angie told me."

A flash of embarrassment hits me. Millie told Angie, of course she would have. She still has people close to her, and I have teammates that I barely know. I get why Gramps wanted me to work on the friend thing now.

"I didn't realize you and Angie talked."

"I talk to everyone," Nate shrugs.

"But you are close enough to talk about Millie and me."

"Don't take it the wrong way." Nate claps me on the shoulder. "Angie is concerned about her friend just like I am."

He's right; I need to talk to her. Something this important can't be left hanging in the balance of a passed note. With new ambition, I toss my uneaten lunch and head to Millie's locker to wait for her.

The bell rings five minutes later. The hallway is so crowded Millie doesn't notice that I'm standing next to it, or she is ignoring me. "Millie," I hope she can't hear the desperation in my voice.

Green eyes, devoid of their usual sparkle, fix on me. I swear all the chaos around us stops while we are trapped in a staring contest. But all too soon, Millie drops her gaze and focuses on her task at her locker.

"Did you get my letter?"

She nods, still looking anywhere else but at me.

"Did you read it?"

Again, she only nods.

"And?"

Sighing, Millie says, "And it doesn't change anything." Just like when everything was great between us, she hands me the notebooks and textbooks for her next two classes. "We are on different paths. It wouldn't have lasted." With anger tinging her words, she slams the locker door shut as an exclamation.

"No, it can work," I beg, not caring if anyone is around to overhear. "You can spend your summers with me, and I'll spend my winters with you."

"I'll just distract you."

"Those were my father's words. You broke up with me because of what he said, not because there was something wrong in our relationship."

Instead of fighting for us, Millie turns to walk away. As if it's a second thought, she pivots back to grab her books from me. Tears are welling in Millie's eyes, making me feel like an ass for having this argument here, but where else am I going to do it? Dad has my life pinned down.

My father, or warden depending on how you look at it, has taken my phone and my bedroom TV; I'm only allowed to use my laptop in the dining room, where he can monitor why/how I'm using it. And, of course, he is driving me to school and practice because I can't be trusted. I have never seen him so much, and I loathe every minute of it.

Coincidentally, I have never seen my mother less. She makes it to my games, and sometimes I see her before she leaves for work. That's it. It's almost like my parents are tag team partners. Except, she hates him as much as I do.

The whole situation is unjust. So what if I had a girl in my room. That's all he can prove; besides, I'm 18! And if he wants to throw that "not under my roof" bullshit at me, where had he been? Not under *his roof*, that's for sure. As far as I'm concerned, Mom was the one present and in charge, and she sure as shit didn't care.

My only outlet is training. And because I take all my frustration out on the ball or in the gym, I'm playing better than ever. It has made the team better, too. They are all taking the game more seriously. We are neck and neck with only one other school in the state, and we're predicted to meet at the state tournament.

Typically, the only time I only see Millie is in the couple of classes we have together. We don't sit near each other, and we never speak, so much for staying friends.

~Millie

Five long weeks of putting on a fake smile and acting like everything is okay aren't enough. My spring break plans include locking myself in my room because it's the only place I can let go. Unfortunately, Michelle is home from college and can see through my act. Therefore, she is trying everything to cheer me up. Today she's taking me shopping, specifically swimsuit shopping. I would rather hide in my bed, but she tells me I'm sleeping my life away. Gah, it's the only place I want to be.

"This is ridiculous. I don't need a new suit," I complain. I don't add that my boobs are sore, and they don't appreciate being stuffed in small tight places meant to be shown off to people that I don't want to check them out.

"Oh, come on, we are the same size, and I don't want to try anything on because I got my period this morning. I feel all...blah!"

"Then why aren't we at home eating brownies and ice cream, watching Brad Pitt?" I walk out to model for her.

"Because you have been eating too many brownies and too much ice cream. Do you need another size?"

"Ugh, you bitch!" I say half-heartedly. I go back in to change into my clothes and think about what she said. Not the part about overeating ice cream, but about being on her period. I stop,

154

staring at myself in the mirror. My boobs hurt, I am gaining weight, and I am always moping around, wanting to sleep.

And last but not least, when was my last period??? I slap myself on the head, trying to think. Have I had it since we broke up? I can't really remember the last month; it has all been a blur. I put my hands on my tummy and imagine it getting huge. I can't be. I have just been stressed. I haven't been sick...except for yesterday. But that was just a bellyache from too much junk food, right? Oh, and that new incense Mom has been burning would make anyone nauseous.

Oh my God, what am I going to do if I am?

Chapter 19

-Dalton

I don't know why it's a surprise when spring break rolls around, and I am shipped off to baseball camp. After all, I'm grounded from dating, not baseball. I've gone to baseball camp every spring break for as long as I can remember. Why should this year be any different?

This year sucks more than ever, probably because I could care less about being here. And just when I think I can go home, Dad shows up. Once again, he ditches me in the hotel to "have drinks with some old friends." I guess it could be worse; I could be locked in my house, staring out the window, hoping to catch a sight of Millie coming or going.

Michael changes our flight plans last minute, again, causing me to miss two days of school. "Relax, son. Maybe we should enroll you at a private academy here to finish out your year."

"What would be the point? I only have about seven weeks left."

"Private tutoring, then. You've already been accepted to FSU, anyway."

"It's conditional. I still have to graduate on time."

"It's also conditional if you get drafted. And with how well you've been playing this year—I have to say I have overheard how impressed the scouts are with you."

"Then why am I still grounded?"

"You're going to complain about that? Making you buckle down has been the best thing for you."

I want to argue that it has only been good for my potential career, but I won't push it. As soon as he leaves for the bar, I hit the pool. I guess he doesn't care what I do as long as Millie isn't in the picture.

We take a redeye home, and I'm expected to return to school that morning. I'm in the second period when I catch Millie looking at me. I mouth, "What?" Hope blooms in my chest, but she looks away quickly. I try to catch her eye again. Has this been happening, and I just missed it?

I attempt to catch her attention again, but she gets out of the class too fast and avoids me for the rest of the day. I know I have another shot during calc, but she skips our day's last class.

Back to my routine: Eat, sleep, school, and baseball. No girls. No social life. I just exist until the night Mom stops in my doorway before she turns in for bed.

Knock, knock. Since I'm not allowed to shut my door, I turn to see Mom leaning against the doorway. "Hey, Dalton," she says in a quiet voice.

"Yeah, Mom?"

"I just wanted to let you know I have a work banquet Saturday the 12th."

I nod along to be polite because, really, what do I care?

Mom's voice drops to just above a whisper. "I told Michael that he is required to accompany me." She must notice my disinterest because she walks in and opens the daily planner the school gave us to record our assignments and whatnot. Mom flips to the date she is talking about and uses a red pen to write, then circles and underlines it a bunch of times.

"Since you don't have your phone, you can use this in case I need to contact you." Mom places her old pager on the desk next to me before she leaves.

That's odd. Why would I need a pager? I could just use the house line. Unless…. unless I'm not at home. I look at what she wrote on my calendar. Above her handwriting is an old note I had put in about Prom. Seeing it cuts my heart until I realize what Mom is insinuating.

Prom
<u>Mom</u> and <u>DAD</u> out 5-?

How did she know? Did she plan the work dinner? Do I really care? She is telling me the coast is clear. It turns out she is my tag-team partner and tagging herself into play, taking on the burden so I can go to Prom.

School dances have never interested me, but I know Millie is into all that shit. I have to tell her about the escape plan and ask her to be my date before some asshole beats me to it.

This is the most alive I have felt in months. As soon as I hear Michael go to bed, I sneak over to Millie's.

~Millie

I'm startled awake when I hear knocking, even more so when I realize it is coming from my window. Quickly, I check what I am wearing before I open the curtains to see what awaits me there. A T-shirt and gym shorts—pretty much my go-to these days. Pulling back the blinds, I see Dalton standing on the garage roof. I open the window, and he climbs in.

"What are you doing here?" I whisper. Does he know? Who would have told him? I've been meticulous with who I share my secret.

"I can't stand it anymore. I needed to see you—to talk to you," Dalton says.

"So, you chose to scare me half to death? I thought you were a serial killer."

"Why would you open your window to a serial killer?"

I palm my forehead. "I didn't open it until I saw it was you."

He takes a step closer to me. "I miss you, Millie." Then he reaches out and pulls me into his embrace.

I can't help it; I melt into him. For a moment, the world feels right. I feel my eyes filling up with emotion—damn hormones.

He asks, "You haven't already accepted any prom invites, have you?"

"What?" I pull back out of his arms. "Are you high? Why on earth would I go to Prom with someone?" Silently, I add "else."

"Go to prom with me," he blurts.

This sounds familiar. I play along. "Are you asking me if I want to go to prom with you, or are you telling me to go to prom with you?"

Dalton smiles, and it stills my broken heart. His Adam's apple bobs as he swallows. "Millie, do you want to go to prom with me?" His eyes are free of the pain that has been present since I broke things off, and hope shines in them now.

I sigh. Yes. No. Hell, I don't know. "How do you think you'll get to go to prom?"

"Mom's going to distract the warden so I can have a free night."

"Wait, you're telling me you and your mom are planning on sneaking around behind your father's back, and you want me to get in the middle of it. Gee, what could go wrong?" I step away from him and sit on the edge of my bed.

He looks at me with sad eyes. "Well, when you put it that way."

"It hurt too much the last time. I don't know if I want to live through that again."

"I can't even tell you how sorry I am about that," he says.

"I know. I'm sorry, too."

"Please, Millie. I still love you."

"I love you too," disconnected, I add, "just from farther away."

Dalton grabs me, pulling me to stand again, and crushes me to him. His mouth meets mine, and he kisses me with all the pent-up emotions he has hidden for the last couple of months. Dalton's hands travel up my shirt. When his fingers find that I am not wearing a bra, he moans. He pulls my shirt off and throws it on the floor. I pull his shirt off at almost the same time. Our bodies collide back together. My hands explore his arms. He has been working out more, and it shows. He's leaner, too. In the back of my mind, I've known all of this, it shows through his clothes, but I haven't had my hands on him to confirm it. He's losing weight while I'm gaining it.

Palming my incredibly tender breast, he kisses my neck and down to suck my nipple. But it is too painful now. Can he tell I've gone up a cup size since we were last together?

"Ow," I say and push him back. I grab my shirt and hold it against my chest.

"Shit, sorry. I couldn't hold back. I—"

160

I interrupt him. "It's fine, but you should go." Shit why did I say that? My body craves this, but my brain controls my words, not my heart...or libido.

Dalton looks around my room like he is looking for something to say. His eyes stop at my nightstand like something is interesting, but then he looks back at me. "I know you still want to be together, Millie. A love like ours doesn't fade." He bends to grab his shit and pulls it on. "If you decide you want to go, page me 143 at this number," he says, handing me a piece of paper. With one last look of longing, he goes back through the window he came in.

The next day, I tell Angie and Danika at lunch. I'm not at all surprised by their reactions. Angie always cheers for a love story, and Dani has trust issues.

Angie says, "Aw, you have to go, Millie."

"No, she doesn't." Danika glares at Angie. To me, she advises, "Don't go. Or at least don't go with Dalton."

"Dani, I swear you hate men so much I'm starting to think you are a lesbian," Angie snaps. Then in a kinder tone, she asks me, "Millie, why wouldn't you go? I know he is the only guy you would consider going with."

"Number one: I don't particularly want to wear a frickin' ball gown all freakin' night. Number two: my heart isn't mended from our breakup. And, most importantly, number three: I don't want to lose my resolve and tell him about you-know-what."

"You should tell him about you-know-what. Keeping that from him is about the lowest of the low," more sound advice from Dani.

"No. Dalton told me before he wishes his mom wouldn't have told his dad, so I'm not going to repeat that past mistake."

"But Dalton isn't his dad," Angie pleads. "You don't know what kind of relationship they had before Dalton was born."

161

I know more than I care to. "You two are not helping me. Should I go or not?" I ask.

"He said to page him 143? Isn't that the 'I love you' code?" Angie asks.

"I think so, but that's not the point," I retort.

Ever the romantic, Angie says, "If you are in love with him, you have to give it another chance."

Even Dani agrees with that and gives me an idea—a loophole.

Chapter 20

-Dalton

Waiting for Millie to page is killing me. I barely sleep because I'm constantly checking Mom's old pager. Therefore, I oversleep, making me too late to catch her before first period. She avoids me during English, then begs out early to use the bathroom. Like the stalker Dani dubbed me as, I watch every move Millie makes at lunch. Not once does she return so much as a glance. Angie, however, gives me a few withering looks over Millie's shoulder, giving me a shred of hope. I know Angie is a hopeless romantic and my best bet for an ally at that table.

"Hey, Nate," I say to the guy who still hasn't let me sit alone.

"What's up?" Nate asks from beside me.

"Have you talked to Angie lately?"

"Not really, why?"

"Just wondering if you heard anything about Millie."

"Somethin' you want me to find out?"

Pausing, I debate how much I want to tell him. Then I suck up my pride because I can use all the help I can get to get Millie back. "I asked her to Prom, but she hasn't given me an answer."

Nate's hand comes down on my shoulder harder than I expect. "YES! It's about time you two work things out. Your dad loosening the reins then?"

"Not exactly," I explain the highlights of the situation to him as Millie pulls out a notebook and conspires with her friends over whatever she is writing.

When I get to calc, I find a note folded up like a Chinese football on my desk.

143—BUT, I will only go if I meet you there. That way, I'm not the one breaking the rules. This is not a date. We will just happen to be at the same place at the same time. I will not face the wrath of "the warden." ~MW

As soon as my eyes leave the paper, they search out Millie. A blush stains her cheeks as she hides a smile. My heart races towards the light shining at the end of this tunnel of misery.

Everyone around me keeps talking about how time is flying by since it's our last month of school, but it is dragging on for me. Mom gets me a tux, and we make a game plan for Prom night. Nate and Angie are in on the details too, and Mom hires a limo for our small group. I thought it was over the top, but she argued that it would keep Dad from noticing my truck had been used, plus it would make the night extra special.

May 12 finally arrives. The day drags until my parents leave, and I rush to get ready as soon as they are gone. When I see a limo pull up to Millie's house, Nate, Angie, Dani, and her boyfriend, Lance, unload and go inside for pictures. I hate that

164

I'm left out of that, but Millie didn't want to do the date thing, so I have to be sneaky. It's absurd, but I will take what I can get.

Millie is the last to get in. She is surprised to see me. "I didn't think I would see you until we were at the dance."

"Well, we just happen to be two people in the same place at the same time. Does it matter if that same place is at the reception hall or in a limo?" She sighs and rolls her eyes, but I grab her hand, grinning from ear to ear.

First, we go to dinner at an Italian restaurant, then to an old, restored reception hall. I've never gone to a big school dance like this, so I am surprised by everything. Balloon archways, streamers, multiple photo backdrops—one of which has a professional photographer. Millie and I pose for a couple's photo and group shots with everyone we came with tonight. It's fun dancing and goofing off—I didn't expect that, either. Why didn't I break out of my shell before my senior year?

At about 10, I get a page from Mom saying they will be home in an hour. Nate and I planned an escape with his car being in the parking lot if we needed it. I'm grateful Millie and Angie decide to leave early too.

Nate drops me off at 10:16, giving Millie and me a little time to spare.... alone. She has relaxed and agrees to come over and sit on the porch swing.

"This was fun; I'm glad we went," she admits.

I put my arm around her and whisper in her ear, "I don't think I told you how beautiful you look tonight."

"Thanks, you don't look half bad yourself," she giggles. "We were certainly the best-looking non-couple there." Her carefree happiness is the best sound in the world, but her words punch me in the heart. We are still a couple, dammit.

Not wanting to pick that fight, I wistfully say, "I don't want this night to end."

"Me neither, but tonight you are Cinderella, and everything is about to go poof."

"We still have 30 minutes or so."

"Are you propositioning me?" She pretends to act astonished.

"Mmm," I moan in appreciation. I start kissing Millie behind her ear to her collarbone.

"What I have in mind will take more than 30 minutes," she says, relaxing into my touch. "I'll leave my window open if you want to come over after your dad gets home."

I stop and look at her. "I can't. I have to get in trouble tonight." My soul dies a little knowing what I'm missing.

Millie's eyes round into worried saucers. "What? Aren't you in the clear? You said your mom orchestrated this."

"Yeah, but I have to make it look like I was up to no good so he doesn't suspect what I really did."

"Fine," Millie huffs. Rightfully pissed, she stands to leave. "I guess I will get going then, so you can get busy with your charade."

"Wait!" I grab her hand and rise. "One more slow dance." I tug her back into my arms and start swaying.

She hesitates, softening to my suggestion. "But there isn't any music."

"I don't care." I don't have the romantic words to tell her that the night's sounds of crickets, frogs, and the rustling of leaves, are all the music we need. I'm sure if I try, it will come out corny. Instead, I reiterate, "I'm just not ready to say goodnight yet."

My pager goes off in warning; 15 minutes. I hold my love's face as I kiss her goodnight. We walk across the street, and I kiss her again at her door. Before she goes in, I say, "Please tell me tonight changes things. I know we can't go back to what we had, but at least at school, can we be more than just two people in the same class ignoring each other?"

166

Millie bites her lips together and nods.

"I know you're thinking about something else, but I am taking that as a yes." I kiss her one last quick time and run across the street.

Part of prepping for tonight was leaving a mess of food around. I even left my dirty gym socks on the couch, just the way Michael hates. I run past all of that, undressing as I go upstairs to hide the tux in my closet. Then I go back downstairs to the liquor cabinet for Dad's whisky and start drinking from the bottle. It's stronger than I expected, so I end up dumping more of it down the sink than down my throat.

I didn't think twice when Mom requested that I dump the liquor. Dad's tongue gets extra mean when he drinks, and he boasts about buying the fine stuff. Since he has been back, he has had a better relationship with the glass bottle than with his family.

Next, I make my way to the hot tub out back and get in with only moments to spare before they get home.

"What's going on here?" My sire's stern voice booms when he gets inside and sees the mess in the kitchen.

Mom calls out to me, "Dalton?" Then she says to him, "I think I hear the jets on outside." They walk out and see me in the tub with the whiskey bottle in my hand.

"Oh, my God! Michael, he is going to kill himself! Dalton, you can't drink like that in a hot tub!!" My mom is good at this farce.

"He's not going to kill himself, Evelyn."

"He could! He's going to have heat exhaustion, and he could pass out and drown!"

"Don't be ridiculous; he will probably just have a nasty hangover from dehydration." He walks over and takes the bottle out of my hand. "He has better chances of dying at my hand for drinking all of my whiskey."

167

"This is all your fault, Michael! You push him too hard. He doesn't have any friends anymore, and you are the reason he's broken-hearted."

"I am the reason he is going to make it someday!" he shouts back.

I know I have to do something to break this up, but I don't know what. "Guys, I'm fine," I slur. I start trying to get out. Honestly, I don't have to fake it too much; I chugged as much as possible before they got here.

"Michael, help him!"

He reaches to help, but I growl at him, "I said I'm fine." I get out and trudge through the house. I don't even dry off. I just leave a trail of water as I walk to my bedroom. They continue to argue, but it all fades away as I fall asleep.

Tonight was fun, but I know my head is going to pay for it tomorrow.

~Millie

I was afraid going to Prom with Dalton would break my heart all over again, but it helped me heal. I'm still not whole; I'm fractured, but the pieces are put back together. Dalton and I find a new rhythm as school comes to an end. We aren't exactly a couple, but we are more than friends. Some days it seems like a fragile balancing act that we are trying so desperately not to fall off.

I spend the following weekend with Michelle in Columbia. I have a meeting with the admissions department at the University of Missouri to explain my situation. Together, we come up with a new plan for college. I'll start classes this summer to get some credits before the baby is born. My sister and I look for housing to accommodate the soon-to-be three of us and sign a lease on a small two-bedroom apartment close to campus.

I thought my dreams would melt away when I found out I was pregnant. Luckily, my family is exceptionally supportive, and they all agree to help me succeed with school and single parenthood.

Yet, I still can't bring myself to tell Dalton.

Chapter 21

-Dalton

This season, from the standpoint of the game, has been the best of my life. I'm hitting everything, unstoppable on the field, and I mesh well with everyone on the team....well, everyone except Bobby Stevens. Lately, he has been mouthy in the locker room. Usually, I tune him out, but I've had enough of his shit.

"I am so glad I never fucked the slut. Have you seen how fat she's getting? What a total cow. No wonder DJ hit it and quit it," he says to some of the underclassmen since none of the juniors or seniors put up with him anymore.

What the Hell? He's not talking smack about Millie, is he?

"Why don't you shut the fuck up, Stevens," I say.

"Oh, so you didn't quit it? You like a little more cushion for the pushin'?" he jabs at me.

He's gone too far; I cannot believe he has the balls to talk like that in front of me. Generally, I don't have a mean bone in my body, but he knows better than to breathe her name around me.

I stand up to my now full six-foot-one. I have also packed on quite a bit of muscle since the last time I taught him a lesson. I get right up in Stevens' grill and say, "I told you to SHUT. THE. FUCK. UP!"

My lunch buddies: Nate, Jason, and Kyle, are standing around me, ready to jump between us. Nate says, "Come on, guys, you don't want to fight. We are too close to the championships."

Jason tries to tug me away, saying, "He's not worth it, man."

The underclassmen, Luke, Chris, and Dave, laugh nervously while my friends walk me out to the fresh air to cool off. I don't hear what Bobby says next, but there is a loud "BAM" as a body hits the lockers. I turn to see Luke, one of the sophomores, jogging to catch up to us.

"You don't want to know, but I took care of him for ya," Luke says, holding his hand. "It's too bad he won't be seeing too well for tomorrow's game."

"Like Bobby would do much more than sit on the bench anyway," Kyle quips.

"I think I should get some ice and maybe an x-ray," Luke says, looking at his swollen hand.

"Well, isn't this great," Nate mutters. "I hope we aren't down two guys now."

~Millie

Angie picks me up early to go to the game. We get seats a few rows back, just off the dugout near first base. I'm always hungry, but today I'm stress-eating. Ballpark food is the best, anyway.

We are tied 2:2 at the bottom of the 7th. Dalton is up to bat. Memories from going to the cages with him filter through my mind. We did more than make-out there; he tried teaching me the mechanics of getting a perfect hit. As someone wanting to study kinesiology, I've been a critic of everyone's technique since those cold days.

The first throw gets past him; a swing and a miss. The second is called a ball. The third pitch is a fastball right down the middle; Dalton swings, crushing it into center field. The two guys on base make it in, and Dalton is rounding second. I can't believe it, but he keeps going and has to dive for third. Afraid he is out or hurt, I cover my face with my hands, fingers spread open to peek through—just like how I watch horror movies. The base ump signals safe, and the crowd goes wild. I am the only one not on my feet cheering. I need more candy and to pee again, but I don't dare move until Dalton is back in the dugout.

Kyle's up next. He hits a grounder to the outfield. It takes the centerfielder a brief moment to scoop up the ball and throw it to the catcher, reaching home plate half a second after Dalton's foot. This game is going to give me a heart attack.

I get up to take care of my needs and literally bump into Evie when I come out of the bathroom.

"Oh, excuse me," she says.

"Sorry, Mrs. James."

She takes a second look at the girl she ran into. I'm in a hat, but also wearing a lot of baggy clothes these days. I'm not really showing yet, but I have gained weight everywhere.

"Millie?" She pulls me into a hug. "It is so good to see you, dear. And you stop that Mrs. James BS. You know better."

"Yes, ma'am."

"None of that either. How have you been? Did you have fun at Prom?" she asks.

"Yes. Thank you. Did you see the pictures?"

"No," she says with a pout.

Dalton only wanted a wallet when the professional ones came in, so I kept the rest. "Here, you can have this one. I have more at home." I give her the small one I keep in my purse.

She looks at it, rubbing her finger across the photo. A tear forms in her eye, and in a rough voice, she whispers, "Thank you."

"I have more; I just have yet to get them developed. I'll get doubles and give the copies to Dalton."

Nodding, she says, "I would love to see them, too."

By the time I get all my snacks, our team is in the field. Dalton is the first baseman; nothing gets past him. No runs are made in the eighth on either side, giving my nerves a short break. Unfortunately, they get three runs in the ninth, thanks to an error by Bobby. 6:5—them.

In the bottom of the ninth, our first guy strikes out. Up to bat next is Nate. The pitch goes wild, and the ball hits him in the shin. From the look on her face, Angie's a little more concerned about him than a friend would be. There must be more going on between them that she hasn't told me, but then I haven't been the best company lately.

"Have you seen more of Nate since Prom?"

Shaking her head sadly, Angie answers, "Not really. He told me he isn't much for dating."

"Nate said that?" Haven't I seen him out with girls—I feel like he's always got a girl on his arm, and not in a player kind of a way. He's definitely boyfriend material. "Wasn't he dating someone earlier this year?"

"That's the thing about Nate. He takes girls out, often multiple times, but he doesn't let it get too far."

Nate steals second while our third batter, Tyler, is up. Tyler gets a base hit, and Nate gets in a pickle going for third. He is called safe, and the crowd erupts in commotion. Dalton is up next. I swear he looks right at me just before he takes the plate. The first pitch is a swing and a miss. Strike one. Then the second is called a ball. The opposing team is getting ugly with their jeers. The next is foul. He looks right at me again when he steps back to refocus. The fourth throw looks good; he swings, and the ball soars out of the park.

Dalton's home run brings Nate and Tyler in with him. 6:8 We win with a walk-off victory!!

The place is a madhouse; Angie and I are holding each other and jumping up and down. There is a short ceremony awarding Dalton MVP. The scouts and reporters are definitely in full force. I just know all of Dalton's dreams are going to come true. I am happy for him but selfishly sad.

Sometime since Prom, I got to thinking about telling Dalton my secret and the life we could have as a family. All of my fantasies were of us going to college. I promised myself and our baby I would tell him if he didn't get drafted this year. But there is no way he won't get that call. I can see that now; he is a shooting star on his way to fame.

Angie looks over at me; I know she can read me like a book. Instead of pushing us toward the field with all the others celebrating, she says, "Come on, let's get out of here before traffic is a mess."

Chapter 22

-Dalton

We actually fucking won the state championship! People and cameras swarm the field, and my teammates lift me off my feet with my new MVP award. While they carry me around on their shoulders, I see Millie leaving the stands. She smiles and waves but doesn't join the crowd.

There isn't an end in sight at Coach Thompson's afterparty. Even Michael, dripping in smugness and pride, has let go of the reins and is having a good time. He doesn't seem to care where I am, making me wonder if he'd notice if I left. Because, as good as it is to be here, there is only one person I want to celebrate with, and she never showed up.

It turns out to be harder than anticipated to sneak away. Every time I try, I get pulled into another conversation. Around midnight, the opportunity presents itself.

"Hey guys, I hate to cut it short, but it's my curfew," Nate announces.

"Are you shitting me?" Kyle complains, "They won't care after our VIC-TOR-Y!"

Nate chuckles at Kyle's antics. "Dad was sure to remind me, 'Nothing *good happens after midnight.*'"

"I think I'll call it a night, too," I say, creeping towards the door.

"No way, D!" Kyle answers. "Your dad is here. You, my friend, are staying."

Quickly, I put my finger to my lips, giving the universal signal to shut-the-fuck-up, and wink at Kyle. He rolls his eyes but nods his understanding.

As Nate and I leave, we see Stevens all over some blonde chick. Thankfully it looks consensual□ because I don't want to waste my time dealing with him again.

Nate gives me a lift, pulling up in front of my house. Instead of walking up the path through the front door, I cross the street and climb onto the garage roof to Millie's window. She's probably sleeping, so in lieu of knocking, I check to see if it is unlocked. Bingo!

As I suspected, Millie's sound asleep, curled on her side, facing the wall. The sight makes my heart ache, missing the nights we were free to spend together. Tonight, I'm stealing the privilege back.

I kick my sneakers off and crawl on the covers to snuggle up to my girl. The past few months have been long and hard, and holding her to me makes me feel complete.

She stirs, rolling onto her back. "Dalton?"

"Shh. Yes, sweetheart, it's me."

"What time is it?" she asks.

"About 12:30."

"We have rehearsal at school tomorrow."

I chuckle, "Yes, we do." Of all things, she would bring up school. "If you're tired, just let me hold you while you sleep."

Millie snuggles in close to my chest. This right here is the cherry on top of my day. Breathing in the scent of her shampoo floats memories of the showers we used to take together through my mind. I think about how incredible the nights were when I held her in my arms while we slept.

"Congratulations."

I thank her and kiss the top of her head. She's not a topping making my day better; she is a main ingredient. Suddenly I understand why my father is so threatened by her. I would probably choose a life with Millie over baseball, but what he doesn't understand is that Millie would never make me choose.

"I was there; did you see me?" she whispers.

"Yes. I'm glad you came, but you were too far away."

Hands slip under my shirt, and Millie's piano fingers play against my skin. "I thought you were tired."

"I'm always tired. And horny," Millie admits. "Make love to me, Dalton."

"Are you sure you're even awake?"

"If I'm dreaming, I don't want to wake up." The delicateness of her actions turns demanding as she rolls atop me, tugging at my shirt as she goes.

I can't say I wasn't hoping for this, but I am surprised. I laugh again, helping her undress me.

Millie's face crashes down on mine, covering me in wet kisses. It's not until I cup her face with my palm that I realize the wetness isn't from her mouth.

"Millie," I pull back to look at her in the soft moonlight, "are you crying?"

"Yes," she sniffles, "We graduate Saturday. Then we will both be going our separate ways. This is probably our last opportunity to be like this."

"Don't say that. We'll have all summer..." Shit, she's right. I don't want that to be true, but shit. "This isn't going to be our last night together," I vow.

"Shhh," Millie's lips silence me from saying more. "I don't want to talk anymore."

"One more thing."

Millie answers with a slight whine of annoyance. "Condom?" I ask, kicking myself for leaving my wallet in my bat bag.

Mille pauses before reaching for the little jewelry box on her nightstand—the one with the soda bottle and dried flowers I gave her so long ago. "I only have one."

She passes me the damn thing, but I'm not ready to suit up yet. We've played the "let's see how long Dalton can last before we need the condom" game before, and it usually ends in a close call. But, if this is going to be our last time together, I'm going to make it last as long as possible.

I might be staying half-dressed for now, but Millie doesn't have to. I want to see all of her, but she stops me when I try to remove her shirt, claiming to be cold. She doesn't feel like that to me; she is hot everywhere I touch.

Rolling Millie onto her back, I kiss every inch of skin, whether it's covered or not. When I can't wait any longer, I position myself to enter her, but before I do, I gaze into her eyes. It's too dark to see the shade of green they are—the color that has become my favorite over the years. I can see the whites of her eyes flare when I thrust into her, joining our bodies as one.

I love her body, pouring my soul into what could be our last time together. The memory of this night will be in my mind forever.

178

Chapter 23

~Millie

Yesterday was graduation. Other than a few pictures, I didn't talk to Dalton much. Michael was in the crowd, and I didn't want to have to see or speak to him.

Since Dalton snuck into my bed two nights ago, I've been lying to him left and right. He wanted to spend that day together—I had to pack, but I told him I had last-minute graduation prep. He asked me out for dinner—I said I had plans with Angie and Dani. He wanted to go to graduation parties together—I made up an excuse that I was spending the day with family. He asked about my graduation party—I told him I was doing a joint thing with the girls on Sunday evening. But I'm not having one. The car was packed last night because I'm getting out of town as fast as possible.

My wrongs against Dalton are stacking up, and I pray he will forgive me someday. I don't know how far off that will be. Will it be a few months from now, or will it be years—decades? Will we both be old and gray? Will his beautiful eyes be cloudy with cataracts?

Will he hate me?

I'm sick of lying to Dalton, afraid I will slip up, or he will see in my eyes that I'm holding back on him. So I'm going to drop off the goodbye/graduation gift on his porch swing. I'm too chickenshit to face him one more time.

Just as I am stepping off his porch, the door opens.

"Millie?" Dalton calls me. Damnit, I forgot he's a morning person.

"Oh, hey. I was just dropping that off," I say, gesturing to the two small boxes on the swing, "it's so early I didn't want to ring the bell."

I can see the accusation in his eyes. He looks at the gift and back at me. Then he peers over my head at my car that's loaded for my college trip. Drawing his eyebrows together and frowning, he says, "You going somewhere?"

"Yeah," I confess. I can feel myself breaking in half from all the pressure, but I have no choice but to keep it together one more time.

"What about your party?"

"I… I lied. I'm getting a head start on classes this summer, so I have to go today."

Shock laced with pain shoots through Dalton's eyes. "I got you something, too." He begs, "Please, don't leave until I get back." He turns and runs upstairs.

I guess I'm staying now, so I go back up and sit on the swing. Dalton returns outside and stops, looking straight ahead, shoulders slumped.

"Here," I say.

He turns, and his whole face is frowning. "I thought you were gone." Then he sits next to me and puts his arm across the back of the swing.

"Open this first," I say, giving him a box full of pictures. I had five rolls developed on Friday, and I put all the good ones in a shoebox wrapped in contact paper.

We look through them, laughing and crying—well, I'm the only one crying. He holds me with one arm. We comment on most of them, reminiscing on our short love affair.

"Make sure you share these with your mom," I tell him. "She's looking forward to seeing them."

"When did you talk to her?"

"I bumped into her at the game."

"Oh, she didn't tell me," Dalton says as he opens the smaller box. It is one half of a broken heart charm. Inscribed on it says, **Achieve Your Dreams**, and on the other side, *I still love you, just farther away ~MW.*

"I have one, too," I say, taking mine off. I have it on a long necklace chain. Mine says, **Don't give up on us**, on one side and the other, *I love you -D.* "I had them inscribe it with our handwriting. Mine is from the note your mom gave me." Dalton's never been a big talker, but this unspoken moment is uncomfortable for me. "I guess it was kind of corny. I just wanted-"

"It's perfect," he cuts me off, sounding a little choked up, and takes his charm out of the box. Together they make a whole heart. "I love it. I might even have to put mine on a chain to wear like yours. I like how it sits close to your heart."

"I'm glad you like it. It was either this or matching tattoos," I say, lamely trying to make a joke.

"Matching tats would be cool. We still can if you don't go today."

"I am going as soon as I get off your porch. I already said goodbye to everyone else." Not to mention, I'm pretty sure pregnant women can't get tattoos, I keep to myself.

Anguish is evident in his voice as he accuses, "You were going to leave without saying goodbye to me. That's why you dropped this off so early."

My body trembles with shame. I've already been crying, so a few more tears escape. This is why I was avoiding a face-to-face goodbye. I knew I would be a blubbering mess. "Guilty. You can always call me, though. Let me know how the draft goes."

"I will. And if I don't make it, I'll visit you before I go to school." A light bulb seems to click in his mind. "Hey, I just realized I don't know where you're going."

He can't come; he would definitely see my body changing. He would know and wouldn't continue pursuing his dream.

What's one more lie at this point? I say the first in-state school that's about as far away as I can think of, "SEMO."

"Oh, you do have quite the drive today. You're driving the whole way by yourself?"

"Yeah."

"Millie, Cape Girardeau over five hours away."

I shrug it off, knowing karma will kick me hard for this someday.

Dalton bobs his head while playing with a small box as if he is mulling something over.

"I'll be fine," my tone sounds rude, but I don't mean for it to; I just want to end the lie.

His gaze clears, and it is sharp enough to cut. "I'm sure you will." He swallows nervously, looking back down at the box. "Here, I didn't have time to wrap it." It's covered in velvet— probably jewelry inside.

I take the gift and open it. My suspicions are correct, but it isn't a necklace or a pair of earrings—there's a ring shining in the center of the box. It's simple and elegant; a silver infinity knot wrapped around a band of tiny diamonds. I gasp, "It's beautiful."

"Just like you." Dalton clears his throat and continues, "It's a promise ring."

Now I am crying. "Yeah, I thought so." I wipe my cheeks and sniffle. "And what are you promising with this ring?"

He takes the tiny ring out of the box and puts it on the third finger of my left hand. "I promise to come to you when I can, I promise you the world when I can give it to you, and I promise to *never* stop loving you."

"Those are good promises."

He scoops me up into his arms and holds me while I cry. "Promise you'll wait for me, too."

"I will, I promise."

"Don't go yet. Let's have this day for ourselves." His hoarse plea nearly breaks me.

"Dalton," I want to say yes but can't. I have to get out of here before I tell him the one thing that will ruin everything. I breathe in my resolve. "I can't." I kiss him one last long, deep kiss and step out of his embrace. "I love you." I walk to my car and turn to see him standing in the same spot. It looks like he's crying now, too. I wave as I get in and drive to Columbia.

Tears continue to stream as I drive the hour and a half to start the next phase of my life. I made my decision, and now I have to live with it—regrets and all.

-Dalton

In the hours since Millie left, I have watched three episodes of Pitching Hard, pounded out a workout, moped around the house, shuffled through the photos she gave me half a dozen times, and went to the Batcave to crush some balls. But once I get in the familiar, safe space, I crumble. I'm not a man that cries, but I bawl like a baby. It's like I'm being torn to pieces by the two things I love most in life—baseball vs. Millie.

She should have made it down to Cape by now. Why hasn't she called? At the ten-hour mark, I cave and phone her. She doesn't answer until the fourth ring and keeps the conversation short.

She sounds optimistic about her new digs, but it doesn't make me feel better.

I wish I were with her. I want to see where she is and know that it's safe. This doesn't feel right.

Three days go by without a word from Millie. Am I on her mind as much as she is on mine?

No moping around today, though, because I'm a ball of anxiety. It's draft day, and Dad is hosting a small party. Unbeknownst to me, an agent shows up as well. However, Dad isn't the least bit surprised to see him, and I know it's a good thing. I'm kind of in a haze from all the chaos, and when we hear my name, everyone cheers—like at New Year's when the ball drops.

New Year's. Fuck, what I wouldn't give to go back to that night. Although, after the hell I've endured this week, I'm kinda pissed at Millie. How could she just leave like that? Why did she jump on my father's plan for my life so easily?

And now I hate myself for feeling that way. I love Millie and will prove to her that we can beat the odds. If only she would try a little harder.

Once the celebration has calmed down, I call Millie to tell her the good news. I'll be going to Ohio to play on a farm team until I work my way up.

I can tell she is happy for me, and she wishes me the best. But once again, she keeps the conversation clipped. I invite her to come back for my send-off party, but she sends her regrets—killing me just a tad more.

Chapter 24

~Millie

It's late July, and the song "Cruel Summer" by BananaRama is playing in the cold waiting room. The chorus resonates with my soul; I've never felt a song hit me so hard.

Everything is hard: school, pregnancy, my new waitressing job, anytime Dalton contacts me... I either cry myself to sleep or pass out from exhaustion. I can't imagine how much harder it will be with a newborn.

A nurse walks through the door, "Millie Wilkins?"

I stand and follow her back for my appointment. I don't even want to know what my weight is today. Last month I was lectured about normal weight gain because I had already exceeded what I should be at full term. How can I help that food is my only comfort these days??

The nurse takes my vitals, and I get on the frigid table for my first and probably only sonogram. "Dad couldn't make it again?"

"No, he had to work."

"That's too bad. I hope he's around for you after the baby is born."

"Yeah," a tear slips as I look down at my round belly.

"Millie?"

"Hmm?" I wipe my face and meet her eye.

"The father's absent, isn't he?"

Heat rushes to my face. "He wants to be here; he just doesn't live close."

"Sure, sure."

Despite the condescending vibes from the nurse, the rest of the appointment goes well. The student that does the sonogram tells me everything looks good to her, but a doctor will review everything as well. The baby isn't as cooperative as we hoped, but the technician is reasonably certain it's a girl.

As I walk home, there's a pep in my step, imagining all the little girl stuff—dolls, hair bows, dresses. When I get in, I start typing Dalton an email. It's a weird comforting torture writing to him as if he knows the truth. I don't know if it's therapeutic or crazy. Nevertheless, it's a useless email that I can't send; he can't learn the things I have divulged in it.

For some reason, I save it, taking the domain off his address, just in case I bump or click send on it someday.

As I skim over my inbox, my phone rings, and I panic. Did that email actually send? Looking at the unknown number on the screen only eases my anxiety slightly.

Quickly, I double-check that my email is still sitting unsent and answer the call with bated breath, "Hello?"

"Hello," a calm, feminine voice replies. "Is this Millie Wilkins?"

Hearing that it is a woman's voice calms me, but I'm still on edge due to the formality in her tone. Suspiciously, I answer, "This is she."

"Hello, Millie. This is Miranda Ross from James, Kauffman, and Associates. We are representing Carrie Appleton in her case against Robert Stevens. I was hoping to meet with you regarding a similar encounter you may have had with Mr. Stevens."

The adrenaline coursing through my veins turns from panic about the future to dread about my past. "Um, what encounter?"

"Are you denying that he attempted to sexually assault you?"

"I'm sorry; *who* are you again?"

The woman impatiently sighs. "Miss Wilkins, I am a paralegal working on a case in which your name was brought to our attention that Robert Stevens has a history of committing sexual assault. I am hoping you will agree to meet with me to discuss your... experience."

Oh my God. Bobby did it again... to Carrie Appleton.... and now I'm getting drug back into it.

"I don't know, I... it... Nothing happened. He tried, but my boyfriend chased him off. Well, he wasn't my boyfriend at the time, but he was shortly thereafter."

"His name?"

"Dalton James." How does she know it happened to me but doesn't have his name?

"And he can testify that this happened as well?" She sounds optimistic.

"He could, but he isn't really in the picture anymore. He moved away." Shit, why did I give her his name?

"I would still like his contact information. Can you come to our office Tuesday?"

"I don't know. I have class and a busy work schedule."

"Millie," her voice is gentle now, "you aren't in trouble here. We are trying a case against Mr. Stevens. Wouldn't you like to see him punished for what he did to you? To Carrie? There are three more girls on my list to contact."

How many more aren't on her list? Carrie must be the most recent, but how many could have been prevented if I had just gone to the police when it happened to me?

Accepting this is something I need to do, I ask, "Can we do Wednesday? It's my only day off at work this week."

"Yes." She rattles off the address, and I agree to meet with her at 4:00.

Tuesday rolls around with a surprise visitor at the cafe. An unexpected, unwelcome visitor, Michael. And he looks so much like Dalton today; I want to cry.

"Mr. James, what are you doing here?" Without realizing it, my hand protectively covers my tummy; Michael's eyes follow and widen in shock.

"I heard you talked to an associate of mine." He scoffs, "You aren't going to help the case. They will take one look at that," he points to my belly, "and decide that you aren't a credible witness."

"Excuse me?"

"Millie, don't make me spell it out for you. The last time I did, my son turned violent."

Heat flames my face remembering the night the man before me called me a whore. "I think you should leave."

Contrary to my words, Michael rolls his eyes. "I wish I could, but we need to talk."

"I'm done talking to you."

"You gave Miranda Dalton's name. Now I'm here to fix the damage you caused."

"How do you know any of that? James Kauffman is the attorney representing Carrie Appleton."

"No, his name is Stuart Kauffman. It's a common misconception, but I am the James in the partnership. If you saw it printed out... never mind. When Stuart heard that you name-dropped my son, he called me into their meeting."

Michael takes a seat at the closest booth and glances down the menu. "You just can't help but derail Dalton's career, can you?"

"You think I'm trying to derail his career? I had to push him away so he would go fulfill *your* dream."

"Doesn't look like you wasted any time finding someone to take his place," Michael concededly sneers.

"What are you talking about? I left town to go to school."

"Millie, it's obvious you're knocked up; I would guess about six or seven months along." Michael pauses, and I watch his mental calculations. His face goes ghostly pale, and then it turns reddish purple. "Does Dalton know?"

"Do you think he would be in Ohio if he did?"

Michael swallows that bit of info. "Why would you keep this from him?"

"Because I wanted him to achieve his dream." My body is tired, physically and emotionally, and it's taking everything left in me to keep it together in front of this man. I will not break down in front of him.

I'm just about to add, *you were right—I love Dalton enough to let him go,* when he pisses me off by saying, "You little gold digger."

Appalled, I raise my voice to a level that startles the other patrons. "Excuse me?"

"You're waiting to tell him after he's made it. Then you can sue him for back child support and muddy his name even further than this little fiasco with your pal Stevens."

"Don't call Bobby Stevens my friend. And if anything, Dalton will come out as a hero over what happened that night."

My boss, a rather large Latino man, comes up behind me, interrupting my tirade. "Is everything alright here?"

"Yes, Mr. James was just—"

Michael cuts me off, "About to order."

Fifteen minutes later, my boss, Juan, places Michael's turkey salad and the check on the table.

From my hiding place behind the counter, I hear Michael say, "If Millie has calmed down, I would like to talk to her."

Juan looks over at me, and I roll my eyes in answer, then head over to the booth, taking a seat across from Michael. He isn't someone I can ignore until he goes away; I need to get this over with.

"Let's discuss your case against Mr. Stevens."

"I'm not the one with a case against him, but if I pursued it last fall, maybe I could have prevented the case Carrie has against him."

"I believe my colleagues are hoping to try Mr. Stevens on multiple counts. Right now, most are just a he said/she said battle. They need more hard evidence. You had a witness. Who else did you tell?"

"My two best friends, my parents, grandmother, and Evie."

Michael's fork stops mid-air. "Evie? As in my wife?"

"Yes, Dalton sent her over to talk to me."

"Tell me everything that happened."

I recall my horrible date with Bobby while Michael picks at his salad. "I don't know what happened between Bobby and Dalton after I went inside, but when Bobby returned to school a few days later, he had a broken nose and two black eyes."

"Are you insinuating Dalton physically assaulted Bobby?"

"There was more than one rumor to that effect. Dalton never admitted to me if that was true."

Shaking his head, Michael scolds me again, "You really got your claws into my son. What's it going to take to get you to stop screwing with his life?"

"That's it," I stand, "we are done here. You came to talk about the case, and we did. But I won't sit here and let you insult Dalton or me anymore." I storm off, but Michael remains in the booth for another hour.

He, of course, summons me once again. The lunch crowd has vanished, so I have no excuse not to talk to the remaining customer. With arms crossed as a shield, I stand back from Michael, ready to run.

"Please stop acting like a child."

I take one step to leave.

"Sit," he orders, "I'm going to help you out."

"Define *help*."

"Please sit down. This is not an offer I make lightly or publicly."

Sullenly, I take a seat. "I'm listening."

Instead of talking, Michael stares me down with judgment. After what feels like an eternity, he speaks in a very low voice. "I don't like to tamper with evidence, but there are strings I can pull that will put Bobby Stevens away for the foreseeable future." Michael pauses as if for dramatic effect. "But, you have to do something for me in return."

I knew there would be a catch. I raise my eyebrows silently, waiting for more details.

Not getting the immediate reaction he was looking for, Michael scowls. "You won't tell Dalton about your pregnancy or come after him for child support....ever."

I hold my breath and count to ten. "You don't think Dalton deserves to know he's a father?"

192

"I'm not saying you never tell him. I'm saying you wait. Don't do anything that will ruin his career."

"Aren't you listening?" My emotions leak out. "I've lied my ass off so he would go. I want him to make it."

"Of course you do. And when he gets his big contract, you will come out of the woodwork calling him a deadbeat dad that never gave you a dime of child support."

"I would never!" I hiss. "I want Dalton to make it because it is the one thing he has loved longer than me. I'm your greatest ally, but you see me as an opponent."

Michael quietly takes that in. "I can see why you would say that. You were the only thing that stood in the doorway holding him back, and I have to admit you stepped back and let him go. However, your motives are what worry me."

"I. *Love*. Him."

Michael scoffs, side-eyeing me with his cold gray gaze. Did I really think he looked like Dalton when he walked in today? "I'm not going to get my hands dirty to get you out of the Stevens case unless you sign something releasing Dalton from any responsibility to you or your child."

"I don't care about the case. I'll do what I have to to put that asshole away. You were the one worried about it."

"And if you get called in, Dalton will get called in, and then he will catch wind about that thing growing in your belly."

The smack I land on the table radiates up my arm, but I don't let the pain affect my voice. "That *thing* is *your granddaughter*."

Michael's face doesn't even soften. "Fine. I will take care of the case for Dalton. You have no need to go to Stuart's office tomorrow. In fact, I don't want to hear that you set foot inside the building."

"You promise Bobby will pay for his crimes?"

"Do you promise not to go after the father of your child?"

It's not until we shake on it that I realize he recorded our conversation.

Before going to bed, I receive an email from Michael F. James. It's a document I am required to sign and fax back to him within 24 hours. It spells out our verbal agreement in ink. He added an addendum that if I break this contract, I lose 100% of my parental rights.

Signing the agreement scares the shit out of me. I know I'm not the gold-digging whore he has called me, so I scribble my signature and pray everything will be okay. However, I am extra careful with any contact I have with Dalton.

Chapter 25

-Dalton

The baseball program is amazing and grueling. The guys on the team are great, except for a couple of assholes that think they can haze the rookies.

I'm assigned to an apartment with three other guys, Pauley, Jake, and Cain. For the most part, we get along well. I imagine it's what having brothers would be like.

Pauley is living the life I thought I wanted. His girl lives nearby and travels to all of our games.

Actually, there are a group of girlfriends that follow the bus on our road trips. Pauley tells me it's because they don't trust their men not to get in trouble while away. And from what I see, it's got to be true. Take Jake, for example. He travels from girl to girl more often than we travel from city to city. It's so easy because the girls "flock to the jock," as he likes to say.

Despite Pauley having the relationship status I long for, Cain is the teammate I feel the closer connection with. He doesn't chase tail as much as Jake, so we usually have deep conversations about life. He avoids conversations about his family but has no problem bitching about his father. We debate who is the bigger asshole, his dad or mine.

As the summer goes by, I watch Pauley's relationship fail. My conversations with Millie are declining, too.

The little free time I have is spent chatting on the computer with Millie. Unfortunately, between my schedule and hers, it isn't as often as I would like. I feel Millie slipping through my fingers, and it's devastating. I hate to admit it, but sometimes concede my father was right. I shouldn't have grown attached to anyone. But I couldn't help falling in love with Millie, and I don't know where I'll find the strength to live without her. My head and my heart are at war over it. Somedays, the brief contact I have with her is all that keeps me going.

Mille never calls me, and she seems distant when we talk. Her emails still come, but they have slowed down to weekly updates. It's all fluff, nothing personal. It almost feels like an obligatory log.

Despite my better judgment, I call her towards the end of my season. "Hey, Millie,"

"Dalton. Is everything okay?"

"Yeah. I just wanted to hear your voice for a change."

"Oh. Okay." Per usual, the line goes silent.

"I could hear it better if you talked more."

"Dalton, I…. I know I said we could talk more. I just can't. I thought I would have more free time."

"My season's almost over; I could come to stay with you for a while."

"No! You can't!" Millie bites out. She takes a moment, and in a calmer voice, she says, "Sorry. That came out wrong. I don't think you should. I have a lot on my plate right now, and I think you should just…. stay in Ohio."

"Millie," I croon. "I need to see you. I want to be with you again."

"No, you don't. I'm not what you need in your life right now, Dalton. Just stay where you are. Focus on your dream." She doesn't even say goodbye; she just hangs up.

To cheer me up, Jake hosts a party at our apartment. The tiny space is packed with teammates and women. Cain is on the verge of losing his shit, and it's the straw that breaks the camel's back for Pauley's relationship.

Pauley storms out after his girl, and Cain turns to me to ask if I want to get the hell out of there too.

Cain drives us to a nearby hotel and checks into a suite. Even though we have shared hotel rooms before, I feel a bit awkward doing it now. But when we get to the room, I'm surprised to see it's bigger than our apartment.

I ask, "Was this the last room they had available or something?"

"Or something," Cain replies, going straight to the overpriced minibar. Scratch that; it's a full-size bar. Cain drinks from the bottle and passes me another.

"Fucking, Jake. A wild party is the last thing you need right now."

"Thanks, but something tells me Jake's never been in love to know how I feel right now."

"I can't say I've ever been in love, but there was someone special once; her name was Gabriele." Cain takes another long pull from the liquor bottle. "And I will tell you from personal experience, fucking someone else to get over her didn't help."

Chapter 26

October 1999

~Millie

It's my parent's 26th anniversary weekend. Grandma Bea, Michelle, and I celebrate with them this year at their home. I'm happy we're only having a small family gathering because I'm as big as a house.

I couldn't be one of those women who only carry the baby-weight front and center. No, I have to put it on everywhere. And I still have five weeks to go!

Even my fingers are fat, so my ring doesn't fit me, and I have it on my necklace chain. My mother assures me that it's normal. She said both times that she was pregnant, she wore a fake ring because her wedding rings never fit in the third trimester. Thanks for the reminder that I am doing this without a husband, Mom.

But I'm not going to be doing this on my own. I have my sister for the rest of this year, and then Grandma Bea promises to move in for as long as I need her, even if it's for years. She is so sweet. Certainly, I won't need her that long.

The worst thing about this weekend is I am back home, on the same weekend it all started. A red "for sale" sign is in his parent's yard. It pains me to look at it. The house sits empty, and I imagine it's as lonely as I feel.

We are all sitting around playing an aggressive game of Scrabble when things get warm and wet. I don't see anything on the table that spilled, and no one else seems alarmed. Oh my gosh, did I just pee myself? I look down. That's too much for my bladder.

Then it dawns on me. "Um, Mom? I think my water just broke."

Everyone jumps into action. How can this be happening? It's too early. Mom wanted me to try a home birth, but we are worried about the early arrival.

It's too soon; I'm not ready—my baby can't be either. Is she going to be okay? What if something terrible happens, and Dalton misses the chance to hold her? Great, now I'm crying.

I should have told him.

He should be here.

I want him here.

And with that last thought, I feel my first contraction, and I'm loaded into my parent's car with lots of towels under me.

At the hospital, the doctors are concerned about my preterm labor. Apparently, my body isn't because I am having regular contractions now. I'm scared. This isn't how I imagined having my first baby. I mentally prepared myself to feel a lot of physical pain; I just didn't expect any emotional pain.

Another round of regrets hit me. Dalton would have been so good, holding my hand, feeding me ice chips, telling everything is going to be okay. Instead, I have my mom dancing around, placing crystals around the room, and my sister reading twisted fairytales. Dad and Grandma Bea are playing a card game at the other end of the room. I'm in a room full of people, yet I feel utterly alone. All because I was adamant about not telling Dalton.

Twelve hours of labor go by. The doctors tried to keep it at bay, but now I am at nine centimeters. According to one of my nurses, it is almost "magic" time. I want to punch that nurse but decide to conserve my energy.

At 11:05 a.m. on October 10th, I am pushing new life into this world. The doctor announces, "It's a girl!" and puts a slimy, wet, mewing baby on my chest. Her skin is so pink and soft.

My mom and sister are oohing and awing over my baby, telling me how beautiful she is and how good I did.

They clean my daughter up a bit and give her back to me, all wrapped in a white blanket with pink and blue stripes. All the pain I felt for the last 15 hours or so melts away. She is so tiny to me. Despite being early, she is a healthy five pounds four ounces.

"What are you going to name her?" Mom asks.

"I've been playing around with a few ideas, but I'm leaning towards Ruth." I'm mesmerized, staring into her blue eyes and holding her tiny hand. The nurse was right about magic time. I thought she was teasing me about all the pushing I would have to do, but this moment *right here* is the magical part.

"Aw, Baby Ruth," my sister says. "Leave it to Millie to name her kid after a candy bar."

That's not why I named her Ruth, but I don't correct Michelle. I chose it because of her father's favorite baseball player.

200

The baby nurse tells me they are taking Ruth to the nursery to finish cleaning her up and do a few tests. I send my sister to watch over her and take any pictures she can get.

She gets done at about the same time the doctor finishes all the after-birth stuff. And another nurse comes in to give me my first breastfeeding lesson.

Just as I'm getting the hang of it, when there's a knock at the door and Mom welcomes the guests into the room.

"Mom, I'm kinda hanging out right now."

"Oh, psh! You are feeding a baby, not walking around naked."

"Yeah," Dani's voice carries from behind the door, "maybe if you had a bit more modesty nine months ago—OW! Shit, Angie, that hurt."

"Can we come in?" Angie asks sweetly. "We want to see the baby."

"And you," Dani interjects.

I look back down at Ruthie; she fell asleep and is no longer latched. "Just a second," I tell my friends, slipping back into my hospital gown.

My two best friends walk in with lots of bags in tow. "What's all that?"

"We knew you didn't have anything here with you," Dani says.

"So, we went shopping!" Angie finishes Dani's statement with flair.

"Oh, thanks. I love you guys." Damnit, when are the weepy hormones going to stop?

The room is crammed with my friends and family. They all pass Ruthie around and fight over who gets to change her diaper. Dani and Angie didn't forget me while shopping, and I am happy to change into pajamas.

With an almost full heart, I start to doze off, and one by one, my guests say goodbye. A nurse comes in to bring me dinner, but I am too tired to eat. She takes Ruth back to the nursery so I can rest.

I'm not sure how long I have slept when the nurse wakes me to try and feed Ruthie again. "Hi, Mama. I have someone here to see you." I recognize the outfit Angie dressed Ruth in. "I want you to try and feed her again, but then we are going to take her down to NICU because her bilirubin levels are high."

She hands Ruthie to me, and I hold her to my chest, trying to get her to latch the way they taught me. "What's a billy-ribbon?"

"Bil-ih-ROO-bin," she enunciates. "It means we are worried about jaundice. Do you see how her coloring has changed? Her skin is starting to look more yellowish?"

"She looks perfect to me." I've heard about jaundice before, but I've been too busy to read pregnancy books. "Will she be okay?"

"It's very common, especially in these little early birds. She needs to be under a UV light for a few days, and she should be fine. But it could be a sign of something more serious."

I swallow that news. This is all so much, too much. I feel tears start to flow down my cheeks. Did I really think I was cut out for this?

The nurse lets me go to the NICU and watch as they strap monitors and a face mask on Ruthie, and then they turn a special light on above her. My heart breaks as she cries and fusses at the intervention, but the nurse encourages me to reach in and soothe her with my hand and voice. Ruth calms down some and eventually falls asleep.

Feeling completely useless, I return to my room. It is so empty now, eerily quiet. I should straighten up the mess we made today, but I curl up in the most uncomfortable recliner in the world to process everything that has happened in the last 24 hours.

All I can think of is who would willingly sit in this chair? Would they actually recline and sleep in it? Then it dawns on me; this is where the dads sit and sleep because mom has the hospital bed, and this is the only other cushioned piece of furniture.

The dads. As in the new dads, not the grandfathers.

Should I call Dalton? I could talk to him without telling him what's really going on. I find my purse and fish my phone out.

A little voice in my head says I could tell him the truth. His season is over; he would come, and we could be a family... at least until spring when he would have to go back. Would he go back?

Shit! I'm forgetting one major part of that problem. Telling Dalton now would put me in breach of the contract I have with Michael. I can't lose Ruthie.

And yet, my fingers press send, calling Dalton. It rings and rings, but he doesn't answer. I leave a short message telling him he doesn't need to call me back.

-Dalton

The season is over, and I feel like I'm in limbo. I don't know if I should go back home or stay in Ohio. The problem is, I don't exactly have a home to return to. Mom and Dad each have their own places now and are trying to sell the house I've always known.

Mom calls weekly to remind me she has a room for me at her apartment. On the other hand, Dad has offered to help me financially, but only if I stay in Ohio. There is no common ground between them anymore. I don't want to pick sides, but I don't want to go back to the KC area. Millie isn't there, not that she has given me any indication she wants to continue our relationship. So, I stay in Ohio, where I have made friends.

Pauley goes home to work as a mechanic at his father's shop. Jake gets a local job delivering packages. Cain is also sticking around, but he's taking college classes online to finish his degree.

A month goes by, and I'm still in the same place. I make a little money working on the equipment and stuff at the field, but there's not enough to keep me employed for long.

Pauley's been living up the single life since his breakup, and he's back for the weekend to party at the club a lot of the team frequents. After all the razzing I get from him and Jake, I cave and go with them.

The club is loud, and not one person working seems to care that we are underage. Well, Cain is 21, and Jake has a fake ID, not that we get carded.

"See, man, I told ya they don't care," Jake assures me.

"Yeah, bro, we're pro athletes," Pauley adds.

"I get that we're more filled out than an average 19-year-old," I reply.

"It's not that," Jake answers, "it's because the cool radiates from our skin."

"And I bet the cool will draw everyone in when we are locked up in jail," I mutter to myself.

"Relax," Pauley claps my shoulder. "Look, aren't those the hype girls?"

"Hype girls?" Jake perks up —as if he needed an extra boost. "Dalton, you need to spend a little time with the short one on the left."

I look over at the petite brunette and dryly ask, "Why?"

"Because she can do amazing things with her tongue, and I'm going to go tell her you're looking forward to meeting her tonight," Jake pats me on the chest and walks towards her.

Spitting beer from my mouth, I shout, "What, Wait!" I reach for him, but he's already gone. The guy is just as fast in his Docs as he is in cleats.

I have repeatedly told them that I am not interested in meeting anyone—that I already have someone special in my life. They either don't believe me or don't care. I'm leaning towards the latter.

The group of hype girls come over. Luckily, the petite brunette, Soyna, is more interested in hooking up with Jake than getting me to open up. Her chances are pretty damn low either way. If Jake has played in her fields once, he won't return for a rematch.

After my one and only beer, I head out. I walk back to my apartment, enjoying the autumn night without checking my phone until I go to bed. I'm surprised to see I missed a call.

A call from Millie.

"Holy Shit!" I jump off the bed. "Nooo, fuck no. How could I miss the one time she's called me?" I say out loud to myself.

I play the message, "Hi, it's me…. Millie. I just wanted," I hear her inhale deeply. "I wanted to hear your voice," she says softly. Then she rushes the rest of the message. "I hope everything is well. You don't need to call back. I'm not sure when it will be a good time to talk. Love ya. Bye." I don't care what she says, I'm going to call her back.

A groggy voice answers, "Hello?"

"Hi, sweetheart. Sorry, I missed your call."

"Oh, it's okay," she sounds tired.

"Did I wake you?"

"Yeah."

"Sorry. Is everything okay?"

"Yeah. I just had a hard day."

"Okay," Shit, she needed me, and I wasn't there for her. "I'll let you go back to sleep. Love you."

"You, too. Bye"

I can't believe she called me. And it was when I was out on some stupid set-up. Without thought, I start packing. There is no rhyme or reason to what I'm throwing in my duffle bag. I'm about to head out when my roommates come home and talk me out of leaving before dawn.

"Dalton, you can't start driving until you get some sleep. Just a couple of hours, then you will be refreshed, and the sun will be up." Jake almost sounds sober with his reasoning.

"We can get some pancakes and take off together," Pauley suggests. Fat chance he'll wake up before noon.

Cain is the last to interject, "They're right. Sleep on it. And if you still want to go when you wake up, I'll pay for your flight."

I choke back a laugh at that. We get paid peanuts playing in the minors, and he's taking college classes; where does he think he's getting the money to buy me a ticket?

Chapter 27

~Millie

As soon as I wake up, I return to the NICU, nursing Ruth in a big rocking chair in her cubicle. "It's just you and me, baby girl," I tell her like I did so many times when I rubbed my pregnant tummy.

The staff starts bustling around and talking to someone of importance, walking through the unit in heels.

"Hello, Millie. May I come in?" I look up to see Evie. Oh shit.

"Hi, Evie. Yes, come in."

She comes and takes the stool next to me. Evie is speechless, but I can feel her judgment filling the room.

"How did you know I was here?" I finally ask.

"Millie, this is my hospital. I see a list of all the patients that are admitted. When I saw your name, I wanted to check on you. How are you doing?"

This is formal, Evie. She hasn't been like this with me in quite some time. I'm not sure how to take it. "I'm fine."

"Just fine? What can I do to make you more than fine?" she asks.

I look down at Ruth. Biting my lips together, I'm ashamed I kept this secret. I'm sure Evie understands my reasons, though. Ruth has fallen asleep, so I put her up on my shoulder to burp her.

"I'm sorry I didn't tell you, Evie. Or do you prefer Mrs. James now?"

She looks like she might cry. "Evie, please." Evie raises her hand to her collarbone like I've seen her do when trying to hold her emotions in check. "And that's ok. Honestly, I was watching for your name. I thought, well, you just weren't acting right when I saw you the last couple of times. And I recognized the look in your eye." Her hand creeps up her neck, and two fingers nearly cover her lips. Her eyes are pools of lavender blue, reminding me of when she visited me at home after the break-up. "Can I see her?"

"Of course. Do you want to hold her?" I offer.

"I would love that."

I pass her granddaughter to her. She certainly has a tear or two now. "She's lovely. Have you named her?"

"I'm thinking Ruth Jane Wilkins."

"How did you pick it?"

"Well, Ruth, because of Babe Ruth," I laugh nervously, "and Jane, because it is close to James."

Evie closes her eyes and nods. Several tears are coming now. Choked up, Evie asks in an undertone, "Does he know?"

"No, I don't want Dalton to know, so please don't tell him. Besides, I can't tell him anymore."

Alarmed, Evie asks, "What do you mean you *can't* tell him?"

"Michael will take her away if Dalton finds out."

"Michael?" Evie says his name with venom. "What's he got to do with it?"

"He came to see me about something else, and he wouldn't believe that I wasn't out for money, so I signed something to prove that I won't screw Dalton over."

"You're telling me Michael knew for a fact that you were pregnant. AND you signed some kind of deal with him?"

I nod, "Yes, ma'am."

"I'm going to kill him. What were the parameters of the contract?"

I shrug. "He'll take her away from me if I break it."

"He can't do that."

"That's not a chance I'm willing to take." Ruthie continues to sleep as if nothing in this world could ever harm her. "Besides, I won't go after Dalton. I want him to make it because it's his dream, not because I want a paycheck."

"Of course you wouldn't. Michael doesn't know the first thing about love. But Dalton does. I won't tell, but you should." Evie calms down, admiring Ruthie and counting her tiny fingers and toes. "You should just give her the name James instead of Jane."

"But that's a boy's name," I half-laugh.

"It should be her name. She deserves to carry it." When she says this, Ruth opens her eyes, and Evie smiles for the first time this visit. "Hi, Ruthie, I'm your," she pauses to think for a brief moment, "I'm your Mimi." Then she looks at me, "Is that ok? Can she call me Mimi?" I can tell she is holding her breath at what my answer will mean for her status in Ruth's life.

"Yes."

She sighs and goes back to cooing at Ruth for a few more minutes before putting her back under the lights. "I'm going to see what I can do to get you both the best care here." She kisses the top of my head and takes off on her mission.

Fifteen minutes later, a new doctor comes in to examine Ruth. He tells me he looked over my prenatal charts and doesn't hide his disapproval of the clinic I was using. He also gives me the good news that they are setting up a private VIP room for Ruth and me. She will need to stay under the light, and if her levels keep dropping, she will be able to go off of them tonight. But that doesn't mean we can leave until she is completely out of the woods.

Evie checks on us again that evening to see how we are adjusting to our new room. While she has a business-like nurturing side, she is extra pissed off tonight.

"The room is great, but you didn't need to go to all this trouble."

"The room was no trouble. I can handle everything that happens in these walls…on these grounds. It's the man I'm still legally bound to by paper that is the problem." Evie peers down at Ruth in the bassinet. "Your grandpa is the biggest asshole to ever walk this earth. And I hope you never have to meet him."

I snort in laughter at her comment. "I can agree with that. But, Evie, I don't think this extra care is going to be covered under my insurance."

"Don't worry about that. I told the hospital you are my family. Anything your insurance can't cover, I will."

"Evie, I can't accept that."

"What's a little insurance fraud compared to Michael's list of blackmail?"

"What?"

Evie sighs, "Nothing you need to worry about." She scoops Ruthie up, taking a deep inhale of baby scent. "Just know there is more holding me to this secret than my promise to you."

My phone rings. BOYFRIEND CALLING lights up my screen. Instantly, I freeze, "It's Dalton." I stare at the phone until it stops ringing. "Do you think he knows?"

"Who would have told him?"

"Everyone that I've told has been sworn to secrecy."

Dalton continues to call long after Evie has left. Eventually, I break and answer, hating myself for his breaking heart but knowing I have to do it.

The next day at lunch, Evie comes in with several bags—I forgot how much she loves to shop. Most of it is for Ruth, but she did get me a few things, too. Then she gives me a card with a generous check in it.

"Evie, this is very kind of you, but you don't have to give me anything."

"Yes, I do. I told you before, I love you like my daughter, and I want the best for you and Ruth. I know you are still in school, but you don't need to worry about a job on top of everything. Your only job is to take care of this little one," she says, picking Ruth up from the bassinet.

"Evie, I don't want a handout. I have it all worked out. It's going to be hard, but my family is very supportive."

"Listen to me. Don't think of it as a handout because I am your family now, too. If you need anything at all, you are to let me know."

"Yes, ma'am."

"What did you decide on her name?"

"Ruth-Ann James Wilkins"

"I love it. It's a good, strong name. Would it be okay to come visit you next weekend?"

How can I turn her down? "Sure."

And just like that, Evie becomes a fixture in our lives.

-Dalton

It takes until 1:28 before I finally fall asleep; it lasts until 1:44. What? That wasn't even 20 minutes! I put my watch down and try again, with about the same results. This loop repeats from 3:14 till 7:20!

I jump out of bed, sling my bag over my shoulder, and head for the door.

Jake's voice startles me. "Don't you want to take a piss and brush your teeth before you leave?" He's casually sitting on the sofa reading. I swear the guy only naps at night and can still function at 100%. "Maybe take a shower. You don't hear about the hero rushing in to save the day with bad breath and BO."

"I, ah… yeah, that's probably smart."

"Here, have some oatmeal, too." He tosses me an oatmeal cream pie.

I scarf it down instead of arguing about the empty calories in junk food, and hit the shower. I don't wait for the water to warm, so the coldness pulls me out of my foggy brain. As I get dressed, I reconsider what I have packed and what I have not. I seem to have stuffed my entire top two drawers in the bag, meaning I have 15 T-shirts, 10 pairs of underpants, and a variety of socks. Not a single pair of pants made it in the bag, nor do I have any toiletries save the deodorant and toothbrush I keep packed at all times.

An hour later, I walk out the door without anyone stopping me. Pauley is still snoring; I have no clue where Cain is, and Jake waves me off so I don't disturb whatever book he's engrossed in. Sometimes, he duct tapes the covers, so we can't see the photo and title making us wonder what mysteries lie beneath Jake's surface.

As I'm tossing my bag in my truck, I see a shopping bag full of snacks and cash. Where in Babe's name did that come from?

It's a long drive to Cape Girardeau, and I have to stop several times for fill-ups. Thankfully, I have the mystery cash—there had to have been a grand, all in 20s, when I found it.

I want to surprise my girl, but I am clueless about where to start. I imagine I will find her in a group of people, or she'll be studying alone under a tree.

It's ridiculous to think I can just magically find her, so I give in and call when I get to town. As usual, she doesn't answer.

I park by a sign that points the way to the student union. I walk around, searching the faces of every woman I see. I ask around, but no one seems to know her. Someone points to a hall that has a lot of science classes. When that fails me, I ask for directions to the dorms. No one there knows her either.

I'm constantly checking my phone, but she doesn't call back. The only voicemail I have is from my mom telling me, once again, to come home.

Some girl offers to call campus information for me, and they don't have Millie listed as a student. I phone Millie again, and it rings to voicemail.

It's getting late, so I find a bistro to eat at and call a third time. When I don't get an answer, I immediately call back, determined not to be ignored.

She finally answers in a hushed voice. "Dalton?"

"At last! I was starting to wonder if you would ever answer."

There is a long pause, like she is waiting for me to say something else. Eventually, she says, "Sorry, I'm busy. Can I call you later?"

"No way. There's no telling how long that will take."

I hear her muffle the phone with her hand, then she comes back on with a strained voice and says, "I don't know what to tell you, Dalton. But I *really* need to let you go."

Is she crying? Her distress puts me on high alert. "Millie, is everything okay?"

All too quickly, she exclaims, "Yes." I hear her suck snot back up her nose. It's an awful sound, but I hear much worse living with a large group of guys in our close quarters. "Everything is fine, great even."

"I don't believe you. Millie, where are you?"

"I'm at school…. in Cape."

"Then why can't I find you?"

"What?"

"I'm here, just off campus."

I hear her sharp intake of air. "No, Dalton, I told you not to go there."

"Well, I'm here. And you're not. You aren't even in the student directory."

A door shuts, and Millie mumbles incoherently to herself.

I keep my calm, just as my father taught me. "What's going on, Millie?"

She doesn't even try to hide her blubbering now. It tears me up. I gather my things and head to the truck. "Where are you, sweetheart? I want to see you."

"You, you can't."

"Why not? Millie…."

"I'm a mess. I don't want you to see me this way."

"That's ludicrous. I love you."

She sounds like she is weeping now. "No. Dalton. No. You have to go back. Go chase your baseball dreams."

My stomach drops; my whole world with it. I sit behind the wheel, knowing I am so close to Millie, yet she is pushing me away. "Millie, you don't mean that. Now is our chance to be together again."

I hear her breathing, but she doesn't speak.

"Millie?"

She sniffles. "Yeah?"

"Do you still love me?"

"Yes, Dalton, I will always love you." She takes a deep breath, and when she speaks again, she has more resolve in her voice. "But now is not the time for us to be together."

I hate that I'm going to ask this next question, but I have to know. "Why do you keep pushing me away? Is there someone else?"

"No...yes...I don't know. I'll tell you everything someday, but you have to make it, Dalton. You have to let me go..... but don't forget about me."

"You aren't making any sense."

"Good. Bye. Dalton."

The other end of the line is silent, too silent. I look at my screen to make sure my battery didn't die. I still have power, but the call has ended. Did Millie hang up on me?

I call back, but it goes straight to voicemail. I drive around the entire town, looking for any sign of her—the whole time calling every ten minutes. When I get tired, I pull into a truck stop and sleep in my car.

The following morning is the same. I finally give up and drive home, like Mom has been begging me to do since my season ended. I have her new address, but that's not home. My truck takes me to the house I grew up in, across the street from Millie.

I still have a key, but when I get out of the vehicle, I don't get past the porch swing. This is the last place I held Millie. I sit here all night and into the next day, feeling hollow inside.

"Dalton," a familiar male voice calls from the bottom of the stairs.

I look over at Millie's dad's casual appearance and worried expression. I simply reply, "John."

"Come to my workshop. Problems seem smaller when your hands are busy."

I have no clue what he is talking about, but I follow him just the same.

The inside of his workshop is full of his creations. Most of the time, he has furniture, like the old-fashioned rocking chair that sits in one corner. There is a smaller child-sized one next to it that hasn't been treated with stain or paint. In the middle of the room is what looks to be a highchair in progress. None of that is out of the ordinary, but on the back wall, he has dollhouse plans hung. Several in fact, like he is getting ideas from multiple sources before building a masterpiece.

"Have you ever turned wood before?" John asks.

"Um, no? My dad never wanted me to carve with Gramps because he was afraid I would cut myself." I'm not sure if that was for my safety or because he didn't want me to be too injured to play ball.

"It's easy; I'll show you how to make a bat." John takes me to the lathe and explains what to do. I get busy, but with all my mistakes, the bat gets smaller and smaller.

When I think I'm done, I turn the machine off and turn to find him behind a clear tarp, painting the highchair and little rocking chair pink.

"What do you think?" John asks.

"The color doesn't impress me, but your craftsmanship does."

"Well, I didn't pick the color, but when my girls were little, they wanted everything pink." John smiles broadly like he likes the color, too.

I nod, not really caring one way or another. "I think I'm done."

John shows me the next steps of sanding and finishing it off. When there's no grit left on the sandpaper, I hand it to him.

"Nice job." He offers it back to me, "Here. take it with you."

"Nah, it's a little small for me. Go ahead and paint it pink to add to the collection."

John chokes up at my suggestion, making me feel all kinds of weird. "Look, I know the situation between you and Millie. I can't say I agree with her choice, but she's my daughter, and I have to stand by her. Just give it some time."

"Yeah, she made it pretty clear that seeing me make it in baseball is more important to her than seeing *me*."

"That's not it. Millie has a knack for making the wrong decision for all the right reasons. This is hard for her too, but she's doing it *for you*."

After I leave the Wilkins's home, I call Mom. She answers, and I tell her I'm in town. Instead of inviting me to stay with her—like she has been begging me to do for the past month, she suggests I call Dad! What the hell is with the women in my life? Yet, I take her suggestion, spending one night with him before driving back to Ohio.

Now that Missouri is off the table, I start working with Jake at the shipping company. Seasonal work is perfect to keep a constant flow of money until ball picks up again.

Millie continues to avoid my calls and emails, and so does Mom. I was planning to return at Thanksgiving to pack my stuff since my parents sold the house, but Mom says she'll have it shipped to me.

Christmas is the same. Mom is busy, and Millie doesn't call me back. I'm so lonely, I make plans with Dad. He insists we take a beach vacation rather than a traditional holiday celebration.

Before I know it, spring training starts, and I quickly move up the ranks to the triple-A team. I wrap my life around the game. I haven't seen Millie in a year, and I've given up calling her. I still email her from time to time, and I'm surprised one day when she replies back.

Nothing personal, not a word about the last night we spoke on the phone, just basic stuff you would tell an outsider in line at the grocery store.

Chapter 28

October 10, 2000

~Millie

Ruthie is a year old today, and we have a small party with only the closest people in our lives. When Evie gets here, she doesn't look so happy. She puts on a good act in front of Ruth and my family, but I know her better than anyone. She has become my number-one go-to person.

"I was hijacked by Michael on my way here." She tells me after all the guests leave.

"How?" I say, cringing at the thought of running into him.

"I had Dalton on the hook to come with me today."

"Wait," I interrupt, "Dalton was going to show up *here*? *Today*?"

"Yes. He stopped by my office to say hello before going on vacation with his dad. I was on my way out and asked him if he wanted to come with me to a family reunion. He agreed, and as we were getting to the car, Michael calls and talked him out of it." Evie is spitting mad, and I'm glad the cup she is holding is disposable when it crumbles in her hand. "I swear that man has cameras on me."

Holding back tears, I ask, "How *is* Dalton?"

"He's good," Evie answers bluntly. She's never said it, but I think she holds back what she tells me about Dalton. She knows we don't talk any more than an occasional email, and she hates that I still haven't come clean.

"I'm sick of lying to my son to protect his daughter," a distraught Evie says.

We both know losing Ruth-Ann is too big of a risk. Evie tells me there is no way the contract I signed can hold water in court, but Michael is sneaky. I'm sure he has judges on his side…or worse. What if he kidnaps her? "I'm sorry, Evie."

"You can still tell Dalton." The hand she was holding to her chest reaches out and grasps mine as she pleads once again. "You have to."

"Millie, think about it. Dalton's already missed her first year. Soon, she will be walking and talking. He's going to miss all of that." She holds both of her hands around mine.

I brush her off. "We've talked about this a hundred times, Evie. Even if I didn't have to worry about what Michael would do, I won't. Dalton always told me how he wished you would have raised him without Michael. And I have no plans to turn Dalton into the same kind of asshole his father is."

"And I have told you a hundred times; Dalton is not Michael." A single tear slides down her face. "Michael's dream was bigger than his reality."

Ruthie starts crying. "I'm sorry. I'll tell him someday. Maybe when he finally makes it," I tell Evie, then go pick up my baby.

"I'm sorry, too. I guess I better head out." She is rightly upset with me, but she still hugs us before she rushes out the door. "Oh, I heard back from the Grace Burke Foundation, and you are a shoo in for the scholarship."

Somehow, the news doesn't cheer me up. "That's great. Thanks for your help finding it."

"Well, you wouldn't let me pay for anything, so I had to find you someone who would," Evie half laughs as she heads to her car.

I pick up my crying daughter. She doesn't seem hurt or need anything—just comfort. I think she's over-stimulated from this whole day. I grab the bottle that is lying discarded on the floor. It has dripped into a puddle. Great, I will have to clean that up. But for now, I'm going to hold my precious daughter and hum while rocking her back to sleep.

As she drifts off, I look around our tiny apartment. I cleaned as much as I could before everyone came over. Between my full-time job and being a single parent, I am zapped. The place is still relatively clean. I have extra trash from all the gifts. And I have a ton of laundry to fold and put away that's been dumped on my bed. I've been sleeping next to it for what feels like a month.

I look out the window, heavy with handprints, and see a family walking by. The mom is pushing a stroller, and the dad has a kid on his shoulders. They are smiling and happy, not exhausted like me. But then again, she isn't doing everything on her own. She has a partner.

I could have had that, but I put his dream first. I'm silently crying, having a pity party for one. And it was all my doing.

Looking down at my daughter, I think about how all the books say to lay your baby down before she falls asleep. Not to let her get used to being held, or she will be spoiled. But the laid-back, experienced moms say the housework will wait; babies don't keep. I like the second bit of advice better, but I'm the only one to do the housework. I have to do everything on my own.

Sometimes, I miss living with Michelle, but she graduated and got an amazing job in Des Moines. I couldn't hold her back from her life any more than I could Dalton.

I get up and carry Ruthie to her crib. Then I start folding and matching all the tiny socks that have been looking for their mates. My feet ache, so I sit while I work. The next thing I know, I'm waking up to my morning alarm. I'm face first in the stack of unfolded laundry that I never finished.

Chapter 29

Summer 2001

-Dalton

Coach calls me into his office before practice. "You've just been called up. Pack your stuff because you're heading to *the show.*"

I can't believe it. I finally made it. As I head out, I think about who I'm going to call first. Dad? He has wanted this as much as I have, if not more. Mom? She will say all the right things and ask all the right questions. Millie? I am closer to fulfilling those promises I made a couple of years ago. I don't know when the last time I called or emailed her. I dial Millie's number so fast because she is exactly who I want to tell first.

"Hello?"

"Sultan of Swat, it's good to hear your voice," I tell her.

"Dalton? Is that you? Did you get a new number?"

"Oh, yeah. About six months ago, my roommate, Jake, had a stalker, and it was so bad even I had to change my number."

"Wow."

"Right? But that's not why I called. Guess what?" I don't wait for her to even breathe a response. "I made it. I'm on my way to sign the contracts right now, but I'm the new rookie for the Cleveland Tribe!"

"Really? Congratulations, that's wonderful! Have you told Evie? Or your dad? I am sure he is on cloud nine right now."

"Sweetheart, you're the first one I called," I say, expecting a tender, loving comeback.

"I'll be right there," she tells someone in the background. "I'm going to have to let you go. But, Dalton, I am so happy for you."

I get out a "Yeah, thanks" before the line goes dead.

This news is what I have worked for my whole life. I thought she would be happier for me—for us. Then it hits me; there isn't an "us" anymore. There's her, and then there's me.

She wasn't alone. I fear she has found someone else because she certainly pushed me away. I should have fought harder for us.

I sigh, refusing to let this dampen my day. I have other people to call who will be happy to celebrate for me.

~Millie

I'm surprised to hear from Dalton, and per usual, his timing sucks. I just got to my softball game, and Ruthie's vocally eager to get out of her car seat.

"Who was that?" Stephanie, my boss, asks.

"Oh, just a blast from my past. I can't believe you all talked me into this," I tell my coworkers as I get in the dugout.

"Girl, you got this," Stephanie tells me. "And I want to know more about this blast from your past." She gives a pointed look to Ruth-Ann, then back to me, wiggling her eyebrows.

"Maybe later," I put her off.

My scholarship covers everything from classes to childcare, but I found a clinic looking for a part-time office manager that I couldn't let pass. They have all kinds of athletes coming in from injuries. The owners are obviously very into sports and encourage us to play in city leagues. It's softball season. And somehow, they found out that I can hit a ball; at least they don't want me to run and kick one simultaneously.

So here I am in a softball league. Ruthie hangs out with whoever is in the dugout unless I have a sitter.

I take a bat and go to the plate. I foul a couple, and then I hit one just over the shortstop. Now, it's the easy part. I can run and steal the bases, no problem.

After the game, a guy from the other team comes over.

"Hey, it's Millie, right?"

"Yep, that's me. Outfield extraordinaire."

"You were cute out there. I especially liked it when you started to trip and turned it into a cartwheel."

Embarrassment washes over me. "I thought I was going to catch that one, but...yeah."

"Wana get a drink sometime?"

"Oh, well, I'm not sure. I have a lot on my plate right now," I say. Then I go start packing up Ruthie's stuff.

Stephanie chimes in, "I got this. Go have a drink; you can pick Ruth up when you're done."

I turn back to the guy, and his face is shell-shocked. "I didn't realize the kid was yours."

Toddlers are man-repellent. "She sure is," I say as I swing her up on my hip.

"Maybe some other time," he says before leaving.

"What an ass. How could he not know? Ruthie looks just like you." Stephanie mumbles.

"He was too busy laughing about my ass in the air. I'm not looking anyway."

"Hoping that pregame phone call leads to something else?"

Grinning, I answer, "More than you know."

If Dalton's signing a new contract today, my deal with Michael is over. Well, the half that I was worried about. I don't need his money; I just need him.

I was the first one he called to share the news with—take that, Michael! Dalton will be knocking on my door at the end of the season. Like today's jerk, he may turn and run when he finds out about Ruthie, but I doubt it.

That night, I watch the Tribe game, searching Dalton out. I see a few brief shots of him, but he spends the game on the bench.

The sight of him stops my heart. He looks chiseled in his uniform. "That's your daddy," I whisper to a sleeping Ruth-Ann.

It's late when the phone rings. I answer it in a hurry, expecting it to be Dalton. It's not. Michael's cool, calculated voice. "Do I need to remind you that I set Bobby Stevens behind bars for the next ten years?"

Taking a play from Evie's book, I answer Michael's threats with calm conversation. "Hello, Michael, how have you been?"

"Don't think you can blow the whistle now. Dalton still has to prove himself."

"Yes, I was excited to hear the good news. Did you catch the game?"

"I mean it, Millie. He still has a long road ahead of him. His goal isn't only to get to the majors but to become a Hall of Famer."

"I don't think I saw that in the paperwork you sent over."

"Don't test me, Millie." Michael still scares me. "Don't blow this too early. Besides, can you imagine what your life would be like if Dalton was in Ruthie's life? He will hate you for keeping this secret from him. Then you will have to share custody of her, and with all of his traveling, she would be flying off in a different direction every week."

That stops me in my tracks. I have worried about Dalton's reaction to Ruthie, but not once have I imagined he would try for custody.

"Goodbye, Michael. I would say it's been nice chatting with you, but I wouldn't lie to you like that."

"Lies, lies, lies. Dalton isn't going to like finding out all the lies you have told him, is he?"

Rattled, I hang up before he can get farther into my head.

Chapter 30

Fall 2001

-Dalton

As I walk into the dark room behind my father, a crowd shouts, "Surprise!"

Dad chuckles, "I got you so good."

"What's this?"

"I invited everyone to celebrate your successful season."

"I don't know if I'd call it successful; we didn't get past the second series in the playoffs."

"The team didn't, but you're out there, kid. I'm so proud of you," Dad says, hugging me.

This is not my father. Michael James never hugs his son or says he's proud…ever. I'm tempted to ask him if he's dying or something, but there are a lot of people here. I vaguely recognize half of them and know maybe a quarter after that.

Nate, Kyle, Tyler, Luke, and a handful of others from high school are here. There is a distinct absence of Millie and her closest friends.

When I ask about Millie, the guys tell me they haven't seen her since high school. How can that be? Doesn't she come back for holidays and summers?

"Sorry, son," Dad tells me when I ask him, "I knew you would want her here. I sent her the invite and called her when she didn't RSVP. She was very rude on the phone—said some very cruel things that aren't worth repeating. Let's just say she won't be coming tonight."

"Millie was rude?" Kyle asks, "Are you sure you didn't talk to her friend, Danika?"

"Yeah, that doesn't sound like Millie," Nate confirms.

"I couldn't get her here anymore than I could get your mother to come," Dad confirms. "Some women just can't let go of the past."

The last time I called Millie was the day I got promoted. She didn't sound angry with me. "Maybe she couldn't come because of school?"

"School?" Dad informs me, "I don't know what lies she has told you, but there is a reason you couldn't find her when you went to SEMO."

"Why would she lie?"

"Let it go, Dalton. Women aren't worth the time it takes to figure out what makes them tick. Am I right? Dad jokes, and those closest to us laugh in agreement.

The next day, Dad and I take off for our annual trip to celebrate the end of my season. This year, we hit the Cancun sand.

The whole time we are there, he bashes women and relationships. The lectures on how it's not the time to get serious are endless. Shit, Dad and Jake subscribe to the same ideology.

When we get back, I break my plans to visit Mom and take a secret side trip to look for Millie at SEMO.

Once again, no one on campus knows who she is. Sick of this shit, I call her.

Millie picks up on the third ring, "Dalton?"

"Yep."

"This isn't a good time."

"It never is, is it?"

"I'm between classes. Can I call you later?"

You could, but something tells me you won't. "Just a quick question then."

Millie hesitantly says, "Okay."

"Are you going to school at SEMO?"

There is a long pause before she answers, "No."

"Have you ever gone to school here?"

"Here? As in, you're *in Cape Girardeau*?"

"Yes, for the second time in my life, I'm in Cape, looking for you. So, I'm going to ask you one more time: Have you ever gone to school here?"

"No."

"Fuck, Millie, why would you lie to me?"

"You wouldn't have left if I told you the truth."

"God, Millie. I guess my dad was right."

"You're going to believe *him* over me?"

"Why shouldn't I? You just admitted to lying to me, AND you broke up with me because you agreed with him."

"Dalton, this isn't a conversation to have over the phone."

"Right, because you never talk to me on the phone. You dodge my calls, and the last time I saw you, you had no problem lying to my face."

"Dalton," Millie's voice is stern, "I can't talk about this right now."

I end the call before she can hang up on me.

With rage burning in my blood, I drive up to St. Louis and catch a flight to Arizona. Last year Cain and I moved out here to work our asses off, and I plan to do the same this year.

I hunt for a bigger apartment this year; that way Jake can move in, too. Sometimes, I miss Pauley, but he never came back to the minors after our first year together.

I put a hefty deposit down on a three-bedroom place in the middle of Phoenix and buy everything I need instead of wasting time moving shit from Ohio.

"Do you like it?" I ask the guys when they move in.

"Hell, yeah," Jake replies. "This is going to be awesome. We're going to train hard and play hard."

"Some of us already do. That's why we're pros," Cain says.

"This is going to be my year," Jake claims.

"The only reason they haven't called you up is because Kovac is almost as fast but can out-hit you," I reassure Jake.

"True, but I heard he screwed the GM's daughter, so he's going to be in the first round of trades," Cain informs us. "Good thing Jake knows how to keep it in his pants."

We all bust out laughing. "Speaking of the trouser snake, I think we need to find some ladies," Jake suggests. And for once, I don't protest.

Chapter 31

July 2004

~Millie

We are watching the KC vs. OH game at work. The girls know that nothing turns me on more than watching a guy in the batter's box. Well, a man who knows what he is doing, not the out-of-shape guys in rec league. There's just something about how he pivots his hips when he drives with his back leg. Sigh.

Dalton is up to bat and makes a base hit. "That man is fine. Do you like his swing, Millie?" Stephanie teases, stretching out the "I" in fine.

More than you know, I think to myself. Since I can't tell my boss that, I just wink at her. The phone rings, and I drag myself from the TV to answer. I'm scheduling an appointment for a patient when I hear a lot of excitement from my coworkers watching the game. Luckily, I'm ending the call when I hear Omar arguing with the TV, "He's out! There is no way-"

"Oh no, that doesn't look good," Stephanie says.

"Looks good for KC. James is a threat to us," Omar says.

What? I rush in to see the replay. Dalton was sliding home, and now he isn't getting up. "Oh no! Get up, Dalton. Get up, get up, get up," I say.

I thought I was only talking to myself, but Omar asks, "Hey, whose side are you on?"

I watch as the medics come to help him off the field and feel water dripping on my shirt. Tears. Great, I am crying at work. As the game takes a break, the announcers show Dalton's mug shot along with a recap of his stats. They even mention that he grew up in the area and call out our hometown.

"Hey, isn't that where you're from, Millie?" Lisa asks. She looks over at me and notices the tears on my face.

"Mmm-Mm. Look at those baby blues," Stephanie comments. She's always admiring men out loud.

Then Lisa turns back to me, eyes popping out of her head. Lisa watches Ruth enough to recognize her eyes and combines that with how distraught I am that the person who shares those eyes is hurt. I know she puts two and two together.

I go to the bathroom to clean myself up. While I'm in there, I hear Lisa and Stephanie come in the door.

"Spill," Stephanie says. "Is that the *blast from the past?*" I nod, and she continues, "So, that's the deadbeat that knocked you up and left." Lisa slaps Steph on the arm. "Ow!"

"He's not a deadbeat dad. He doesn't even know. And please don't tell *anyone*. I don't want to ruin his career; that's why I never told him."

"Go to him," Lisa says. "He is only a couple of hours away!"

"Wouldn't that be nice? 'Hey Dalton, I know I haven't talked to you in a while, but I saw you were hurt. Instead of bringing balloons, I brought your long-lost kid," I joke.

"Don't put it like that. And I will pick up and watch Ruthie tonight," Lisa offers.

The idea is tempting. I would love to see Dalton again. I could call Evie to find out where he is.

"Go. I'm giving you the rest of the day and tomorrow off." Stephanie says.

It doesn't take more arm twisting than that. I hop in my little car and zoom to the hospital. When I get close, I call Evie, and she tells me what hospital he's at and his room number. She is excited that I'm going up and promises to keep Michael distracted.

Butterflies swarm my tummy as I park the car and walk to the elevator. How will he react to seeing me? I should have stopped at home to put on something cute and freshen up my hair. But I rushed right here because—shit! How bad is his injury?

I get to his floor, but the nurse won't let me go to his room. She's an older lady and a rule stickler. She says, "Mr. James doesn't want any guests right now." But I recognize the tall blonde man walking down the hall. It's Jacob Antonius, the second baseman on Dalton's team.

"What about him? Isn't he a guest?" I ask. He turns to smirk at me before he walks in the door, dark eyes full of mischief.

"*He* is listed as family," she tells me.

"I'm family, too, then. I'm Dalton's fiancé." I lie. Then again, I am still wearing his promise ring.

She snickers at the tiny ring I'm wearing. "I wasn't told about you. What's your name?"

"Millie Wilkins," I urgently tell her.

"I'll just check with Mr. James to ensure you're telling the truth."

She goes into his room and quickly returns. "YOU need to leave NOW, or I am calling security."

234

"What?" I am astonished. I'm sure Dalton would agree to see me.

"I know Mr. James is a high-profile patient. We will respect his privacy and not let any fame chasers bother him. Now go. This is your last warning," she says as she picks up the phone.

Stunned, I leave without argument. Feelings of rejection and loss consume me. I bawl the whole drive back to Columbia. When I pick up Ruth from Lisa's, I don't have to say anything; the words *it didn't go well*, are written all over my face.

When we get home, I tuck Ruth to sleep in my bed with me. This isn't a habit I want to start back up, but I need to hold her tonight. I need to remind myself that Dalton's love for me was real once. If he has given up on it, then it's time I should, too.

I take my ring and necklace off, stringing the gold band through the chain so it falls to join the charm. With shaking fingers, I close the chain forever and put it on the soda bottle that is still on my nightstand. The pendant is too big to fit, so it dangles out with the flowers. I can't get rid of it yet. Someday, Ruth will ask about her father. I will tell her about the most incredible romantic love I have ever known—the love from which she was created.

-Dalton

This is the first time I have seen both of my parents in the same room since I lived at home. I remember them arguing behind closed doors, but I guess they have pushed past that.

"Dalton, let's get you transferred to my hospital, where I can have the best medical staff KC has to offer."

"No! This is where the league sent him, this is where he stays," Dad protests.

"Who do you think knows the doctors in this area better? Someone who lives here and runs a hospital or a national organization? I guarantee he was only brought here because it's the closest to the stadium."

"I know you just want your own *people* to get their hands on him. And that's not what he needs right now. He needs to focus on getting back in the game." Maybe it's the drugs, but Dad's rebuttal doesn't make sense to me, but Mom has no problem understanding him.

"My *people* have his best interests at heart."

"Would you two just stop? Please," I cover my face with my hands, "you're killing me."

"Are you still in pain? Is it your head? Maybe we should have a CT scan, too," Mom suggests.

"It's my damn knee that's fucked. My head hurts because the two of you can't put my problems above your hatred."

"We are both concerned for you," Mom states.

"Then leave before I have an aneurysm, too."

"You heard him, Evelyn, get out," Dad smugly says.

"BOTH of you! GET OUT!"

The oldest nurse in the country comes in because of my shouting. Mom and Dad leave, still bickering at each other. "I think I need to adjust my guest list."

"Yes, Mr. James. Who would you like on it?"

I give her Jake and Cain's names but tell her if it's one of my coaches or trainers–basically, anyone with a league badge is welcome. We already talked about fans and press need to stay the hell out.

Shortly later, Cain strolls in. "How are you doing?"

"Better now that my parents left."

"I saw them in the lobby still arguing about something." Cain chuckles, "Made me feel right at home." He points to my leg, "I was actually wondering about your knee." Waving his question off, he adds, "Actually, wait and tell me when Jake gets here."

"Why? You got money on it?"

"Of course. But if he doesn't get his ass in here in ten, I will tell you what to tell him."

"Where is he?"

"Flirting. There was a group of nurses heading to the cafeteria."

"Hey man, there is one fine piece of ass trying to get past your nurse to see you," Jake tells me when he walks in 20 minutes later.

"The last thing I want right now is a woman. Did you bring me anything to eat?" I ask, and he tosses me a bag of greasy fast food–not my first choice, but anything is better than hospital food. "This was in the cafeteria?"

"Yeah, they had a couple of chain restaurants in there," Jake answers.

The nurse knocks as she walks in. "Sorry, Mr. James, but there's a young lady out here who says she is your fiancé."

Sitting in the chair by the window, Cain happens to be taking a drink when she says this and starts laughing, causing it to spray all over himself.

"I don't have a fiancé," I deadpan.

"A Molly Wilcox? I believe she said that's what her name is," says the old lady.

"I don't know anyone by that name. I already told you, don't want any reporters or bat-bunnies in here," I state, try not to shout. She abruptly turns and goes out of the door.

Laughing, Cain says, "Fiancé? What some women won't do or say to get a piece of fame. It's pathetic."

"She was hot, though. I wouldn't have pegged her for that type. She was more the girl next door variety," Jake says.

"Whatever," I grumble as I hoover the cheeseburger he brought me. Jake knows that is exactly my type of woman.

I had the girl next door, or rather, across the street. I haven't even heard from her since I exposed her lie. I left the ball in her glove, so to speak, but she didn't call, nor a single email popped into my inbox.

"Dude, you need to get laid. You're always so uptight. Maybe I should go get Molly and bring her back here for you," Jake says, looking towards the door like he might really go after her.

"Yeah, because your track record with setting me up has gone so well."

"Hey, now, you dated that last one for like a month."

Yep, and that was last winter. She was the last time I got laid, too. He's probably right. "Sorry, I'm not the womanizer that you are. I prefer to feel a connection with the person I'm sleeping with."

"Right. If you feel that connection, then why do your relationships not last more than a month?" Jake jokingly asks.

I glance up at him, "You know why." I have vented to them my frustration about Millie before. How one-sided it was before it fizzled out.

"Yeah, yeah, yeah. The one that got away. You ever gonna get over that?"

Nope.

Chapter 32

October 10, 2005

~Millie

To: daltonjames88@
Cc/Bcc, From: longrungurl@email.com
Subject: _____

> Dear Dalton, How've you been? I've been watching all of your games. The save you made last night was incredible! I jumped out of my chair, cheering so loudly that I woke up Ruth.

Scratch that part about Ruth. And *I watch all of your game*s????? Really, Millie, could you sound more like a fangirl? No wonder he didn't want to see you at the hospital. I sigh and start again.

To: daltonjames88@
Cc/Bcc, From: longrungurl@email.com
Subject: _____

Hello Dalton, your season looks like it's going
well. How have you been outside of the game?
Having any fun-

Nope—not going there. I don't want to know about the fun
Dalton has outside the game. Evie told me he was dating
someone, but it ended badly. I didn't ask any of the questions
that made me want to die.

To: daltonjames88@
Cc/Bcc, From: longrungurl@email.com
Subject: _____

Hey Dalton, sorry it's been so long since I have
written. To be fair, I barely have time for myself.
Raising our daughter takes a lot out of me. I hope
you can meet her someday. She is so beautiful;
she has your eyes and my crazy hair. Her teachers
are amazed at how well she reads for a 6-year-old.
Today is her birthday. All she wanted was a
unicorn. That's right, a real live unicorn. I couldn't
find that in stores, so she has to settle for a stuffed
unicorn that she can sit on and pretend to ride. Of
course, everything else she got was some sort of

> unicorn thing, too. She loved all of it. She is
> thoughtful and kind—thanked everyone for her
> presents.
>
> She asks about you. She wants to know who you
> are and what you look like. Most of all, she wants
> to know why you aren't here. It comes up more
> than I ever expected. I don't remember "Daddy-
> Daughter Dances" when we were growing up. Or
> the "Donuts with Dads" annual breakfast at
> school. And it's all my fault that you aren't here for
> all this crap. I know I should have told you by
> now. I had planned on telling you years ago. You
> deserve to know, and she deserves a father.

I stop because tears are flowing so hard that I need to find a tissue. I can't write that either. Every time I email Dalton, it's like this. I've gone from telling him he's a father to just pretending like he knows and carrying on with my day-to-day stuff. But I never send them; they sit in the folder I created years ago. I'm not sure the last time I sent him so much as a Happy Birthday, let alone anything of substance.

This is not the life I thought I was choosing. Ignorantly, I believed it would just be a year or two of single parenthood. Now I'm looking for full-time jobs because I'll have my degree soon.

Amazingly, we have both accomplished the goals we set out for after high school. Now, I'm looking down the barrel of when and how to confront him.

Evie regularly reminds me *nothing's holding you back*. Unlike with her, Michael's threats to me are invalid. Dalton made it to the big leagues and fought his way back after an injury that could have ended his career. Will he be a Hall of Famer? Only time will tell. He has been voted as a fan favorite more than once, so I would say his chances are good.

I still don't know all the details that hold her to this secret, and I fear I'm the root cause that tied her down.

With that last thought, I shut my computer down and go to bed.

Chapter 33

November 2009

-Dalton

I can't believe it's time for my ten-year high school reunion. I missed the five-year because they planned it in the spring, but they're having it over Thanksgiving this time.

I debated coming back. The clincher was when my old baseball coach found me on social media and asked if I would come to give an inspirational speech to the high schoolers. I agreed because I always liked Coach Thompson, and working with kids has always been a passion of mine. One I haven't been able to indulge in very much with my busy schedule.

Walking through these halls again brings back so many memories. As images flood my mind, I'm surprised to see my old friend, Nate, standing before me.

"It's good to see you," Nate says, clapping me on the back.

"King of Swat, is that you, Nate?"

"Sure is. I got old and became a teacher."

"Hey, now! Be careful who you're calling old. If I remember correctly, your birthday is a week after mine."

"Age is just a number; trust me, math is my specialty."

"Your's the one calling himself old."

"Didn't you always think teachers were old when we were students?" We chuckle, "Speaking of, the kids are so excited you came. And fair warning, you'll be signing stuff and taking selfies all day."

"That's okay; it goes with the territory."

"Good, then I can be the first to geek out." Nate pulls out my rookie card, and I pose for photos with him and the other coaches.

We don't get to chat more than that because the gym starts filling up with the baseball team, and then more and more students fill the bleachers, making me wonder if anyone is still in class.

After school lets out, I'm back in Nate's classroom catching up on life and hearing about most of my old teammates. I haven't brought up Millie, and neither has he. I want to ask what he knows about her, but I hope he gives me a good segue way—or just tells me without my prodding.

"I would invite you over for dinner, but my wife has already told me no," he says, a little embarrassed.

"What? What did I do to piss off your wife? And, by the way, when did you get married?"

"Ha, well, you left her best friend in the dust," he says. When I look confused, he says, "I reconnected with Angie after college. We got married a few years ago." He shows me the picture on his desk. It's from their wedding. Then he scrolls through his phone, pulling up a more recent one that shows she is pregnant.

"Congrats on the wedding and baby," I say.

"Thank you. Baby's due in January." Nate smiles down at the picture with a mixture of pride and love. "I know you didn't really leave Millie in the dust, and she defends you when your name comes up, but Angie won't let it go."

"Oh, I see. How exactly does my name come up?" I use this as an opening to fish for details about Millie.

"We hang out with her on occasion. She's been giving Angie a lot of advice about the pregnancy and baby stuff," his face freezes like he said something he shouldn't have.

"Millie knows about baby stuff?" I ask.

"Yeah," he hesitates, "she has a kid." The stupefying information causes me to only hear bits and pieces of our conversation. "She moved back recently," and, "We've watched your games together."

It's all I can do to add words here and there, hoping it sounds like I'm following along. We say our goodbyes, and I drive around town in a daze.

Naturally, I go by my parents' old house. Of course, that just leads me to see the Wilkins' home, too. Then I drive to the places where I spent most of my time, like The Batcave, which Dad sold, and the land has been developed into a strip mall.

Eventually, I find myself at the field where I gave lessons. The playground there has been updated, and the unseasonably warm day has coaxed lots of families out.

Families. Millie started a family with someone else. Of course, she did. I've been gone, living my dream for the past ten years. I should have come back sooner. If I did…No, I can't think that way. She pushed me away, and lied to me so I couldn't find her.

As if I conjured her out of thin air, I see Millie. She's holding a baby. She looks great and… happy. A man comes up to her with a baby bottle. She looks like a pro at mothering.

I have to go; I can't watch this. I rush out of the parking lot. There's no way I am going to the reunion dinner tomorrow.

I blow off this town, the reunion, the holiday plans I had with each of my parents. When my flight lands in Arizona, I lock myself in my condo, not wanting to see or talk to anyone.

~Millie

It is almost Thanksgiving. Instead of a winter storm, Mother Nature has provided us with a 65-degree day. Because it's so beautiful, Michelle and I decide to take the kids to the park.

She did things more traditionally than I did. She got a husband first, then bought a house, and now has kids. Piper is three, and Gabe is six months.

On the other hand, I had a baby, went to school, and now live back at home. Well, not quite at home. Grandma Bea needs live-in care, and here I am. Having a physical therapist at her beck and call kept her from going into a rehab or nursing facility. And it just so happened that Evie's hospital was hiring. I don't like it as much as the clinic in Columbia, but it pays better.

Ruthie loves her school and has made a good friend, Mikaylla. They are the only girls on their baseball team. I thought it was crazy at first, but Evie buys all of Millie's equipment and even has her go to lessons.

I'm getting my baby fix holding Gabe; I miss these days. If I had a stable man in my life, I would have another kid. Unfortunately, I don't find much time or interest in dating. When I do, I hardly ever date the same guy twice.

Michelle's husband hands me a bottle for Gabe. My nephew coos and helps me hold the bottle. I can already tell what a handful he's going to be.

A loud car pulls out of the parking lot in a rush. Don't people realize they need to slow down? There are little kids everywhere. I look at the driver as he goes by and become paralyzed because there is no way that's who I think it is.

The next night at the reunion, I find out that it was who I suspected. Dalton James is in town and expected to come tonight. So far, there hasn't been any sign of him.

I wait nervously, my two best friends by my side. Angie says, "He sent a yes on his RSVP a month ago, and yesterday, he told Nate he would be here tonight."

Danika asks, "Are you going to tell him about Ruth?"

I bite my lips together, thinking of my answer.

"He deserves to know, Millie," Dani condescendingly says.

"I know. I'll tell him. I just don't know how to drop that kind of bomb on him. What if he gets mad? He could take me to court for custody."

Danika points out, "That man is practically a lap dog. He doesn't get mad, especially at you."

"You didn't see him tear out of the parking lot yesterday. He had to have seen me and left. I don't know why he would have been so upset to see me. Nor do I think he would have seen Ruth because she was mixed in with all the other kids on the jungle gym," I ponder out loud.

Angie says, "It's not like you haven't tried to contact him. He had his second chance and sent you home." She crosses her arms over her chest to pout. Her face is all kinds of mad, but with her swollen belly, she just looks cute.

"Wow, where did that come from? I thought you were the one always rooting for them," Dani says in her usual snarky tone.

"Not anymore. He wouldn't even see her at the hospital," Angie says.

"Can you two please stop talking about that? Just help me decide how to tell him IF he even comes tonight."

We hatch up a couple of different scenarios, but it doesn't matter. The reunion is over without us being graced by our most successful classmate.

Chapter 34

February 2010

-Dalton

Cold water spraying my face wakes me from my drunken slumber. "What the fuck!"

Assholes, Jake and Cain, are laughing at their shenanigans. "Wakey-Wakey," Jake says as he shoots me with a large water gun.

I jump out of bed, and, for once, I catch that fast fucker–he must not have anticipated my retaliation. Grabbing the gun, I break the damn thing over my knee, causing all the water to spill on my bedroom floor. Cain is in the doorway, doubled over in laughter.

"HEY!! I just bought that!!" Jake complains.

"GET OUT!" I roar at them. "And leave my key when you go." I should have known better than to let those two have a way in.

When I rush into the bathroom to grab towels to clean up the flood on my floor and bed, I catch my reflection. I barely recognize the man who looks back at me. He has a full, unkempt beard, and his long hair is a greasy rat's nest. The dark circles under his eyes set off the whole drugged-out homeless guy look.

Even though the towel I grabbed smells like mildew, I still use it to mop up the mess. Meanwhile, I can hear Jake bitching in the other room about his broken toy. Serves him right.

Cain tries to talk him down, "I warned you not to do that. What did you expect? He doesn't care about his own life; why would he care about your stuff?"

Ouch. I walk out to them. "Cain, if that's how you really feel, you can get the fuck out, too."

"Sorry if the truth hurts you, Dalton. But take a good look around this place. You have take-out boxes everywhere. By the smell of things, I don't think you've taken out the trash in a month. I haven't seen you change your clothes in at least a week either. Although, I hardly see you to know for sure," Cain chides me.

"Yeah, man. I was only trying to give you a bath," Jake snips in his deep voice.

With cold fury, I repeat, "Get out. Now." I raise my arm and point the way.

Jake storms off. From the hall, I hear him slam his door.

Cain turns in my doorway. He always has to be the voice of reason, "Jake's an asshole, but we're just concerned about you. Spring training is about to start. I know we no longer play for the same team, but you're still my best friend. You're either at the bar or asleep all the time."

I argue my case, "Yeah, well, that's the only way I can stop thinking of," I pause, "*her*. I can either drink the pain away or pass out and sleep through it."

250

"I know how you feel. Gabrielle…" he takes a deep breath and turns his lecture back on me. "You need to wake up. Quit dreaming about your first love. If she moved on, so should you," Cain says just before closing my door on his way out.

I'm so angry I punch the wall. "FUCK!" I shout as pain radiates up my arm. I immediately go to the freezer for ice, noticing that's the only thing in there. I wrap my hand, then open the fridge to grab something to eat. Nothing in there looks safe to consume, and the pantry is just as empty.

Deciding to sit and watch something while my hand is out of commission, I turn to the couch. There is nowhere to sit; boxes and wrappers are littering every surface. Cain was right; this place needs to be cleaned. I could call a maid, but it will be more therapeutic to do it myself.

Just then, a memory slaps me—Millie asking if I clean as well as cook. The pain in my hand doesn't hurt nearly as bad as my heart. Hell, I don't think a heart attack would hurt this bad. I give up on cleaning and head back to bed.

The next time I wake up, I hit the shower, standing under the hot water until it goes cold. Even then, I don't want to get out, but at least it wakes me up. Eventually, I scrub myself down and then the apartment. To be honest, I don't scrub the place. I just pick it up and call someone else to do the scrubbing. Because the therapy wasn't as good as I thought it would be.

There are only three suites on our floor. Cain, Jake, and I each bought them when the place was being built. I avoid the guys the best I can, but our front doors all open into the same ginormous lobby, and we share an elevator.

Jake still hosts his weekly poker game in our lobby. I'm not playing, but I see he invited ladies to join the game this week, and they are playing for clothes instead of money.

Jake calls out to me as I walk by, "Come on, Dalton! Seeing some boobies will make you feel better." The girl on his lap, in a lacy bra, giggles, and he rubs his face against her chest. "They sure make me feel better about losing all my clothes."

The day after poker night, I'm alone, sitting at a swanky bar. I may be a miserable asshole these days, but I'm working through it.

A woman approaches me. She doesn't have to tell me she gets paid to have a good time; I've seen enough of that to spot a call girl when I see one. "Hey there, big guy, you look so lonely."

I try to brush her off, "I prefer it this way."

Not taking no for an answer, she continues to push herself on me. "But this could be the most amazing night of my life."

This shit goes on for another ten minutes, and I turn her down several more times. Finally, I snap, calling her out for what she is. "Look, I don't pay for… companionship."

"Oh, aren't you the sweetest, but you don't have to pay." With her hand dangerously high on my thigh, she leans in and whispers, "It's already been taken care of."

Grabbing her by the wrist, I tell her, "That doesn't make a bit of difference in my book." I shove her away with more force than I mean to use.

When she steps back, she is holding her wrist protectively. Her face has an odd expression, almost like she liked it.

"Go back to your pimp or whoever the hell paid you for this. Just stay the fuck away from me."

That finally does it. She backs away, sulking, to the man in a corner booth. I recognize Jake's profile before she gets there. He looked over at me and shook his head.

For years, he's been trying to set me up with women, often named Molly, because of the incident at the hospital. And now he paid someone to screw me? Fuck that! He's the one that needs help in a more professional sense.

Things between Jake and me continue to escalate, and it starts to affect our work. It may have cost us today's game when I brought my aggression on the field. Good thing preseason stats don't count.

I may have thrown too many balls at him instead of to him. Then, when we were in the clubhouse, he confronted me only to get a face full of my fist. I'm sure he's icing more than a few welts tonight. The asshat just won't shut his hole about me needing to move on.

I pour myself a whiskey and settle in at home. Behind a door with new locks, where he can't send me anyone to cheer me up. It's going to be a long season.

Next, my phone rings. It's either Cain telling me, "It's just how Jake shows he cares," or it's my mom.

She won't leave me alone, either. My voicemail is full of her messages, most of which I haven't bothered to open. She didn't believe–what I saw with my own eyes–last November and tells me all the time that I need to dig deeper to find the truth.

I look at the caller ID and see Dad's name on the screen. That's odd. Why would he be calling? "Hello?" I realize, after I answer, what this is about. Today's game was televised. I'm surprised my agent didn't call first. I look at the missed calls list and see his name five times. Shit.

"What the hell is going on with you?"

"Jake and I were just having a little fun."

"It looked more like you were throwing a tantrum."

"Jake's been acting like a child, too."

"I've talked to Jake and Cain."

"Why would you talk to them?"

"I talk to a lot of people. I've heard about what you are going through, and you snap out of it."

"But," I don't get to answer.

"That girl has done nothing but mess with your career ever since you were a kid."

"I didn't know I had a career when I was a kid," I mutter, but he continues talking over me.

"I've also talked to Evelyn, and I think she's right." Whoa, he *agrees* with *Mom*? "God, I can't believe I'm going to say this. Maybe if you had some closure…."

It's my turn to be heard. "NO! I'm not ready to go down that road. Besides, I don't have time. Kudos to you for finding something to agree on with Mom, though."

"Dalton," he tries to get more of his thoughts in, but I'm not having it.

"Can we just go back to when you only cared about my career and not my personal well-being?"

"Your personal well-being is affecting your career!"

"Thanks, *Dad*. I'm so glad you care. I'll be sure to make you proud out there. Talk to ya soon, bye."

~Millie

Usually, Evie takes Ruth to her batting lesson. But Evie had to go out of town for a conference, so here I am. This is usually the only time I get to myself. They always make a night of it and have dinner out, as well.

Ruth is consistently a bubbly little girl, but tonight she seems to have a higher energy buzz. I know she really likes her coach because she talks about him often. "Mom, you will finally get to meet Coach Ben!"

"I can't wait," I say, trying to force any amount of enthusiasm in my voice. It's not that I don't want to meet him; I should know someone who influences my daughter. It's just that I remember the last time she was giddy for me to meet someone. She totally blindsided me, trying to hook me up with her teacher–her freshly divorced teacher.

Mr. Newton was a mess. He tried to get handsy; I shot him down. Then, to my horror, he burst into tears because he missed his wife. He was nice to talk to, though, and I confided in him about how much I missed Ruth's dad.

"You will like him. He's super nice and funny." After a moment, she softly says, "And he is cute."

I turn and look at my dear, sweet girl. Half her face is tucked into her scarf. Her eyes are poking out, and her forehead is flushed red with embarrassment. I chuckle. "Oh, he is, is he? And just what is so cute about him?"

Riled up, she swings her hands in the air. "I don't know. I just think you will find him good-looking."

"Ruth, please, don't do this again," I say as we pull into the parking lot.

"Come on, Mom, you need to find someone to go on a date with for Valentine's Day."

Well, shit. Ruthie's heart is in the right place. I didn't even think about that holiday coming up. "Thank you, sweetie, but I'm not looking for any dates." She rolls her eyes and is out the door before I finish my speech.

I trail Ruth into the building. She's already running up and giving a high five to a man--a very young man. I'm not sure if this "man" has even graduated from high school. I'm a bit mortified that she would consider this.

I peruse a magazine while Ruth swings away, looking up occasionally to see how she's doing. I'm trying not to give off the overbearing-mother vibe. Also, I don't want her coach to think I'm interested in him.

When the lesson is over, they walk up to me. Ruth-Ann is beaming, and it reminds me so much of Dalton; it's in the eyes and her smile. "Mom, this is Coach Ben."

"Hello, Coach Ben. How did she do today?"

He answers, "Amazing, as usual."

Something about Ben seems familiar. He looks older than my first impression. Sandy-red hair frames hazel eyes on a baby-face. I cock my head to the side and ask, "Ben. Wait, you aren't Benny Shaefer, Britney's little brother, are you?"

He chuckles and rubs his hand on his jaw. "I haven't gone by Benny in a long time. How have you been, Millie?"

Ruthie gasps. "You know each other! This is great!! Want to come out for dinner and ice cream with us?" she pleads.

Ben looks at me. I'm holding my breath, giving my best at a poker face. "Normally, I would say no, but my next lesson canceled," he says. "Of course, if you don't want me to…"

"Umm," I say and then mistakenly look at Ruth. I can't say no to the look in her eyes. I am such a sucker for her baby blues. I sigh and agree. "That's fine. I think we will just go to that buffet across the street."

"Sounds great. That's where I was going to go anyway. I'll meet you two there."

We sit at a table in the back. It's a weeknight, so the place isn't very full. I was afraid the conversation would be awkward. But I should have known Ruth would never let there be any uncomfortable silence.

Turns out Benny, correction, Ben, has been working his way through college at the city recreation department and will be graduating in May. "I give baseball lessons on the side because," he cringes as he finishes his sentence, "I had a great coach once that inspired me." He sheepishly looks at me, "Sorry, I give the same answer so much–I didn't think…." His gaze switches to look at Ruth out of the corner of his eye.

She doesn't seem to notice because she pipes up to ask, "Mom, did I eat enough to have ice cream?"

It's a good time for her to escape the grown-up talk, so I say. "Go for it, kid," without checking her plate. Once she is far enough not to overhear me, I say, "She doesn't know much about him."

"Yeah, Evie told me that. She said he doesn't know anything about Ruth, either." His voice isn't quite accusatory, but I feel a stab, nonetheless.

"It's complicated, but," I look down, "someday."

Ruth comes back. I think her eyes are bigger than her stomach because the sundae she made is the size of her dinner plate. "You planning on sharin' that with me?"

She shrugs, "Sure."

As we head out to our car, Ruth asks, "So, are you two going out for Valentine's Day?"

We both stop in our tracks. Ben asks, "Ugh…?"

"Ruth!" I grab her hand and mentally scold her with one look before turning to Ben. "Sorry. She seems to think I need help, but I am not looking for anything like that." I scowl at my daughter.

"That's okay. If you change your mind, you know how to reach me," Ben politely says.

I force a smile. "Thanks, Ben. But I'm just not… Well, I have been putting off that thing we were talking about earlier. I think that's why I haven't felt comfortable in the dating world."

Ben nods, then says, "I completely understand. Those are some big shoes to fill. And you should get that all worked out before you take anyone else on."

Chapter 35

June 2010

-Dalton

I've been traded to Kansas City. I should be happy. This is the team I cheered for growing up; it's close to "home." But now it holds bad memories, too. This is where I got hurt; I'm lucky that my knee isn't worse than it is. But most of all, I'm only about half an hour from where Millie and her family live. It has been seven months since I found that out, and it still cuts like a knife. I'm back to the life I led in high school. I only eat, sleep, and play baseball. I have no social life. Gah, what if my parents expect to fight over my time like they do with my holidays.

Mom is the first to call me when she hears the news that I'm moving back to Missouri. She's so excited that she doesn't even let me get a "Hello" out before she starts talking.

"Is it true?"

"Hello, mother dear."

"Dalton, I just heard on the radio that you have been traded to KC!"

I sigh, "Yes, I have."

"Thank God! I can see you more."

I try to dash her hopes away by telling her, "Not as much as you think; I'm on the road–a lot."

"Where will you be staying? I have room if you need a place until you find a house of your own," she offers.

I know the answer, but I ask anyway. "Have you moved in the past ten years?"

"Of course not."

"Then, no. I'll be set up in a hotel by the league until I find an apartment, anyway."

"Apartment? Don't you want to set down some roots?"

"Not really. I have my main place in Phoenix." Not that I will want to stay that close to Jake. I guess I will be looking for a new place there, too.

"You grew up here! This is your hometown. You can reconnect with Mill-."

"No," I quickly cut her off. "I saw her in November. I told you about that, and I don't want to rehash it."

"Awe, sweetie, I'm sure that wasn't what you think you saw. Have you called her?"

"No. Can we please change the subject now?"

"Okay. How about some good PR? The little league here is going to the state championships! How about I organize a meet and greet for you after your first-day game as a Kansas City King?"

"Fine. I'm sure my agent would like that. I need all the good publicity I can get right now." Jake was always my buddy, but things went wrong, and that might be half of the reason I was traded.

"YES!!! I will work out all the details!" I have never heard my mom this excited.

~Millie

Ruth is on fire! She's the number one pitcher on her little league team. A team that is undefeated and will be going to the state championship tournament. Coach Ben informs us that they will take a field trip, of sorts, to Sunday's King's game because of their success. The kids and dads are excited; I am not.

Evie comes over Saturday to give Ruth a gift for the "field trip" tomorrow: a King's jersey, complete with the number 88 and the name 'JAMES' on the back.

I stand up, "No. This is too much."

"Thank you, Mimi!! It has my middle name on it. But I'm number 10," Ruthie says.

Evie glares at me before answering Ruth, "James is the last name of their first baseman."

"Nope. She isn't going," I say as I start pacing.

"You have to let her go! She has earned this opportunity."

"Plleeaassee, Mama. I want to go so bad. Everyone else is going. You can come, too."

"No. I can't... I have my reasons," I say.

"What kind of reasons?" Ruth asks.

"Grown-up reasons." Like people in this town are already catching on to how much Evie is around Ruth-Ann. Stamping JAMES across her back is only going to solidify it. Then, rumors will spread outside of our community and go public.

"Ruthie, why don't you go to your room so I can talk to your mama," Evie reasons with her.

As soon as Ruthie leaves, I sit down on the couch with my face in my hands. My emotions drive me to the brink, and I feel like melting into a puddle. Evie moves to sit on her knees and begs me to let Ruthie go.

About fifteen minutes later, I break down and agree to let Ruth go. I can't say no to Evie's tears. She gives me a big hug and calls Ruthie back in.

"Ruth, she said yes!!!" Evie exclaims.

Chapter 36

-Dalton

My first week with KC hasn't been as bad as I anticipated. The guys have been cool and seem more down-to-earth than my last teammates. Probably the difference between the majority of them being married rather than bachelors.

A few of them are jumping in on the meet and greet with me, and I'm glad since Mom left me hanging. Surprise, surprise, she has to work. She did tell me that Benny, one of the kids I used to give lessons to, will be my contact person in her place. I guess he grew up and works for the town's parks and recreation department.

I get in and see Benny. He shakes my hand and gives me a ball all the kids signed. Well, that's a new one, but I love the sentiment. I start giving high fives and signing stuff. Benny tells me he has someone special for me to meet. Their star pitcher is a girl. This shouldn't be funny to me, but it is. She reminds me of a little girl I knew once. One that was about this age when I broke her arm.

Crouching down to her level, I say, "Hello, what's your name?"

"I'm Ruthie," she says. Then she hands me a marker and asks me to sign her jersey.

"Wow, you have my jersey," I say.

"Yeah, my Mimi gave it to me because my middle name is James." She tells me.

This is rich; I guess her dad was really hoping for a boy. "Tell your Mimi I said thank you."

"You could tell her yourself if she didn't get called into work." Typical girl; loves to talk. She just keeps babbling along. Benny is videotaping us, I guess for Mimi, so I listen and play along. "She said to show you her picture and tell you that you can call her even if she is working."

I cringe at the hook-up offer from Mimi. Is that what she calls her mom, or is it a different guardian? "Mimi must have been really disappointed she couldn't stay. My mom was always running off to work, too."

I attempt to find a way out of this sticky situation, but the ten-year-old girl has a cell phone, and she pulls up the image quickly.

I'm nearly knocked over when I see a picture of this girl, cheek to cheek with *my mother*. They have the exact same eye color, the same shade of blue that mine are. I look back at her. Other than the eyes, she's identical to Millie. Her wild, curly hair is tamed in double braids, and they share the same prominent cheekbones on a heart-shaped face.

I don't get a chance to speak, not that I could form words right now. "Want to know a secret?" she asks.

I clear my throat, "Yes," it comes out more of a whisper.

"Mimi wasn't supposed to be here at all today. She promised Mama she would go to work instead. I think that's why she ditched out early. But she begged Mama to let me come because she said you need to know the truth."

"What's the truth?" I am still whispering. I don't know if it's because she's telling me a secret or if I'm in shock.

"I don't know. I just heard Mimi tell my mama that. I was spying on them." She confesses and hangs her head low like I used to when I got in trouble with my father. Father.

I'm not sure I want to know, but I need confirmation. "What's your mama's name?"

"Millie Wilkins."

That's all I need to know. I pull the girl into my arms for a hug. Then I look at Benny, who is still recording this. "That better be for 'Mimi' and not go public."

He smiles and says, "I wouldn't sell ya out, Dalton. I have too much respect for you to do that. Plus, I had my orders from her since she couldn't be here. She also said if it's okay with both of you, you can take Ruth back to her mom."

I nod, "Would you like that, Ruth?"

"If Mimi says it's okay, then YES!!"

I know I can't drive, I'm too shaken up, so I call a car service. It's going to take them a while to get through traffic, so I leave Ruth with Ben while I shower.

A million questions and thoughts hit me. My last conversation with Millie plays in my mind. I've tried to block it out, so it's a bit rusty, but didn't she say something like *If you knew the truth, you wouldn't have left.*

Fuck! Why didn't I ask her what the truth was? I was too upset that she lied to me about school to hear her out.

Chapter 37

-Dalton

"So, Ruthie, tell me how you got into baseball," I ask. It's going to be a long ride if we sit in silence.

"Well, my mama plays in a softball league," she tells me.

"Wait, Millie Wilkins plays softball?"

"I didn't say she was good, but yeah. She had me in the dugout as early as I can remember. The better players would work with me. When Mimi found out, she started buying me all kinds of baseball stuff and got me real lessons."

Interesting, my mom has been in this girl's life and never told me. I don't know who I feel betrayed by more, my mother or Millie. I'm torn from learning more about Ruth or more about Millie. "How did your mom get into softball? When I knew her, she claimed she wasn't coordinated enough to do anything but run."

"I don't know," she answers, then cocks her head to one side. "You know my mom?"

Loaded question? "I did. I think I have a picture in my wallet," I say, fishing out the old prom picture. I think it's the only one I didn't burn.

She looks at it and laughs. Then. she goes right back to the previous topic. "She doesn't catch well, like at all. But she can hit *good,*" Ruth stresses the double o. It's so cute, I chuckle to myself. "Better than some of the guys on her team. She throws okay, but not as good as me. I'm a pitcher."

Ha. Wait. Guys on her team? Is she with one of those guys? Instead of asking that, I focus on Ruth. I ask, "Ben told me that. Why do you like that spot?"

Prideful, Ruth answers, "I just like throwing the ball so fast the boys can't hit it."

"We'll have to play catch sometime." I should have caught the first ball she ever threw. My chest is so tight, and I can't breathe. "Would you play catch with me?"

Her eyes go wide, and she nods vigorously. "I live right by the park," I bet she lives in Bea's house. "I will get my stuff, and we will go there. Do you have a glove? If not, my grandpa keeps his at my house." She is nodding to herself, making plans in her head.

Ruth has been quiet for the longest period of time since I met her, which is less than five minutes. Then she breaks the silence, "I have a question for you."

I must admit, I'm a little worried about what she will ask. "Shoot."

"Isn't Dalton a last name? And James a first or middle name?"

"Yeah, my parents were hilarious, huh?" I used to tell people that my dad was a big James Bond fan, and that's why he named me Dalton. But the truth is, it's my mother's maiden name—no relation to anyone famous.

"Yeah, I get that. I mean, my mom did give me a boy's name," she says.

"And why do you think she did that?" I ask.

Ruth crinkles up her eyebrows, just like Millie. "I don't know. She told me Mimi convinced her James was okay for a girl." She just shrugs it off.

My traitorous mother has known since Ruth was named! I am itching to call her, but I don't want to argue with the beloved *Mimi* in front of the girl.

"So, do you have any brothers or sisters?" I am dying to know what I am up against when I get to the house.

"Nope. Just mom and me. We live at my grandma's house since she's old."

"I'm an only child, too, but I always wanted a brother," I tell her.

She goes quiet, staring out the window. I can see wheels turning in her brain. Mine are, too.

When I notice she has fallen asleep, I swipe the phone off her lap and find the photo icon. I scroll through all her pictures. There are some of today's game, a bunch with her friends, and then I find the one she showed me of her and my mom–her *Mimi*. Next is a video. It looks like Ruth was sneaking in on a conversation my mom had. Mom is on her knees, begging someone. Is that Millie? I start the video, ready to change the volume if I need to.

"Please, Millie, you need to tell him."

Shaking her head, Millie says, "No, I can't. It's been over ten years. He won't understand."

"Millie, Dalton is so sad and lonely. He needs to know the truth; he deserves to know. You know I can't tell him. Michael will-"

Then, an older woman's voice is much closer, "Ruth-Ann Wilkins, spying is not polite." The video ends.

So, my father knows, too. How many other people have been keeping this from me? I am so angry I could break something.

Deep breath; count to ten.

I scroll through more pictures, finally finding what I'm looking for. It's a photo of Ruth and Millie. They are cheek-to-cheek, just like the one Ruth took with my mother. Millie was pretty in high school; now, she is stunning. I text the picture to my cell, so I have my own copy.

I look back over at the daughter I just found out about and snap this moment on my phone camera. I want to remember it forever. She is as beautiful as her mother. I already know I love her and will move heaven and earth for her. Getting traded to KC was a blessing, after all.

Ruth wakes up just as we get to town and is a chatterbox. I bet she's a morning person, like me. Inwardly, I chuckle, imagining how Millie must hate that.

We pull up to Grandma Bea's beautiful Victorian home. A home that I was lucky to share a few family dinners. I always felt comfortable here. Grandma Bea was always so inviting; it was as if it were my grandmother's house. I only knew one of my grandparents, and he was a cornerstone in my life.

"This is it, right here. The yellow one with all the gingerbread. Isn't that funny? It isn't really like the cookie. Do you like gingerbread cookies? They are my favorite." She hardly stops to hear my response.

"Yes. They're my favorite, too." I pay the driver and get out, and Ruth runs ahead of me, leaving the door wide open.

"Hey there, Ruth, come tell me about the game," Millie calls out.

Ruth is digging through the closet. "It was sooo awesome, Mom."

I am standing in the doorway when Millie walks into the foyer and stops dead in her tracks. Her eyes are wide in shock, looking at me. Ruth doesn't even notice; she just keeps talking, "I made a friend. I need to find Grandpa's glove so we can play catch."

"I see that." Even though her eyes are locked on mine, Millie keeps on with Ruth's conversation. "I don't know where it is."

I have so many emotions running through me right now. The anger that has been simmering inside me for almost a year fades away as my eyes rake over Millie.

She's standing before me barefoot, in running shorts and a tight tank top. Her hair is pulled back in a ponytail with a winded look—like she recently went for a run. Her body has matured and honed to perfection.

"I'm gunna check the garage," Ruth says, giving up in the stairway closet. "Oh, Mom, this is Dalton James! I met him today. He says he used to know you." Ruth dashes off to the garage. Over her shoulder, she hollers, "He even showed me a picture in his wallet." I feel the blood rush to my face.

"So," Millie starts. Her hands are fidgety, and her expression looks like she's preparing for a curveball.

I walk right up to her and pull her in my arms as if it hasn't been eleven years since we were together. Her body quickly deflates, melting against me. Holding her feels so right, like I finally found the missing piece to become whole.

~Millie

Holy shit, Dalton is *standing* in *my doorway*, and he is huge. He's got to be half a foot taller and packed on at least 30 pounds of

270

muscle. His hair is darker and longer than it was in high school, short on his neck but combed back on the top and sides. He also has a full, thick beard.

My heart and libido spring to life at the sight of him, but my brain warns me this could go sour really fast.

I'm not sure how he's going to react once Ruth leaves the room. I don't think he will yell; that was never his way, but he must be angry and confused.

The last thing I expect is for him to pull me into a hug. It takes me a few moments to put my arms around him and hug back. Then I am weeping. "I'm so sorry, I, I," I can't choke out the rest.

"Shhh, it's okay. We're going to talk about everything, and I mean everything, but right now, I just want to hold you again." He puts his nose behind my ear, at the nape of my neck, and breathes me in.

"Okay," I agree. I'm not sure, but I think he's crying too.

"I'm not letting go of you this time, Millie. I hope to The Babe no one's going to try and stop me."

I chuckle. I forgot that he always said different nicknames for Babe Ruth instead of taking God's name in vain. "No, there isn't. Well, maybe Angie, but Nate can handle that." I still have to try to cut the tension with humor. Otherwise, I will cry like a baby.

A car pulls into the driveway, and someone in high heels walks into the house. I know the only person that can be is Evie. "Well, it's about time," she says.

Dalton wasn't joking when he said he isn't letting go of me because he lifts his head above mine and turns both of us to address her, "I will have words with you later."

"Don't be mad at her, Dalton. She's been walking a tight line and helps me out a lot," I tell him.

Then, we all hear Ruth enter the kitchen from the garage, "I couldn't find it out there, either."

Evie walks right past us, hurrying to divert Ruth. "Hey, sweetie, let's go get ice cream."

"But Mimi, did you see who's here? It is *Dalton James*! Just like my jersey," Ruth says.

"Yes, I saw him," Evie says.

"He wants to play catch with me, but I can't find Grandpa's glove for him to use."

"I bet I have one at my house he can use. Let's go get it."

"But- "

"Shush! Your mother needs to talk to him now."

The door to the garage shuts, and it's just the two of us in this big old house.

"Let's sit down. There's a lot I need to tell you." He only releases me enough to grab my hand, and I lead him to the family room, where I'm most comfortable. We sit facing each other on the same sofa.

"Okay, start at the beginning. I want the whole story," Dalton requests.

"Well, I think you know the beginning," I say with a smirk, "so I'll skip ahead a bit. I didn't find out I was pregnant until spring break." I go on to tell him what life was like in Columbia and how his mom had suspicions and was on the lookout for me at the hospital. I don't leave out the threats Michael pulled.

"So that's how he fits into all of this. And it was all to push me out, keep me in the dark," Dalton says with an edge to his voice.

"I didn't do this to push you away. I'm sorry if it feels that way. But I, we, did it to protect you. We all just wanted you to reach your dream."

272

He hangs his head. "What about your dream, Millie? This can't be what you wanted."

"My dreams changed. I worked really hard to get the degree I wanted and wouldn't give up Ruthie for the world. I always wanted to be a mother; it just happened earlier than I thought it would."

"My dreams would have changed, too."

"No, Dalton. I know how you felt about your parents doing that."

"But he never loved her like I love you," he says, standing up.

Did he just tell me he still loves me? Isn't it too soon for that? We don't even know each other anymore.

My oven timer goes off. Talk about being saved by the bell. "Hungry? I guess I have extra since Grandma Bea is at my parents, and Ruth is with Mimi," I pause and let out a small laugh, "I mean your mom."

"I don't know if I can eat, but it smells great." His voice is still sore, but his words aren't.

"It's a new recipe I'm trying. I've become quite the cook since you knew me."

I get the casserole out of the oven, and he grabs the plates. We set up our dinner like we've been doing this for years. The companionship feels nice. He talks about how his life has been living his dream. How it's everything he hoped for, yet empty.

"Can I ask you something?" He nods, so I continue. "Why did you send me away when you were in the hospital?"

He stops moving. The cup that is halfway to his mouth comes down with a loud clunk against the table. "That was you?"

"What do you mean? I told the nurse my name," I'm not going to tell him I claimed to be his fiancé. "She came back out and threatened to call security if I didn't leave right away."

"She told me some woman was claiming to be my fiancé and that her name was Molly, something-or-another! If I had known it was you, I would have jumped out of that bed and ran out into the hall; my knee be-damned."

We both laugh nervously. Then I solemnly say, "I was so mad at you. That's when I stopped wearing your ring."

"I noticed it was missing. Do you still have it?" Dalton tentatively asks.

I nod, "It's on the chain with my broken heart charm."

He reaches inside his shirt and pulls his out. We both still and get very quiet, looking into each other's eyes for a long moment until Dalton breaks the silence. "This was good. I don't remember the last home-cooked meal I've had."

"Thanks, I've had time to improve my skills. Ruth is a picky eater."

"Tell me more about her."

We skip the clean-up, and I take him to look at the scrapbooks I've made. I tell him so many stories about our daughter. We're on the sofa; our bodies have gravitated towards each other. We're sitting much like how we used to, years ago, when we would study from the same textbook.

"How are we," he nervously stutters over his next words, "um, ugh, I mean, are you going to tell her? About me–who I am to her?"

I knew the day would come when I would have to. "Do you want me to? Once I do, you'll have to be part of her life. Are you ready for that?"

He doesn't even hesitate, "Yes. Hell, yes. I want that; I want you both in my life." His arm squeezes around me, holding me securely to his chest.

I'm glad he can't see my face because it's leaking. I am such a blubberer. "Well," I start, but I'm choked up. I wipe my face. "Do you want to be here when I do?"

"I would like that, but you know her best."

We don't get a chance to plan how we'll tell her because, just then, she storms in the door.

Chapter 38

-Dalton

Sitting with Millie back in my arms fills me with a contentment that I didn't know I was missing. I'm happy and sad, looking at pictures of Ruth growing up and listening to stories I wish I had witnessed. I want to be here for everything from here on out. I know I'm going to miss a lot with all the traveling I do since I still have a couple of seasons left on my contract.

The back door slams open. "MOM! MOM, is Dalton James still here? MOM?" Ruth is home.

"Please tell her tonight so she stops calling me by my full name," I quietly tell Millie.

She laughs at me, "Okay, I have an idea. I'll be right back." She gets up, and I am left sitting with empty arms.

"Hey, Ruth," I say, walking into the kitchen where my mom is closing the door behind them. "You didn't think I would leave before you got back, did you?"

"Maybe." Ruth's eyebrows crinkle. "Mom is good about chasing guys away." Interesting. "Look what we found at Mimi's house." She shows me my old catcher's mitt. "Do you think it will fit? It's an old one she had packed away. I also found this old hat," Ruth rambles, putting her hand on her head in reference to the hat she is wearing.

"I remember that hat!" I say, reaching for it. She looks at me, a little confused. "I mean, I used to have one just like it." Quickly, I act like I was just adjusting it on her head.

"No. He means it was *his* hat." Millie says, walking in with another scrapbook under her arm. "And the glove should fit because it was *his* glove,"

"Why does Mimi have a box of your old stuff?" Ruth asks, looking up at me with questioning eyes.

Here we go. I look at Millie for approval before slowly answering, "Because... Mimi is my mom."

Ruth looks back at Mom for confirmation. She nods. I think she might start to cry.

"Does that mean we are related or something?" Ruth says, starting to put some pieces together.

Millie answers for me, "Ruth, I want to show you some pictures and tell you a story."

We return to the couch, with Ruth sitting between us—like a family. Mom sits in a chair across from us. I know she takes a couple of photos while Millie tells Ruth the story of when we fell in love. Well, the PG version. Millie saved every movie ticket and note I passed her in class. She put a lot of time and work into this book. The last pictures are from graduation. I can see it now that I am looking; her pregnancy was starting to show. I can't believe I missed it until now, probably because I am looking for it.

Ruth is a smart girl; I can tell that. She starts to ask the next question slowly and thoughtfully. "So, Mom, is Dalton James my, um, dad?"

"Yes," Millie says, with tears she is holding back. Then, in true Millie fashion, she has to lighten the mood with a joke. "And you are going to have to stop calling him by his full name before he goes crazy." She laughs; so do I.

Ruth looks over to me, "Can I call you Dad?"

The weight of this moment is magnificent. "I would like that very much."

Ruth jumps up and wraps her arms around my neck. *My daughter is hugging me.* "I always wanted a dad."

I put my arms around her, too. "I didn't know about you, or I would have been here."

Millie moves over and kneels on the couch next to me. She brings her arms around both of us. "That's my fault, Ruth. I should have told him before now."

I pull one of my arms out and include Millie in the embrace. "That doesn't matter now. From here on out, we are a family."

I hear my mom sniffling. She gets up and leaves the room. I guess this moment is too much for her.

"Can we go play catch now?" Ruth asks, breaking the intense moment.

Millie gives permission, "It's close to bedtime, but yes. Go have fun."

I hug my mom before I go outside to toss the ball with Ruth. It doesn't take many throws to see why she is their star pitcher. She has quite an arm on her for a 10-year-old girl. Of course, I might be biased. The only other time I have played catch with a girl her age led me to play catch with this girl. I smile to myself. I give her a few pointers, and her aim improves.

We are also throwing out questions to each other—stuff like favorite color or food; what is better with chicken nuggets: barbecue or honey mustard. It surprises me when Ruth goes for a more profound question. "Is that why Mama gave me a boy's name for my middle name?"

I stop before I throw the ball again. "My guess is she gave you the name James because it should be your last name."

"Oh," is all she says, but I can tell she is thinking more.

Cautiously, I ask, "Would you like that? Do you want to change your last name to match mine?"

She grins, "Yes!" As an afterthought, she adds, "If that's okay with Mama. I don't want her to feel bad that I don't have the same last name as her."

My heart squeezes at my next thought; I say it anyway. "Then we'll have to change hers, too." Now, I am the one grinning.

~Millie

I take the fastest shower of my life and clean up dinner. I'm still standing in the kitchen just watching Dalton and Ruth play catch. The windows are closed because the air conditioning is running, so I can't hear what they are saying. I can tell by their faces that they are both happy. It fills me with something I can't name. Joy? Love? Fulfillment? Yep, all of that plus more.

Evie comes up and watches with me. Her eyes are still red and puffy from all the tears she has shed. Happy tears. I know today has taken an enormous weight off of her shoulders.

"You were right; I should have done this a long time ago," I admit and put my arm around her.

She does the same and says, "Yeah, I should have meddled long before today." She gives me a look with a little mischief in her eyes.

"You're responsible for this?"

She nods, blowing her nose. "I may have arranged for her team to go to the game and do a meet and greet. I wanted to be there so badly, but I knew it would have played out differently if I had. But I did have Ben record their meeting."

I gasp, "I want to see it." She pulls out the video camera, and I watch as Dalton unknowingly meets his daughter. She shows him something on her phone. Then he really looks at her. You can see the moment he realizes who she is. It's like a Mack truck hit him. Now I am crying again. I whisper, "Thank you."

If she hadn't organized today's events, Ruth and Dalton wouldn't be having this perfect moment.

"But wait a minute, what about Michael?" I ask.

"I didn't tell Dalton. He figured it out on his own. Besides, Dalton's made it now. His career isn't in jeopardy. And this," she points out the window at father and daughter, "is worth prison time."

"You've never told me what he has on you."

"Let's just say I *found* the hard evidence the prosecution needed to lock Bobby Stevens away."

"Nooo," I reply, in shock. "I had no idea you did that for me."

"It wasn't just for you. Michael didn't have to convince me, but he asked because he was afraid Dalton would get pulled into the case. I had no idea Michael was more worried about Dalton seeing you pregnant. Then, after Ruthie was born, he was ready with the blackmail to keep me from telling Dalton about her."

"Do you really think he would have turned you in if you told Dalton?"

"Yes. I've seen him do worse for less."

The sun has set, and it's past Ruth's bedtime, but I don't want to break their game. Dalton seems to have the same thought. He puts his arm over her shoulders and walks her in. They are deep in conversation about something but stop when they enter the house.

"Did you have a nice time?" I ask them.

A cheerful Ruth says, "Yep!"

"Good. I don't want to break this up, but it's after 9, young lady," I say.

"But Mom,"

"No, buts unless you want yours swatted," I half-jokingly say. I don't have to spank her; she's a pretty good kid, but I need to keep her on her toes.

Ruth hangs her head and puts her gear away before starting up the stairs. I'm strict about bedtime because she's an early riser, no matter how late she stays up, and lack of sleep causes my kid to be a whiny crab the next day.

Ruth pauses and asks Dalton, "When will I see you again?"

"Uhh," he looks at me, then back to her. "I'm not sure. I have a late game tomorrow. I would get you tickets, but I know it'll go past your bedtime. The same is true for Tuesday. Maybe we can hang out earlier in the day because I will be heading out east for about a week."

This is going to be a problem. Dalton's schedule is crazy and doesn't coincide with ours.

Ruth doesn't look at it that way; she only hears that he will make time with her in the next couple of days because she skips up the rest of the stairs. She shouts, "Goodnight, Dad!" before shutting her door.

Dalton seems to stagger back a step and puts his hand to his chest. It's like she shot an arrow straight to his heart. I feel it, too.

"I'm going to head out, too," Evie says. She walks to Dalton and asks, "Are we good?"

He hugs her and says, "Yes. Mom, I'm sorry I didn't listen to you before."

That's interesting. Once all the goodbyes are done, I ask Dalton, "What didn't you listen to your mom about?"

"She kept telling me to call you or come visit. I always had an excuse. You don't know how much I regret that now." He reaches out and tucks one loose lock of hair behind my ear. "I did come back once in November. Nate told me you had a kid; I never imagined it was mine," he lets out a nervous chuckle. "I even saw you at the park holding a baby. Some guy was with you..." his voice trails off like he is looking for an answer.

"I knew that was you peeling out of the parking lot! You can't drive like that next to a park full of people," I scold him in my mom voice.

"Who was the guy, Millie?" Dalton sounds stern, and I detect a bit of anxiety. "Tell me if there's anyone else."

"I was holding my nephew. Ruth and I were spending the day with Michelle's family. I'm guessing you saw her husband and jumped to conclusions." I barely have the last part out before I'm enveloped in his embrace.

"So, there is no one else? Since that day, I've had the worst time, thinking you, you-" he can't even finish his thought.

"I don't have time for relationships. I have Ruth, my job, and Grandma Bea."

"Will you make time for me? For us?"

"I don't think *you* are going to have the time. How often will you even be in the area? I work 8-4, five days a week. Sometimes more if I can get the hours. We'll barely see each other."

"We'll figure it out as we go. All I know is I don't want to lose you again."

282

Dalton's so close, close enough to kiss me. And I'd bet he's thinking the same thing. He doesn't even pull away when a car pulls into the driveway.

"That's my dad dropping off Grandma." She doesn't need my assistance anymore, but Dalton doesn't know that. The moment was getting heated, and I needed to take a step back.

Grandma comes in and welcomes Dalton back to her home as if no time has passed. My dad shakes his hand, and they start catching up while I help Grandma to her room. She's in pretty good shape for a woman in her late 80's. I just need a chance to think.

"Lovely to see Dalton again. I knew he would come back," she tells me. "Why are you in here with me? Shouldn't you be out there planning your future together?"

"I don't know how it's going to work, Grandma. And besides, we don't know each other anymore."

"Your head might not know the answers yet, but your heart does. Stop telling me what you know or don't know, and tell me what you feel," the wise old lady tells me. "You may have changed a little, but that was just growing up. Your perspectives have shifted; you think like a mother, not a child. Deep down, a person doesn't change who they really are." She puts her fingertips on my chest, over my heart. "You loved him once and sacrificed much so he could have his happiness. If it was true love then, it still runs through your soul." She turns as if to dismiss me, shutting the door behind her.

I go back to the men talking in the kitchen and lean against the doorway. I don't join the conversation because I am thinking about what my grandmother told me. When Dad says goodbye, I only wave.

Dalton asks, "What's wrong?" He walks over to me but seems hesitant to touch me. I can tell he is holding himself back.

Could Dalton and I pick up where we left off? I'm definitely still attracted to him, and the passion is still there. "Nothing, just tired. It's been a long, emotional day." Not untrue.

"Okay, I'll call for a ride then and head out."

"You didn't drive?"

"No, I was a little shaken up and didn't want to get behind the wheel." That was smart of him. Is it wrong that his putting Ruth's safety first is such a turn-on?

"You can stay here tonight if you want." Did I just say that?

He teases, "That depends; would I be sleeping on a pull-out couch?"

"Only if you want to," I banter.

Chapter 39

~Millie

Abruptly, I turn so he can't see my face go red and start my nightly routine of locking doors, turning off lights, and picking up what has been left out. There isn't much, just the scrapbooks–Ruth's goes in the entertainment center, but Dalton's belongs in my room. He follows me along, watching me like the stalker Dani always liked to call him.

When we get upstairs, I pause at the guest room/den. "What did you decide? The pull-out is in here," I say, turning on the light and nodding to the room.

"I can sleep here, but I would rather have you in my arms," he says in a deep, quiet, hushed tone. His hands have found their way around my waist. Since he towers over me, he has to lean down to speak in my ear, "I'm kinda afraid if I'm not touching you, I won't see you for another eleven years."

"So, you think we are going to go 'POOF!' and you won't be able to find us?" I joke.

"Yeah, something like that," he says. Dalton takes the opportunity to kiss me for the first time since I left for school. Wow, he's gotten better at this, whereas I'm rusty as hell.

I drop the scrapbook in favor of putting my arms around his neck, purely for support because I'm melting into a puddle of sap. There isn't much room between us, but Dalton closes the small gap, pushing me into the doorframe. "Ugh," I grunt.

"Sorry," Dalton retreats slightly, but I protest.

"No," I grab the collar of his shirt, yanking him back to me while on tip-toe. "More. Closer." In my lust-filled mind, climbing him is the only way to get closer. My arms are already close to his neck, so I pull myself up, and my right thigh tries to find a gripping point on his hip to boost me up and tug him closer at the same time.

Dalton doesn't leave me to struggle in my quest; he's on the same page. His hand shifts from my waist to my thigh, caressing my ass in the process. Needing more contact, Dalton bends at the knees, grips the back of my other leg, and boosts me up. When he straightens, I feel everything I've been missing.

I've been going through such a dry patch lately; I haven't even taken care of myself in six months. It's not going to take much for me to explode.

We come up for air and rest our foreheads against each other. Looking into Dalton's eyes, I say, "My bedroom is the next one down."

He pulls back, letting me slide to the floor, and takes my hand. "Lead on."

I almost leave the scrapbook where it lies, but I have treasured it for so long, and it's already bad enough that I carelessly dropped it. I grab it, and we walk into my room—the "master suite."

It was remodeled years ago, so a smaller bedroom that was next to it is now an attached bathroom and closet. When I moved in, my grandmother insisted I take it since stairs have become difficult for her. We changed the old den into a main-floor bedroom for her. It's still kind of makeshift, but she is more comfortable. Ruth has a massive room on the third floor.

The air is thick with tension and anticipation. My body aches for everything that might happen. I haven't had a man in my bedroom since Dalton snuck through the window in high school. But my mind won't stop all the "what ifs." Not to mention that even though I have been abstinent for the past decade, he probably hasn't. I don't even know if there is another woman in his life. He bluntly asked me, but stupidly, I never asked him.

Dalton immediately shuts the door behind him, and I'm yanked back to him by the hands we are still holding. He doesn't waste time looking at my room; his complete concentration is on me: one hand at the base of my skull, fingers in my hair, and the other, still holding my hand, is pressed against my lower back.

There is a hardness between us, and I don't mean his erection. It takes me a minute to realize I'm still clutching the scrapbook to my chest.

Dalton realizes the problem, lets go of me to grab the scrapbook, and tosses it to the floor to free our hands for something more useful—like removing clothes.

Dalton makes quick work of undressing me. I don't own sexy underwear anymore. I have on plain pink panties and a white sports bra, and that is all I'm wearing right now.

All his muscles distracted my progress of undressing him. I have only removed his shirt, but I have managed to walk us back to the bed.

The backs of my knees hit the edge of my bed, and I take a seat so that I have a front-row view to unbuckle his belt. Good lord, his abs continue below his waistline into that perfect V pointing down while something else points up.

Taking his erection in one hand, I lick the length of him. He groans loud enough to fill the room and possibly beyond.

"Shhh, Dalton. This is an old house, and the walls are thin."

He chuckles, "Sorry, it's been a long time since I had to worry about being quiet."

And there it is. I freeze at his words. When I don't go back to sucking him, he looks down to see what is wrong. It feels like forever before his words register back to him.

"Millie," Dalton starts to speak, but I stop him.

"No, it's okay. It's been over a decade, I couldn't possibly have expected you to—well, you know."

He takes a seat next to me. "Do you mean after all this time, you haven't?"

"I've dated but haven't even gotten to first base with anyone."

Dalton smirks, "Well, that is my job, keeping people from getting to first base."

"Meanwhile, you've been getting home runs with—you know what? It doesn't matter." I stand up and pull my T-shirt back on. "I don't have any condoms anyway."

Dalton leaps into action, pulling one out of his wallet. It looks a little worn like it's been in there a while. He inspects it closer. "Damn, it's expired."

"Just as well. That's probably how I got pregnant."

"They got used too often to have expired." The joke lightens the mood. "I don't understand; we were always so careful."

"No, we weren't." I pick up the scrapbook. "We were horny kids that couldn't wait to cum. And having sex in a hot tub is not safe."

"We didn't have sex in the hot tub."

"No, but we got awfully damn close." It was the one time he entered me without one. If I hadn't insisted on getting out and finding some lube, we would have probably finished in there, believing that the heat killed sperm.

"Yeah, I guess you're right. When we first started having sex, I didn't really know what I was doing with them. And then, as we used them more, I thought we would be safe as long as I got it on for the finale."

I put the scrapbook back in the cabinet part of my nightstand. The top still displays the old soda bottle and dried flowers. I've tried to throw it out or even tuck it out of sight, but I always put it back here.

"Do you need anything? Towels? A glass of water? I don't think I have any clothes that will fit you, maybe a T-shirt." I start searching through my dresser.

"Millie," he tugs at my hand until I look back at him, "We don't have to do anything but cuddle."

I let out a deep breath I didn't know I was holding. I nod and head to the restroom. I decide to ditch my bra and sleep in the shirt and panties I already have on.

When I come back out, Dalton's sitting on the edge of my bed with his boxers back on. He's holding the soda bottle of flowers, looking at the bottom intently. When he sees me, he lowers it and sadly looks at me. "Millie, are you still mad at me about the mix-up at the hospital?"

I walk to the bed and sit next to him. "No. It's water under the bridge."

Pulling the flowers out, he carefully puts them on the nightstand and tips the bottle to dump it out into his palm. "Then will you wear this again? I still have promises to keep."

I nod and wipe the new tear that is coming down my face. Dalton takes the ring off the chain, wraps the necklace around my neck, and centers the broken heart charm. I hold out my palm for my ring. Instead of dropping it in, like I thought he would, he takes my hand in his, turns it over, and slides the ring back on my ring finger. Then he brings my hand to his mouth and kisses it.

"Does this mean we are going steady?" I try to joke.

"Something like that," he answers.

"Dalton, just to be clear, you asked earlier if I have anyone else in my life," I don't even get to ask my question; he knows where I am going with this.

"I don't either. You don't know how much I regret the handful of women I dated. But know that you've always been the only one I wanted. And there will never be another."

"Okay." That's one weight off my shoulders.

Dalton holds me close. The hug is healing and rapidly becomes much more than a friendly gesture. It doesn't take long for the mood that I ruined to return.

My shirt is back on the floor, and we lay on our sides, face to face, on the bed. Dalton's hand is kneading my butt cheek, fingers ready to tear my panties off.

"Millie," Dalton says, almost like a prayer. "I was tested for everything under the sun at the beginning of the season and again when I was traded. I swear on Babe Ruth's grave I don't have any STDs. The doctor even joked that I'm the cleanest player in the league." He swallows hard before continuing, "And I have a lot more control now; I could just pull out."

Knowing where he's going with this, my head is shaking before he finishes. "No. Did you forget we are a very fertile combination?"

"Would that be so bad?"

"YES! Today is the first day we have seen each other since high school!"

"Dry humping like it's 1998, it is then," Dalton says, rolling on top.

"I'm sorry. It's just a…" Every thought in my brain vanishes when he drops his hips and rocks against my core. "Ohhh," I exhale in revelry.

Dalton lifts his lips from my neck to whisper, "Now who needs a reminder to stay quiet?" He silences the rest of my moans with his mouth on mine.

Good God, I have missed this. How have I made it so long without Dalton's touch? Tears form in my eyes, and Dalton kisses each one when I blink them away.

I'm right on the cusp of orgasm, just waiting for one little thing to tip me over the edge. Dalton must sense it, too, because the hand that has been holding my breast to his mouth skims down my body, to my inner thigh, and into my panties. Without breaking the delicious motion of his hips, he inserts one finger inside me. A little wiggle, and I am cumming harder than a freight train.

When I open my eyes, Dalton's blue-lavender eyes are shining with pride. "What?"

"Nothing," he smiles as if he has a secret he can't keep in. "You're just so beautiful, and I… I really wish I had a condom."

"This again," I mutter.

Dalton hops up and starts getting dressed with a full boner that is obviously begging to be released. After that fantastic friction play, I should suck it down. But now he's slipping his shoes on, sockless.

"Where are you going?"

"Is that gas station," he scrunches his face in concentration, "on Pine still open all night?"

"Yeah, but that's like a half-mile away."

He gives me a quick, unsatisfying peck on the lips, "I'll be right back."

-Dalton

Thankful to be in the best shape of my life, so I can literally run to get condoms at 11:27 at night. I feel like a horny high schooler, and I'm not even ashamed. Maybe this would have been better motivation to break Dad's 50-yard dash record.

I run straight past the little car filling up and into the convenience store. The condoms are on a rack next to the cashier like they are a hot commodity that needs surveillance.

"No frickin way! Dalton James is back in town," says the man behind the counter.

Hearing my name snaps me to attention. I look at the cashier, vaguely recognizing him. "Hey man, how's it going?" I grab a box, no, better make that two boxes just to be sure, and put them on the counter.

The man takes them but doesn't look at them, let alone ring them out. He just keeps talking like we were old friends. Maybe if I wasn't in such a stupor when I left the stadium today, I would have worn a cap... and socks.

How the hell did I forget to put on socks when I left? Oh, that's right, I had just been thrown a life-altering curve ball and knew I would finally see Millie again.

The bell on the door jingles, signifying another customer, and I look over my shoulder, praying this person will help me get away.

The woman is also slightly familiar. She pauses, telling me she recognizes me. Shit, I hope I don't get pulled into some kind of fan freakout. Instead of nerding out like the cashier, she walks to the aisles.

"So, now that you've been traded back to KC, are we going to be seeing you a lot more?"

"I don't know, maybe."

"Gaw, Jason. It's 11:30ish on a Sunday night," says the woman, who is now way too close in line behind me, "and the man is buying condoms. Do you think he wants to rehash high school glory days?"

Jason! Yes, now I can see it. He's put on some weight and has a receding hairline, but I remember him now.

I mouth, "Thank you" to the woman, but she still has a resting bitch face for me.

"Only a few blocks away." She asks, "Can I assume those are for whom I think they are for?"

"Umm." Warning lights are flashing in my brain that I should know her. Shit, is this Danika? She definitely has the scary man-hater vibe working for her.

"I'm going to assume yes since I saw you run your ass here."

"You're getting back together with Millie?" Jason interrupts. "That's great!"

His enthusiasm gets the better of me, and I grin sheepishly. "I sure am. I've waited too long to get her back in my arms." And I would love to get back there, so if this happy reunion could just wrap it up.

Dani smiles. A real honest-to-goodness "I'm happy for you" smile. She isn't as beautiful as her best friend, but I can see how someone might find her attractive. "Good for you. The condoms are on me. And grab one of the flower bouquets. Only a pig would show up with rubbers and nothing else." There's the Danika I remember.

"Thanks," I take the bag from Jason and the suggestion of flowers from Dani.

"If you can wait a second, I'll drive you," Dani offers, but I'm out the door and running before Jason rings up her soda.

Millie's curled up in a rocking chair when I arrive. Her hair is blowing in the light wind, and she has a bathrobe wrapped around her. It's sexy as fuck.

"Hi," she stands and greets me with amusement in her eyes. "Did you get me flowers?"

"Umm, kind of. I brought you flowers. They were Danika's idea."

"You bumped into Dani?"

"Uh-huh," I have no interest in talking about her friend, so I start kissing her the way I was before I ran out.

A car slowly approaches and beeps. "GET A ROOM!" Dani yells.

That's a great idea. I scoop up Millie's legs and carry her into the house. I would carry her all the way to the bed, but she insists on taking the stairs on her own, and we race down the hallway to her room.

Ditching my clothes as fast as possible, I tumble onto the bed, grabbing Millie in the process. I'm surprised that she has no objections to completely naked foreplay. I could cum just like this, on the outside of her body, but I want to be physically connected when I do.

After all the fuss about condoms, I plan on making a show out of putting it on. Rolling Millie onto her back, I take the top position, straddling her. I tear into the box, fish out the strip of small plastic packages, and rip open one, tossing the other two.

"Hurry up, Dalton."

"Hey, now, this is what you wanted."

"I know, but it's taking too long."

I chuckle. "We have the rest of our lives to do this," I tease.

"We also have a lot of time to make up for."

"Fair point." I shift so her legs can wrap around my waist and slide home. She is so tight I have to ease my way in and wait a moment.

Millie is the first to buck against me, and I answer in like. Our bodies slide together and apart, finding that perfect rhythm until a title wave hits me, and the only thing I can do is submit to the orgasm that washes over me.

Fuck, did I cum before Millie? I open my eyes to see her panting, and I feel her muscles contracting around my member as if there is any extra room.

I almost blurt: *How can you be so tight after having a baby*, but by the grace of The Babe, I can't form words.

I hate the moment I leave her body to toss the condom, and I know she was right to insist on it. There is no way I could have pulled out pre-orgasm. However, I would rejoice in any additions to our family.

We both crawl under the covers. I'm on my back, with my arm around Millie, who is curled up on my chest, using my shoulder as her pillow. This is the most content I have felt in as long as I can remember.

With all of the tears, excitement, and sex, I expect Millie is already asleep. But to my surprise, she asks, "Did you buy a place yet? Where are you staying?"

"No, I'm supposed to go look at condos with a realtor tomorrow. I'm set up in a hotel until then."

"You would have probably fit in that bed better than this one; it's only a full size." She giggles, "I bet your feet are hanging over the end."

"I'm happy to trade that big empty king for this. My feet don't even mind." I wiggle my feet that are indeed hanging off the bed. "Just a little extra airflow so they can breathe."

"Well, I'm sure breakfast here will be better. I will make pancakes and bacon, or are you still on a protein shake breakfast diet?"

"I love pancakes and bacon," I confirm.

"You will have to fight Ruth for the bacon. She could probably eat the whole pound," she warns me. "We should probably wake up before her anyway."

I'm not sure how Ruth will take waking up to having me here. I think she will be tickled pink, but I don't know her well enough to place that bet. Besides, she is ten; is she old enough to understand what Mom and Dad were up to all night? What conclusions will she jump to?

I ask, "Do you have to work tomorrow?"

"Yep. I usually pack my lunch, but I can come home if you're still here."

"I can stay until then," I promise. I might not get to stay wrapped up with Millie, but at least I can spend time getting to know my daughter.

Millie yawns, so I kiss her on the forehead and whisper, "Goodnight."

"Goodnight," she answers and starts to drift off.

The last time Millie and I were together like this, I gave her a piece of my soul. And at some point before that, I gave her a different piece of me. One that I unknowingly left behind, leaving her with all the responsibility of a single parent.

I'm still mad about that, but I know she isn't to blame. I will bring that anger to my father the next time I see him.

I sit up with a start, "SHIT!" I was supposed to see him after today's game for Father's Day.

A sleepy, confused Millie asks, "What," looking around for the cause of my distress.

"Was today Father's Day?"

Her brow crinkles, "Yeah. I think that is why-"

Not needing anything more than confirmation, I cut her words off with a long, hard kiss. "This has been the best day of my life."

Chapter 40

-Dalton

Monday morning, I wake up slightly earlier than usual because of a cramped sleeping position. An inhale of woman's shampoo reminds me why I'm not in my overpriced hotel bed. Millie. I finally got her back.

Pulling her close, snuggling in, but the movement startles Millie awake. "Wha-what time is it?"

I check my watch, "4:51."

Millie's head crashes back to the pillow, "Why do I have to have a kid that wakes up so damn early?"

"What time does she usually get up?"

"A quarter after five, like clockwork."

"That's not so bad."

"Not so bad? Are you kidding?"

"Nope, that means we still have 20 minutes for," I slide my hand down her front and between her legs.

"I'm never going to get to sleep in again, am I?"

"She's ten. You don't really need to get up with her anymore, do you?"

"No, but chances are she will come find me this morning to ask a million questions about you. Plus, I want us to both be downstairs by the time she is up."

"Does that mean sex is out of the equation?"

"Let's be quick."

The rest of the morning is perfect. We have breakfast as a family before Millie goes off to work. I know she's trying to keep what is happening between us just between us. But I want to tell the world. I take her lead, though, at least in front of Ruthie.

I spend the next few hours with my daughter. She wants to play ball, but I'm sore from not icing after yesterday's game. So, I make her a deal that she can hit off the tee and talk her through some stuff while I ice. I don't think I was as excited about baseball as she is when I was her age.

Ruth usually fills her days with Grandma Bea and Yaya Kathy. So, I tell her about my Grandpa Jack and how we liked to go fishing every morning all summer long.

"What kind of things do you like to do with Grandma Bea and Yaya?"

"Yaya makes me read…during the summer!! Can you believe that?" She doesn't let me answer. "But we also garden, and when I'm lucky we bake cookies."

"Let's do that then," I suggest.

"Do you really know how to make cookies?"

"I sure do, Mimi taught me. I used to make them all the time for your mom." I don't make them as much anymore. In the past few years, they started to make me melancholy, but that is sure to change now.

"Mom is going to flip when she sees this mess."

"I guess we'll have to clean it all up before she gets home because I don't want her to get mad at me." I wink, "Besides," I tell her, chuckling, "there will be cookies to soften her up."

"Is that why you broke up?"

"Uhh…" Shit, I'm not prepared for those kinds of questions. Why is this the one time she waits for an answer? Treading carefully, I say, "We broke up for a lot of reasons, but not because she was mad at me."

Ruth wraps her arms around my waist and squeezes tight. The hug is so out of left field that I'm frozen for a moment before I reciprocate. "Don't break up again."

"Don't worry about that, Ruth. That was all old stuff that has worked itself out." I rub her back. "And even if your mom and I can't make it work, there is no way you are going to lose me again." I hate to think that way, but this girl needs to know that.

"You promise?" She holds up her pinky finger.

"I promise; pinky swear."

While we wait for the cookies to bake, I call the realtor I'm working with to tell him I decided against condos; I'm more interested in houses or land for sale. It's time to have a permanent place. Maybe I'll even get a dog. I've always wanted a pet. I bet Ruth would, too, one that likes to play fetch.

At 11:30, we walk to a sub shop, and Millie meets us there. We have lunch and get several surprised looks from some old classmates we bump into. It thrills me that the gossip train will be filled with our news.

After we eat, she drives us back to Bea's house, and I call for a ride back to the stadium to get my car.

Once I get back to the city, I drive to my father's office.

"Well, hello, son. Thought I would have at least gotten a text from you yesterday."

Oh, this is rich. He has so much room to talk. "Sorry, Dad. I met someone. I was so wrapped up in her I didn't even realize it was Father's Day."

"Well, good for you. It's about time you start thinking about your future."

"This girl is my future, all right. I wish I would have known about her *eleven years ago.*"

He perks up, "You know. How? Did your mother-"

"No. Although I have spoken with her, so I know about your little deal."

"Listen, that girl you were with would have ruined your life," he says, rising to his feet.

I stand, too, towering over him even though I am only a few inches taller. I speak my mind to him for the first time since we clashed in our hallway when I was in high school, "No, Michael, *you* ruined my life. You call me a son, but you never really wanted me. I never had a childhood; all you did was push me to be some perfect version of yourself that you were never able to achieve. Then, you tore me from the one person in my life that I truly loved.

"So, I'm sorry that I didn't call you to wish you a happy Father's Day when you have made damn sure I didn't know I should be celebrating it *as* a father."

"You ungrateful son of a bitch! Do you have any idea how much I have given for you to reach the top?"

"Thank you for helping me with my career, but I won't be needing you to work on any more contracts for me because I am thinking of pursuing a family life as soon as possible. I want to finally have a place to call home with people who know what it means to be a family." I turn my back on the cruel man to leave.

I hear him yelling behind me, "Just as well, because I never got my cut of those contracts. It all went to Millie."

301

I reach for the door handle but pivot to hear this new information. "What?"

"Oh, you didn't know that. Millie isn't as clean from our deal as you would like to assume. Ask her about it; ask her who paid her way through school. How she never struggled to make ends meet."

"Millie would never take *your* money."

"I couldn't have her going to you for it."

"That's who she should have gone to–me! I was the one that should have been held responsible! And what about the relationship that I should have had with my daughter? All the time I missed?"

"Oh, give it a break. She had her mother; she didn't need you."

"You don't know that!"

"Sure I do. Alyssa turned out just fine without me."

"Alyssa? Who the fuck is Alyssa?"

"The beauty queen I introduced you to at FSU."

"The girl you tried to set me up with in Florida?"

"Set you up?" He laughs, "More like a playdate for two children so their parents could have some time alone! Why the hell would I set you up with your sister?"

"I have a sister? I thought I was an only child because you couldn't have kids!"

"Surprise! The two of you sure were, so I ensured there wouldn't be any more brats begging for my money. And then I get hit with your problems. But, like the good father that I am, I took care of everything, so you didn't have to ruin your life over a little mistake."

"A child isn't a small mistake!"

Michael's secretary knocks on the door. "Is everything alright? Should I call security?"

302

"No, I was just leaving." Michael keeps yelling, but I just don't care anymore.

I call Mom as soon as I get in my car. She confirms the Alyssa thing–I'm relieved she already knew. And she tells me Millie knows nothing about where her "scholarship" money came from.

Am I supposed to keep that secret from her?

No. No more secrets. I fucking hate secrets. I'll find a time to talk to her about it. But first, I need to make sure she isn't going to cut communication with me again. Even though we had one night together, and I think we are headed in "'til death do you part" teritory, I need to make sure she feels the same way.

I text Millie.

> **Me: U sure no game 2nite?**
> **Millie: No sorry**
> **Millie: U hangin w ruth 2morrow?**
> **Me: YES 10?**
> **Millie: K**

I wish I was going to wake up there again. But I don't want to go barging in after they've all gone to bed. Besides, I have an early appointment with the realtor that I blew off today.

The following day, Millie surprises me by taking a half-day. She got tickets to come to my game, but they won't be staying the whole time because Ruth will need to get home before the end. I will take what I can get.

~Millie

I haven't checked my phone since Dalton showed up at my house yesterday. I'm on my way to meet Dalton and Ruthie for lunch when I check it and see 27 texts from Angie, one from Danika, and one from Mom. Before number 28 can come through from Angie, I call her.

"Oh My Gosh, Millie!!!"

"Good morning, Angie."

"Well??"

"Well, what?"

Angie groans in frustration. "What took you so long to get back to me?"

"I was too busy to check my phone."

"Too busy? Doing what?"

I snort, "What do you think?"

"Oh, I know. Dani texted me to tell me who she bumped into and what he was buying."

"If you know, why are you asking?"

"Because! How could you just jump in bed with him after he rejected you?"

"It wasn't his fault. The nurse told him the wrong name. Called me Molly."

"Oh, please. How could he not figure that out? Who else would show up with a similar name?"

Even though she can't see me, I shrug. "I don't know, but I believe him." I hear her sigh through the phone. "He didn't know where I was living, and I don't know how far fangirls would go—what he's had to deal with."

"What about-" Angie starts, but I cut her off.

"You are starting to sound like Dani. What happened to the friend who always rooted for love?" I laugh, "You swapped! You are unforgiving, and she was rooting for Dalton last night."

"She wasn't rooting for love; she was rooting for lust. That's nothing new."

"I've forgiven him, Ang. And he definitely has more to be angry with me over. But he's not holding it against me. Anyway, I'm about to have lunch with him and Ruthie."

"They're together?"

"Yep, they spent the morning together."

"Aw, that's so sweet. How did he find out?"

For the rest of the drive, I tell her all about yesterday. "He took it better than I expected."

"So, are you two going to make it work? I watch the two most important people in my heart walking towards where I am parked. "I really hope so."

That night, Ruth and I watch Dalton's game. There is a different aspect to it now that she knows. She has been quite inquisitive about him and what life is going to be like now. I wish I had all those answers to give her. I don't get a break until she goes to bed.

Maybe we can go to tomorrow night's game? I look up tickets online. It's not an early game, but we could catch part of it. In a snap decision, I buy two tickets, and I email my boss a request to take a half-day vacation so I can spend more time with Dalton before the game.

Chapter 41

-Dalton

Life on the road has never sucked more. We win some; we lose some. But losing a game isn't as bad as losing out on time with my family. Finding out I have a ten-year-old and I have missed out on her whole life is Hell. Knowing what I am missing now is torture. Her big tournament was yesterday, and I'm in Texas. At least Millie taped it so that I can watch it later. I've only had them back in my life a few weeks, and I already know I would rather be there watching her than here without them.

The All-Star game is coming up. I have gone several times before, both as a participant and a spectator. It's the most fun week of the regular season. This is the first year I'm not stressing about getting voted in because I'd love to have that time off.

Millie and I haven't gotten as much alone time as I would like. Because of Millie's job, I spend more time with Ruth. I've been trying to convince Millie to take more time off and come on the road with me, and the All-Star game would be perfect.

I know Cain and Jake will be there whether they play or not. I need to mend the rift between us; introducing Millie to them is a perfect way. Once they meet her, they will understand why I was so hung up and unable to move on.

I know she is probably still at work, but I text her the invite anyway. She'll get back to me when she can, but she still hasn't responded to my earlier message.

The clubhouse is full of the usual banter, shenanigans, and strategizing. But I'm staying out of most of it by looking at house magazines.

I've been looking at house plans so much they are running together. I haven't talked to Millie yet, but there are two houses I plan to take her to look at and one piece of land that we could build on.

I've also started looking at engagement rings. I don't care if it's too soon; I don't want to lose her again. I'm determined to fight harder for us this time. Diamonds and gold will be my weapons—not really. But I am concerned when I don't have any notifications on my phone after my game.

I hope she isn't shutting me out; I couldn't live through that again. We had a day game today, a night game tomorrow, then a travel day. Maybe I will book a red-eye and surprise her when I get back early. Then again, that won't help because it'll be a weekday, and she'll have to work.

The one good thing about life on the road is that I've gotten to know some of my teammates better. The catcher, Darius Jackson, has been in the game for a long time. He noticed how often I was checking my phone and called me out on it.

"Hey man, ya look like that thing's offending ya, just 'cause it ain't ringn'," he tells me in his southern drawl. "I swear, ya look at it more than the scoreboard. What's got ya so distracted?"

"Just making sure it works," I say.

"Ha. It's gotta be a hunny. No man in his right mind looks at a phone the way ya doin'."

"Yeah. It's just that she's blocked me out before, and I don't want that to happen again."

"Shit." The way he says it, it sounds more like "she-it."

Finally, she texts me back.

Millie: Sorry n car ttyl

"What does 'T-T-Y-L' mean?" I ask no one in particular.

One of the younger guys pipes up, "Talk To You Later."

"Least she answered ya back," Darius states.

"Not helpful," I grunt.

Then he goes on, "Tell ya what, why don't ya join me," almost as an afterthought, he adds, "and my wife tonight for dinner. Take your mind off the phone, or ya'll go crazy."

"Yeah, sure," I answer indifferently. He simply laughs at me.

We meet at the hotel restaurant at 7:00. We are seated, and Darius asks, "Did ya ever hear from ya hunny?"

"Yes. She was getting ready for dinner, so she couldn't talk long," I tell Darius and his wife. I think she is keeping something from me, but maybe I'm just suspicious.

"This life doesn't suit everyone," Ria, Darius's wife, says. "I know we had our problems figuring it out. It will be even harder once this little guy comes." She is rubbing her small baby bump and looking affectionately at her husband.

"We'll figure it out, always do," Darius tells her while he rubs his thumb over her hand. "Now, I gotta go figure out where the men's room is. 'scuse me." He gets up, pushes in his chair, and leaves us.

"I didn't know you were expecting. Is this your first?" I ask, trying to make a polite conversation.

"It is," she says with a big smile. "We've been trying for years now. Do you have any kids?"

"A daughter." I don't add in that I just found out about her. But I do tell her all about how Ruth likes to play baseball. I have her laughing about Ruth's comment, "I like to throw faster than the boys can hit," when the hostess comes up extremely flustered.

Chapter 42

~Millie

I miss Dalton so much it's crazy, and this is only the second time he has had away games. It's not like we get to spend much time together when he's home, either. I'll have to get used to our schedules clashing, or it is going to get unbearable.

I finally found the missing piece of my life. I guess it makes sense, but I still feel silly.

Evie sees it, too, and talks me into doing something insane. Now I'm flying to Texas to surprise him. Evie told me what hotel he's at and assured me he'll dine in at their swanky restaurant. She even booked me an appointment at a salon to get my hair, makeup, and nails done.

I was planning to sit at the bar and wait for him to come down, but when I arrive, I see he's already seated—with a beautiful woman. She's dressed in a tight black dress that shows off her ample cleavage. I can't see the rest of her, but it doesn't matter.

I nearly choke, watching her smile and laugh at what he's saying. She's practically glowing.

I have two options: cower and run or stand up for myself. I'm nearly at their table when I realize I made the second choice. The hostess tries to stop me, but I won't hear it. I have waited too long for my family to be complete.

"Ma'am, Ma'am, you can't," she says, trying to cut me off. She turns her back to me, trying to block me out, and addresses Dalton, "Sorry, Mr. James, I know you don't like to be disturbed. I can call security if you would like."

"Yes, Mr. James, would you like to call security?" I echo in my stern mom-voice, coming up to her side.

He pops up, "Millie!" he reaches for me, but I pull back. That's right, you're busted.

A large black man with a serious face comes up. I think he's undercover security; only he takes the seat between where I'm standing and the other woman. That's when I realize there is a third-place setting. And I feel like a fool for jumping to conclusions. "Oh!"

"No need for security, ma'am. My girlfriend will be joining us, and please have her travel bag taken to my room," Dalton tells the hostess. I forgot I was even carrying it.

Dalton insists I take his place and takes the empty spot once another chair arrives. "Millie, this is Darius and Ria Jackson."

"I'm sorry, I thought," I don't need to finish; they all know what I thought. I am so embarrassed. Surely, my face is scarlet.

"No worries, sugar. I've been there," Ria says to me with a wink and a pat on the hand.

Dalton takes my other hand under the table. "I can't believe you're here! Is that why you were ignoring me all day?"

"I wasn't ignoring you. I was traveling and then at the salon," I admit, gesturing to my hair with my fancy nails.

"Beautiful," Dalton whispers.

"So, this is the hunny that's got ya all tore up this week," Darius rats me out.

"It's been going on a lot longer than this week," Dalton says almost under his breath. But he squeezes my hand to let me know he is acting playful.

They both give us looks that say they are curious, so I fill them in, "Dalton and I were high school sweethearts. We only just recently reconnected."

The rest of the dinner goes well. I find out Ria is expecting, so we start talking about babies and kids. She is shocked to learn we have a ten-year-old daughter. I wonder if she picks up on the fact that Dalton is about as new to parenting as they are.

When dinner is finished, we share an elevator up to our floor. Dalton doesn't stop touching me—a comforting reaffirming hand on my back or stroking my arm. But as soon as we are in his room and the door is shut, he grabs my hand and spins me around. He has me pinned to the wall as he kisses me with a hunger I wasn't expecting. Then he's ravishing my neck as his hands travel south until he palms my bottom and pulls me against himself.

"We really need to talk about your lack of trust in me, but right now, I am so happy to see you, and I would rather use my mouth in other ways," he says low, right into my ear. He's sending tingles through my body just thinking about his mouth working me over.

"I'm sorry, I kind of lost my mind, um, down there," the double meaning was not intended, but undoubtedly true as I can feel how much he wants me through our clothes.

His mouth has found its way to my chest. The spaghetti straps of my dress have fallen over my shoulders, and the front is sliding down. My once small breasts never went back down in size after being pregnant, so I can't go without a bra anymore. They are all pushed up in a new, uncomfortable, strapless number. Dalton seems to like what he sees because he moans and sucks my nipples through the lace.

"Oh, Millie," he moans.

He picks me up with both hands on my rear. I wrap my legs around his waist and my arms around his neck. He walks us over and lays me on the bed. Our mouths have molded together again, and he nestles himself between my legs like it's a gift.

-Dalton

I finally have the woman I have been pining for in my arms and on my bed. Her ass fits in my hands perfectly. It thrills and surprises me that she's wearing a frilly thong. She's never worn sexy underwear before. I continue to slide my hands up under her dress, removing it over her head. Dear Colossus of Clout, her bra and panties match. They are black lace trimmed with little red flowers that match the red dress she was wearing. Her rosy nipples strain out, making the fabric pucker, begging for attention.

"You are so beautiful," I tell her, coming back down from admiring the view. I cover her again, and this time, her hands make a similar assent, taking my shirt off. Her hands trace over my arms and chest. "I couldn't believe my eyes when I saw you tonight," I say between kisses. Next, I unclasp her bra. "This is *all* I could think about during dinner."

"My boobs?" she giggles.

"Getting you naked and in my bed, and definitely, these fine boobs," I say as I grasp one side and suck on the other. I use my tongue to play with her nipple. Then, I give the other side the attention it's due. My other hand pushes her thong to the side and gets busy warming up her pussy. She's already slick and ready, but I play with her anyway. My finger plunges into her and twirls as my thumb finds her swollen clit. She moans with pleasure, so I add a second finger; she spreads her legs even more open for me.

Her hands find their way to my belt, button, and zipper. Delicate fingers trace the waistband of my boxer briefs. She raises her knees and uses her feet to push my pants off. "Resourceful," I praise. "Scoot back, let's use the whole bed." She moves back, but I don't. I step out of my shoes and pants.

I remember she has a thing about no socks in bed. So, I try to be sexy, taking them off for her. I put one foot up on the bed at a time and do a striptease of my feet. I successfully make her laugh. It's the best sound in the world.

"Good! You can't trust someone who wears socks to bed. It's a sure sign they are hiding something," she tells me.

"I don't want to hide anything. I want us to be open and honest about everything. No more secrets between us," I tell her.

"No more secrets," she agrees.

I crawl up on the bed and trace the lacy panties. "Don't lose these; you look great in them, but I sure am going to enjoy taking them off of you." My face is already so close, and she took such care getting primped for me; it would be a shame to skip over this opportunity. Bending down, I rub my nose in the crease between her leg and pelvis, inhaling the scent that is unique to a woman–loving Millie's scent most of all.

I hook my finger under the thong, where it starts getting very narrow so that my knuckle teases her opening.

Millie's panting fills my ears, and I feel the need to remind her we aren't at home. "Do you like that?"

"Yes," she breathes.

"What's that?" I press a little harder while making little circles.

"Yes," she repeats a little louder.

"I want to hear you, or I'll stop because I think you don't like it."

Since she doesn't answer, I start to retract my hand. "Don't stop," Millie's hand slaps the back of my head.

"Ow," I chuckle.

"Sorry," she rubs my hair where she struck me. "I like it. Don't stop."

I smile into the soft flesh of Millie's thigh and tug her thong to the side. "Do you like this?" Languidly, I brush my lips to hers.

"Yesss."

"What about this?" I ask, adding a little tongue to the mix.

Millie gasps. "Yeah."

Inserting one finger, I ask, "And this?"

"Uh-huh."

I don't have to ask if she likes it when I start sucking on her clitoris because she lets me know in no uncertain terms. The sound of my name being called out while she climaxes is better than a stadium full of fans cheering from a grand slam.

"I fucking love how easy you cum for me."

I would continue licking her while she cums, but I might explode before I even step to the plate.

I put on an act for my socks, but I am all business taking my briefs off. Soon, I'm over top of her again, rubbing my penis to her opening. "Shit," I say as I pull back quickly.

"What's wrong? Don't stop now," she complains.

"I don't have a condom," I tell her.

Still glowing from her orgasm, Millie smiles almost mischievously. "I recently went on birth control. If you want to put it to the test, we don't have to stop."

"You're saying I don't have to run downstairs and buy a box of rubbers at the nearest convenience store?"

"Yep."

"We're done using them… for good?"

She rolls her eyes at me, "Are we stopping?"

"I love you, Millie. I would never put you at risk if I thought there was anything to worry about."

"I love you, too, Dalton. I never stopped."

With that, I sink into her. It is like sliding home.

Chapter 43

~Millie

Dalton and I stay in bed, wrapped in only each other and the fine sheets. We talk, sleep, and make love all night and half the next day. We even order room service because we can't be bothered to leave the room for food.

"I heard you tell Ria you wished you had more kids," he says as a statement, but I can tell he means it more as a question by the way he doesn't elaborate.

"Yeah, I always thought I would have a big family like Grandma Bea, but I'm happy with only having Ruth. I am closer to her since it's just been the two of us."

"I hated being an only child growing up. Do you still want more?" he asks.

This conversation is going more in-depth than any of the others tonight. "I don't know." I feel like I am being put on the spot. I'd be lying if I said no, but I don't want to have a family with someone who isn't around half the time.

He says, "I ask because I would love to have more kids. Maybe you could tell me before the baby is born next time." I know he is half-kidding, but it strikes a nerve. I start to sit up, but he reaches out to rub my back. "Shh, shh, we are only talking. Don't get all upset."

"It's not as easy as you think," I say, throwing my hands in the air. "It's a serious time commitment. Babies need you almost all day and night. They depend on you for everything. And do you know how much childcare is? I barely made anything after paying for daycare. I am lucky for all the support I got from my family, but it's not the same as what my sister has. Her husband is there all the time to help her."

"You won't have to do it all by yourself again. I will support you. I can cover the cost of any daycare, or you could stay home."

"I worked really hard for my degree. And I'm proud that I earned it," I defend my work.

"I didn't mean to upset you. I'm amazed that you earned your degree. If you like your job, you should keep it. It would lighten your load not to have to work outside the home and raise kids. But I've been thinking if you didn't work as much, we would see each other more," he says to calm me.

I lay back down but not curled up as I was; we lay shoulder to shoulder instead. Dalton turns his body into me. Playing with my hair, he says, "I'm all in, Millie. I have a couple properties around KC I want you to look at with me. I want us to live as a family. I understand if you aren't ready for that yet. But I want it all, and I want it as soon as possible."

That stops me. He's all in? Live as a family? That would make things easier. I'm pretty sure Grandma is only keeping the big house so I can live there. Mom and Dad have been looking for a single-story home with two master suites so she can move in with them. Ruth could have a semi-normal family life if we moved in with Dalton.

Dalton starts reasoning with me again, "I'm still under contract for the next two seasons, but I will retire after that-"

I interrupt him with a gasp. Turning to him, I say, "Dalton! You can't do that; you're at the top of your game."

"Shh, just hear me out. I've missed so much of Ruth's life. I want to be there for everything else. I hate that our schedules conflict so much. Also, my knee is worse than I let on. Who knows what shape I will be in two and a half years from now?"

I put my hand on his knee, the therapist in me coming out. I like my work, but not so much the job. I have been taking off a lot of time since he came back in my life because if I don't, I won't see him. Case in point: this trip. I sigh, resigning to the thought, "I could see about cutting back to part-time."

He gives me a big, knowing grin, "See, now we are compromising. That is step three on Dalton's list for a long, happy relationship." He kisses my temple.

I tease, "What makes you such an expert? Is step one talking in the third person?"

"Dalton is an expert because Dalton has seen firsthand what doesn't work," he answers sarcastically.

I know what he means. I witnessed enough of his parent's fights. "Then what are steps one and two? Is there any hope for us?"

He props himself up over me. "Love," he says, kissing me just below my left ear, "and communication," kissing the same spot on my right side. "I would say we're off to an excellent start." Then he kisses my mouth feverishly.

Chapter 44

-Dalton

A couple of weeks later, I'm taking Millie to California for the All-Star game. Tonight, we have dinner plans with Cain and Jake. They were my best friends from minors until Jake and I had a huge brawl in spring training. I warned Millie what a lady's man Jake is and how Cain comes from old money and, ever since he proved himself to his dad, likes to throw it around. But once you get to know them, they are loyal to the bone. It's just getting there that's the hard part. I also told her how we didn't leave on the best of terms the last time I saw Jake.

"We are really hitting a club after dinner?" Millie asks as we walk to the corner booth.

I put my arm around her lower back as I guide her to the VIP section. "It wasn't my idea. They always hit the clubs. We don't have to stay out late," I reassure her.

Jake's already there, with a woman on each arm. I was hoping this night would be different, that he would be the man I know he is under the facade. He sees me and looks somewhat surprised.

"Oh my God, you really did bring someone! I thought you were just telling me that, so I brought an extra date for you!" Jake says with a boisterous laugh.

Millie says quietly to me, "Why would he think you would lie about that?"

"Because in the past, I have." The memory makes me cringe. "I knew if I met him stag, he would make it his mission to set me up for the night," I tell her under my breath. "Jake, this is Millie," I tell him.

"No, shit! *The* Millie?" Jake asks and half-stands to greet Millie. Instead of shaking her hand, he kisses the back of it and looks into her eyes. "My pleasure." Then I notice the sleaze makes it his pleasure by checking out her chest. This is going to be a long night.

I tense up, but Millie shakes it off. She looks at me and rolls her eyes. "Nice to meet you, Jake."

Jake and the women have to slide down to make room for two people. When we are all finally situated, he introduces them. "This is Molly," he tells me with a wink, "and this is…" Jake stalls out, proving to all of us that he doesn't give two shits what her name is. Therefore, remembering it isn't a priority.

"I'm Amanda," she giggles.

"That's right. I was just about to say that. Well, I guess I have two dates then. Don't worry, ladies, I will take care of both of you tonight," Jake says, laying it on thick.

"Cain still planning on joining us?" I ask Jake. "Or is he making some grand entrance in half an hour?"

"You know his style," Jake laughs and gestures to the man walking up to us from the bar. Damn. I thought I had dressed up for tonight, but Cain takes getting dressed to a whole new level.

"Well, hello, stranger," Cain's quiet confidence fills the space. I stand to greet him, and he gives me a one-armed hug. Then he asks, "Who do we have here?"

"This is Millie," I say, introducing them. "Millie, this is Cain Alexander, the third baseman for the Chicago Stars."

"So, this is the elusive Millie. I've heard so much about you, and I mean *so much*," Cain says, shaking Millie's hand.

"Nice to meet you," Millie greets Cain. As Cain pulls up a chair, Millie asks me, "So why doesn't Cain have a date brought for him?" It comes out a little louder than I think she intended.

"Because Cain can get his own dates; thank you," Cain answers. He winks and smirks about it, but his voice betrays him. He sounds perturbed.

"Cain has a long-term, on-again, off-again girlfriend," I tell her.

"How is Gabby?" Jake asks. "I would have brought you some company, too, if I'd have known she wouldn't be here tonight. But, I guess I can share." The girls on either side of him eat it up, giggling.

"Gabrielle is fine. Last I knew, she moved to Santa Fe," Cain tells us, his voice trailing off at the end.

After we place our orders, Jake starts up again, "I can't believe you found her, Dalton. How in the world did that happen?" he doesn't wait for an answer; he just switches his focus to Millie. "He was such a bore. Always checking his email, never wanting to go out, just in case you called."

"That's because the one time she did call, I was out with you," I tell him.

"*Riiight*," he says like he doesn't believe me. "It took me two years and a lot of Patronne to get this one loosened up enough to even have a lap dance at Lucky 7's. You don't even want to know what it took to-"

I cut him off because I know where his next story is going. "Millie was busy raising our daughter." That shut him up fast.

He lets out a low whistle. "Wow, I did not see that one coming."

Cain's eyebrows raise. Then he signals to the waitress to refill his lowball glass.

Amanda giggles, "Isn't that, like, backward? Aren't you supposed to get pregnant because you want him to stick around?"

"Well, I guess the whole situation was backward. But I wouldn't suggest getting pregnant just to get a guy to stay with you," Millie says very carefully.

"So, you have a daughter?" Cain directs the conversation back on track.

"Yes, tell us more about her," Jake requests.

"We do. And she is too young, even for you," I tell Jake, knowing his history.

"Touché. But that's not where I was going with that," Jake says. He directs his next comment to Millie, saying, "I was going to ask why you didn't come and put this sorry excuse for a bachelor out of his misery before now?"

"Well, I tried once," Millie starts.

"Millie was the 'fiancé' that came to the hospital when I hurt my knee. The old batty nurse got her name wrong," I say, laughing.

"What? You mean I have been looking for women named Molly for you this whole time, and that wasn't even your stalker? Man, what a waste." Then, as an afterthought, Jake turns to the Molly he brought for me, "Sorry, babe."

The rest of the dinner goes smoothly. Jake isn't putting up his front. He seems genuinely curious about my life in KC. Cain is quiet but attentive.

We hit the club, but Millie and I stick to ourselves, including making out on the dance floor for a couple of songs. Jake's dates act more interested in themselves than the rest of us. He seems to have gotten bored with them, too.

When we are about to leave, Jake and Cain walk us out so we can talk without shouting. "Man, I am happy for you," Jake tells me. He claps me on the back in a bro hug, then continues, "I can tell you are out of the singles game. Hell, I don't think you ever really were in it. No matter how much I tried."

"You're right about that," I confirm.

Just before we get in a cab, Cain shakes Millie's and my hands. "Night, you two love birds. Make sure you invite me to the wedding. Hell, I better beat Jake out for best man," he says with a side nod toward Jake. We both wish him goodnight, but the ride back to the hotel is quiet. I know what's weighing on my mind, and I wonder if Cain's hint of a wedding in our future has Millie nervous, too.

"Let's walk in the garden before we turn in," I suggest. Millie follows my lead hand-in-hand.

The courtyard is beautiful. Its landscaping is as classy as the hotel decor. There is even a little bridge over a pond with Koi fish. The whole garden is lit up with strands of tiny fairy lights.

"You'll marry me, right? You'll be my wife," I say, trying to mimic the first time I called her my girlfriend all those years ago.

Millie smiles and bites her lips together, with a slight blush on her cheeks. Recalling the memory, she answers like she did before. "Are you telling me I'm going to be your wife, or are you asking me if I will marry you?"

I take both of her hands in mine and turn to face her. "Millie, I have loved you since high school. I think my feelings started the first time we played together on your swing set. Your laugh was something I knew I would do anything to hear," I say.

I start to pull the promise ring off. "When I gave you this ring, I promised to find you again. That took some help, but I have done that. I also promised to always love you, so you should always wear it," I put it on her right hand. Before retaking her left hand, I reach into my pocket. "I also promised to give you the world, and now I am offering it to you." I hold out the new ring I just bought her.

It's a 3-carat princess-cut diamond in a platinum setting. When I first began looking, I wanted to get her the biggest stone I could afford. But when I saw this one, I knew it was meant for her.

Going down on one knee, I ask, "Millie, will you marry me?"

"YES!!" she squeals, jumping in my arms.

Epilogue

October 2012

-Dalton

I'm finally home after the biggest after-party I've ever been to. I'm wound up, and I know it will take hours to come down from this high. Millie and Ruth were with me most of the night but left an hour or so ago. I'm sure Millie will be awake—Ruth probably is, too; I can't believe she is a teenager now.

I walk into the house Millie and I built and have made into a real home. I feel the warmth and love inside the walls, unlike any place I've lived before.

Yet, only the dog greets me at the door. Instead of hearing my family's voices, I hear my own on the TV.

"As I promised my wife, tonight's game was my last. I have enjoyed this game my whole life, but it is time to enjoy it from a different position. I couldn't be happier that my career is ending on such an epic win." It's from the press conference after the game. We just won the World Series. How could I ever top that moment in my career?

I come around the corner, and Ruth jumps me. "I still can't believe we won!!!!"

I nearly fall over; she isn't so small anymore. "Careful, I'm an old retiree now," I groan. But I love it more than she will ever know.

Millie comes up and wraps her arms around us. She's crying.

"What's wrong," I ask her.

"Nothing, I'm just so happy!"

"She has been a wreck all day. You should have seen all the nachos and licorice she had at the game," Ruth says, rolling her eyes.

"I can't help it; when I'm stressed, I eat. You had plenty of junk food, too, young lady," Millie banters.

"Speaking of deliciousness, look, Dad, we made you a cake!" Ruth says. It's a round cake that is frosted to look like a baseball.

While we are eating and joking around at the kitchen table, Ruth asks, "So, what are you going to do now that you are retired?"

"I'll be here every night to meet who you go out with and make sure you're home for curfew," I tease her. "Maybe I will even bake your mom some cookies. I know she has always wanted me to be a housewife." I wink at Millie.

"You really are hanging up your cleats?" Millie asks.

I look at her, questioning where she is coming from with this. We've been planning for this, looking into opening a sporting complex. But she isn't looking at me; she's giving Ruth a sly smile. They are up to something, sharing a secret. I hate secrets, but I play along to fish it out of them. I slowly and cautiously say, "Yes, why?"

"Well, I am going to need to find a sub for spring softball," she answers.

I'm not sure what to say, "Why aren't you going to play?" I don't get to watch her play much, but it's Ruth's and my favorite comedy. Spring league is months away; why is she thinking about this now?

"Well, I don't think they will let me on the field looking like I have a basketball shoved under my shirt."

I don't get it. "Why would you-?" Ruth has her hands covering her face because she is laughing so hard. "Oh, Jidge!" I jump up. "Are you saying what I think you are saying?" I tug her out of her seat.

"Yep! I'm due in early June."

I pick her up and swing her around. "I didn't think this night could get any better!" I kiss her long and hard.

"Ewww! I'm going to bed," Ruth says, leaving the room.

I whisper in Millie's ear, "I'm thinking the same thing; let's get in bed. I love you, Millie. I am so happy you helped me achieve all of my dreams."

Continue reading for a teaser of

Alone on Second

book two in the **HOMERUN SERIES** by

Kay Lucas

Alone on Second

Chapter One

December 2010

Jake

The Fireside Tavern. Sure, why not? I have hours to kill before I need to be at the church for the rehearsal dinner for one of my best friends' upcoming doom. Don't get me wrong; I'm happy for them. I just don't think that is the right path for me. There is way too much pussy to enjoy settling on only one for the rest of my life.

Marriage. I know plenty of couples that make it work. Hell, my own parents seem to have a happy union. And it's not like Dalton didn't have one foot in this trap before I met him.

I walk in, and the place is mostly empty. The only table filled is next to a large fireplace. It looks cozy compared to Missouri's December chill, but I choose to sit at the bar.

The waitress greets me. She's cute, young, and petite, with short blonde hair, and she is all smiles for me—I'd do her.

I'm just about done eating when Smiles comes back, refills my beer, and tells me that her boss will ring me up when I'm ready because her shift is over. I watch her clean off the other table then go in the back. A few minutes later, she comes back out, followed by a woman that catches my full attention.

I assume this is the boss. She is a little taller than the waitress, but that's not saying much. She wears a ripped band t-shirt, showing her lean muscular arms, and it's torn at the bottom, displaying her midriff. Her black jeans are almost a second skin.

Dear Lord, her sculpted ass is so compact. I usually prefer a little more junk in the trunk, but damn. I have a hankering to feel that sweet curve in the palm of my hand.

I watch her willowy frame at the jukebox before she turns to the pool table. Black hair with fire-engine-red streaks is so long it reaches her waist. I itch to run my hands through it.

Distantly, I recognize my favorite Aerosmith song playing, but that's secondary to the woman before me. I'm drawn to her like a moth to a flame.

Grabbing my beer, I walk over. I'm fair at 8-ball, so I challenge her to a match. "Hi, care for a game?"

She turns her head to look at me. The first thing I notice about her face is her big, brown doe-eyes against her pale, porcelain skin. Her nose is small and almost turned up. When she gives me a smirk and says, "Sure," my attention is pulled to her lips—lips that are the same red as her hair. I imagine them wrapped around my cock, and immediately try to shake the image off. That's the last thing I need to think about if I'm going to concentrate on a game.

Danika

I'm just finishing payroll when Katie comes in to tell me goodbye.

"Hey, my shift is over. The kitchen's cleaned up, and the bar is all stocked. There is still one customer finishing up; I would wait, but I have class. Can I 86 myself out of here?"

"Okay. Go ahead and clock out. I'll wait until he's done," I say, stretching back in the desk chair.

This is my last shift at the bar for a while. I have to get out of this town so I can heal my wounded heart. At least enough to come back home with my tough-girl shell firmly in place.

It might be more my pride than my heart that needs healing. I never thought Nikki would stab me in the back. We were always there for each other, and that's exactly how we went from friends to roommates to lovers.

"I'm really going to miss you!" Katie gushes.

I wave her off before she hugs me, and God forbid her tears. "Eddie isn't that bad. He can handle things, and I won't be gone forever," I reassure her and myself.

My brother, Eddie, and I co-own this place. It was our father's. When dear old Dad took off, it was all we had left of him.

"I'm sure Eddie will be fine," Katie says as she punches her timecard then manages to hug me farewell. "The hottie at the bar is drinking tap beer. His tab is next to the register."

"Okay, go ahead and lock up behind you. I don't want anyone else coming in before I have to go," I tell Katie.

We close for a couple of hours between lunch and happy hour. Usually, it's delivery time, but that was rescheduled for yesterday since I need to get out of here by four o'clock today.

I follow her out and decide to turn on some classic rock and shoot pool until he's done. As I'm racking the balls, the customer saunters over.

"Hi, care for a game?" he asks.

Katie was right—this guy is HOTT. I haven't been with a man in over two years. I could use a rebound fuck, and I sure as hell ain't gonna go back to the home team for it.

Nikki and I weren't always exclusive. When I broke up with my last boyfriend, she decided to cheer me up sexually. For a long time, we would invite one or two lucky guys home to join us for the night. However, for the last couple of years, I assumed we were monogamous. As it turns out, Nikki was a cheating bitch that was never honest with me.

"Sure." It's only two o'clock. I have plenty of time to *play*.

It becomes apparent this guy is smooth and a little cocky. He's also a huge flirt. Customarily, that combo is a turn-off for me, but today it builds my confidence.

And did I mention how fucking hot he is? He's a good half a foot taller than me and built as if he lives in a gym—not in a muscle-head way—but he's definitely an athlete. The beanie he wears hides his hair, but his scruffy beard is dark blond. In this light, I can't tell what color his eyes are; they just look dark and hungry. He has a prominent Roman nose. It isn't big and hooked like a beak, but it's proud and sexy. By far, my favorite feature is the wicked grin that probably gets him in a lot of trouble.

The first game is friendly; the second is even friendlier—lots of accidental touches and brushing past each other as if the place is crowded. I can't help but bend at my waist and stretch for my shots. I'm having a good time, and best of all, he has me laughing.

334

I haven't felt this free in months, maybe even years. He doesn't know me, so I don't have to be the bitchy Danika everyone has come to expect.

"Alright, we each won one. I think we need to up the stakes for the third round," mister hot-stuff says.

"Like what? You want me to buy you a drink if I lose?"

He walks right into my personal space to say, "I was thinking of making the stakes a little higher than that." His warm breath against my neck gives me delightful chills. Then he plants his mouth on mine, grabs my ass, and arches me back so I can feel how well-endowed he is.

When I come up for air, I say, "If I win, you have to use that talented tongue wherever I choose. If you win, I'll give you the best damn blow job of your life." Either way, this will lead to what I truly want; a good hard fuck to erase the memory of the last four months.

"Now you're talkin'," he says. Then he kisses me once more and slaps me on the ass.

It's so not like me to go along with this chauvinistic attitude. So, when he turns to rack the balls, I whack his ass with my cue stick—not too hard—just enough to give him a taste of his own medicine. "You're on."

He jumps a little in surprise but laughs it off.

The game is rapidly discarded. When one of us is shooting, the other interferes by copping a feel.

Making sure I'm in his line of sight, I take off my shirt, distracting him while he aims for the seven. He scratches; the cue ball almost hops off the table.

He takes that as a green light to start stripping too. Soon the whole game is lost, along with most of our clothes.

Picking me up, he sets me on the pool table. By now, I'm down to just my panties, and he's only in his green boxer-briefs.

"You don't play fair, Firefly," he says, nibbling on my ear, sending delightful tingles down my body.

"You're playing a little dirty yourself," I reply, running my hands down his torso to toy with the waistband of his shorts. His chest and abs are so defined that I can't stop myself from licking the valley between his pectorals.

While my tongue enjoys its adventure, my hand travels south of the border, and I grip the mighty package that I seek. He lets out the most intoxicating moan.

When he lays me back on the pool table, I'm more than happy to comply. Spreading my legs, I provide him full access to my aching body. A thrill of anticipation engulfs me as he suckles on my breasts. I need to move this along faster. "Do you have a condom, or should I get one from the quarter machine?"

"Patience, my little eager beaver." He leans back and takes off my undies. He watches intently at his thumb as he runs it up my pussy to rub my clit. The sensation is phenomenal, and it is apparent that this man knows his way around a woman's body.

Abruptly, I grab his wrist and say, "Enough games. I want it hard, and I want it now."

About the Author

Kay Lucas grew up in southwestern Wisconsin, and now resides in South Carolina with her husband and four kids. Kay was never a big reader when she was young, but now you can't get her to put down a book. She can usually be found at the ballfield cheering on her kids, or at the dance studio waiting for her girls—or taking a class herself! She also enjoys, hiking, camping, gardening, and is a massage therapist by trade. Creative writing has always been fun, but it has recently become a passion for Kay.

Books by
Kay Lucas

Dreaming of First
Alone on Second
Dreaming of Third

Stay continued for more!

www.ingramcontent.com/pod-product-compliance
Lightning Source LLC
Chambersburg PA
CBHW020931260626
47169CB00006B/1672